Night

Night Songs

FINDING LOVE IN THE MIDST OF TERROR

LeRoy Miltner

authorHOUSE®

AuthorHouse™
1663 Liberty Drive
Bloomington, IN 47403
www.authorhouse.com
Phone: 1-800-839-8640

Published by AuthorHouse   02/28/2013

ISBN: 978-1-4817-1836-3 (sc)
ISBN: 978-1-4817-1837-0 (e)

Dedicated to my wife, Freda Ammon Miltner and to the memory of Marine Sgt. William Rogal, my hero and my friend.

CHAPTER 1

S PRING CAME EARLY to France's Loire Valley in 1937, with the rivers flowing fast and full, their waters dark with run-off from the rich soils of the northern French plains. Farmers looked with enlarged hope for bountiful harvests, and herdsmen for lush grasses to feed their cattle.

Nanette Lemond lifted her face to the warm sun as she walked from her parents' home to the dress shop owned by her father Geraud, in the village of Cande. After the cold winds of winter, the sun felt like a gentle hand caressing her skin.

She was the second child of Geraud and Paulette Lemond, born in 1918, three years after her brother, Julian. She had a close relationship with her parents, especially her father, who adored her. Ever since she could read, she came to the shop each day after school, devouring the fashion magazines her father received, and sketching ideas of her own which she kept in a folio she called her 'future design book'. At first she helped by dusting shelves, arranging inventory and offering customers a bright smile and a cheery welcome. Later, she learned how to keep track of inventory, select dresses for display, and dress mannequins. Fashion was her world, and she was never more content than when surrounded by articles of beauty and creativity.

She was half way to the shop when Monsieur Durat, still spry at eighty, waved to her as he peddled his bicycle home from his daily foray to buy bread and a newspaper. In his lapel he wore the muguet, a small cluster of Lily of the Valleys, heralding the arrival of spring. Nanette waved back, remembering how, as a young girl, she would peek into his patisserie on the way home from school each day. She would feign surprise as he asked her if she would come in and eat his last pastry so he could close the shop and go home. It was a pleasant memory, one of many she held in this lovely small town, where people were friendly and cared for each other like a large family.

Nanette crossed the river Edre, its water flowing generously toward a final rendevous with the Loire at Nantes. The cobblestones on the old stone bridge were rutted from the passing of countless carts across the generations. She sang as she walked, about the sun and the verdant fields to which it offered the gift of life-giving warmth. Others on the street nodded and called their bonjours, until she reached the center of town, a busy intersection of six roads, spraying web-like in all directions. In the center was a bronze monument, dedicated to the memory of fifty-one Cande men and one woman nurse, who were killed in the Great War. On one corner of the plaza stood her father's shop, which he named 'La Belle Femme', expressing his desire that women who bought his clothing and accessories would indeed feel like 'a beautiful lady'.

Despite its small town location, La Belle Femme attracted its clientele from a broad area, including the much larger cities of Nantes, Angers and LeMans. The shop's appeal lay in its serious attention to the latest fashions from Paris, and a wide variety of accessories, including a line of moderately priced baubles recently produced by Coco Chanel, which she called 'costume jewelry'. Cande's proximity to the busy shipping port of Nantes, just thirty-fives miles west, enabled Geraud to stock a small adjacent shop with imported goods. Irish linens, Scottish wools, teas from the Orient, and coffees from Brazil lined his shelves. Despite hard times in this decade of the 1930s, those with the means kept his business profitable.

Now nineteen, and in her second year out of school, Nanette often accompanied Geraud on trips to Parish for style-shows and buyers' markets. She developed bargaining skills, and a keen eye for what would sell in her region. What set her apart from other tradespeople were her age, and her rare beauty. Her mother was a Castillian, and Nanette had the same olive complexion and dark eyes, accented by her broad smile and perfect teeth. Her facial features, long, slender legs, and full breasts were not lost on men, wherever she went. Ever since her eighth year of school, boys were attracted to her like bears to honey. More than once, her mother Paulette, no doubt recalling her own struggles of that nature as her body matured, deluged her with advice about how to avoid boys with quick hands. Even so, on several occasions Julian had to come to her rescue, especially from older lads trying to take advantage of her innocence.

Julian, now tall and athletically built, had light wavy hair, which he wore long, and a deep, strong voice. He had also helped in the shop during his pre-teen years, but shied away from having anything to do with dresses as he grew older. Always quick with figures, when his school years ended he took a clerks' position with an import/export company in Nantes owned by the parents of Paul

Moreau, a soccer team-mate. Julian had a small flat in Nantes, but came home most weekends to enjoys his mother's cooking, to see his sister, and mostly, to date his girl-friend, Louise.

Entering the dress-shop, Nanette greeted her father with a kiss and asked about his plans for the day.

"Well, my dear," he replied, "we have a shipment of shoes arriving this morning, so they will need pricing. Then you must decide which to display in the window."

Nanette smiled. She enjoyed the easy partnership she had with her father, who had gradually given her a wider latitude in making decisions and offering ideas. Her confidence had grown to the point where she was certain that, if necessary, she could comfortably carry on in her father's stead.

"These are the shoes I selected at the last show, are they not?" she asked.

"Of course," he answered, also smiling. "The very elegant and exceedingly expensive ones I was reluctant to approve. So let me see what you do with them, and how many of our customers will be as excited about them as you are."

She laughed. "Wait and see, Papa. We will have women begging us to sell them a pair."

As she turned to walk away, Geraud said over his shoulder, "Oh, I almost forgot. Monsieur Terrand is stopping in later this morning for a cup of coffee."

"Monsieur Terrand?" Nanette shrieked. "Emile Terrand is coming here? Oh Papa, why did you not tell me sooner. Look at me. I'm dressed like a—."

"Like a proper sales-lady in a proper dress shop." said Geraud quickly, "And, I might add, the most beautiful and talented sales-lady in all of France."

"But Papa, why is he coming?" she asked, still not believing it was true.

"He is coming to visit the shop which has sold more of his designs than any other in all of France!" he said proudly.

Nanette began to clap her hands and dance. She was proud of her father, and pleased that his hard work was being rewarded.

"And", he continued, "to see the proper and beautiful sales-lady whom he has admired so much and seen so little."

"Now you are being silly," she said, blushing. "I met him only a few times, and he was much too busy to notice me."

"We'll see," replied Geraud, "but now we must get to work. I want to see the women rushing in to by your irresistible shoes."

Emile Terrand swept onto the Parish fashion scene some fifteen years before, shocking critics in the post-war years with his flamboyant and sexy designs. The public, those with money and a free spirit, took to him immediately, making his name synonymous with the cutting-edge of fashion. More recently, with the wave of the 1920s giving way to a growing modesty, Terrand began also designing sophisticated styles for older women. He enjoyed continued success, and his dresses were the top line carried by La Belle Femme.

Nanette hummed to herself as she decided which shoes to remove from the window display in anticipation of the new arrivals. A rap on the glass drew her attention, as the smiling face of her best friend, Sister Danielle, greeted her through the glass. Nanette beckoned to her to come in.

The two women had been friends for years. Danielle was a nun assigned to the Cande parish as a music teacher. Replacing an older and stodgy nun, she was an instant hit with the youth of the parish, with her almost mischievous smile and quick laughter. Nanette met her when she first arrived eight years ago, accepting an invitation to dinner with the Lemonds. Danielle took an immediate interest in Nanette when the young girl played the piano and sang for their guest after dessert. Although five years older, short and a bit pudgy, Danielle's youthful spirit turned a student-teacher relationship into a lasting friendship.

"Bonjour Danielle", called Nanette, as the nun entered the shop.

"Bonjour, Nanette. You are so busy already. I think you have some new merchandise coming, no?"

"Yes, and I am quite worried about what's coming. Over my father's objections, I bought some very expensive shoes, and now I have to prove to him that they will be good sellers."

"Oh dear," said Danielle, "I'm afraid that's something I can't help you with, and I don't think the Lord would want me praying for such a thing."

"Not even a little prayer?" asked Nanette, jokingly.

"Well, maybe as a postscript to another petition."

Both women laughed, as a delivery van drove up, and a man stepped out carrying two large cartons.

"Speaking of the devil." commented Danielle, and they both laughed again.

After some pleasantries, Sister Danielle left Nanette to unpack her parcels. There were a dozen boxes inside, and, as Nanette opened the first box and withdrew the attractive shoes, she wondered again if she had made the right choice.

"Well, too late now for regrets." she said to herself. "Into the window they go. Come, come eager women, and buy my lovely shoes."

The remainder of the morning moved swiftly. A few shoppers stopped in, but it was not unusual for things to go slowly, since most of their clients came in the afternoon or early evening.

At 11:00, a limousine stopped in front of the shop, the uniformed chauffeur hurrying to open doors for its two passengers. Nanette, hearing the car doors close, looked out to see a handsome, elegantly-dressed, gray-haired man of middle age, looking into the shop window. He then stepped back, looked up as if to read again the sign over the shop, and said something to his companion.

Nanette called for her father, who was just finishing with a customer, and who came to the door to greet Emile Terrand. The designer's secretary, or so he seemed to be, held the door for his employer, who entered with a flourish.

Before Geraud could utter a word of welcome, Terrand exclaimed in a loud voice:

"Geraud, Geraud, what a beautiful setting. What a warm feeling your shop gives me. And my dear man, those shoes in the window, where in the world did you find them?"

Nanette trembled inside with the feeling that she had made the blunder of her life.

"The shoes?" asked Geraud.

"Why yes, those incredibly beautiful shoes just by one of my dresses. My God, they are spectacular. I adore them"

"Oh, yes, of course," stammered Geraud, "they have just arrived this morning. We, that is, my daughter, thought they might, ah, be a nice addition to our line."

"Nanette," said Terrand effusively, "of course. How rude of me, Mademoiselle. It is my great pleasure to see you again. The last time was in October, wasn't it? And before that in June? You are as lovely as ever; no, more lovely than ever as I see you in this setting, among these works of art, and you yourself a work of beauty. Oh, I embarrass you. Forgive me, but please, show me around and tell me what is selling."

To his secretary he said: "Jerome, take copious notes."

They toured both shops, had coffee, and then Geraud, Emile, and Jerome shut themselves in the office while Nanette attended to the rush of people, only a few of whom were customers, their curiosity aroused by the limo parked outside.

Half an hour later, the three men emerged, shook hands and said their good-byes. Terrand came over to Nanette and gave a slight bow. She offered her hand, which he kissed and said:

"This has been a delightful morning, Mademoiselle. Your father and I are so alike. He has a wonderfully keen business sense, and a warmth of personality so lacking in most businessmen. I hope we will soon be seeing more of each other. Good-bye."

Nanette was so excited she was hardly able to mutter her farewell. As Terrand went out, greeting the crowd which now recognized him, she wondered what he meant by his last words. Was he and her father entering some new arrangement?

The voice of a customer, asking about the new shoes in the window, brought her back to reality, and she went swiftly and excitedly back to work.

CHAPTER 2

N ANETTE'S LOVE FOR her brother Julian was deep and sincere. She watched as he grew tall and muscular, and noted with pleasure how he interacted with his parents and friends. She found him to be warm, honest, and considerate of others. His name came up one day in a conversation Nanette had with Sister Danielle. The two women were walking along the river on a warm evening, greeting those whom they passed.

"So, Nanette," remarked Danielle, "I have seen how the young men we meet give you that longing look. You haven't told me, have you met someone you like?"

"I like a lot of young men in the village. But if you mean is there someone I want to spend my time with, the answer is no." Nanette replied.

"So, you are being very choosy. I think that is a good thing. You have very much to offer the right man."

"Thank you," said Nanette, but its not that I am so fussy. For one, I am much too busy with my work and hopes for the future, to be thinking about dating. And for another, I have an idea in my mind about the kind of person I want to meet."

"Where did you get this ideal man figure? Surely not from the cinema."

Nanette laughed, and answered, "No. To tell you the truth, I get it from Julian. If I could find someone like him, I believe I would fall in love."

"Ah, Julian. He is a charmer, and I mean that in a good way. He has a girl-friend, not so?"

"Yes, and she is both nice and very intelligent. I worry though, and I think Julian does too, that when she finishes her work on a university degree, she may be more interested in finding someone in the professional ranks.

Danielle stopped, and was thoughtful for a moment.

"Has Julian not considered some additional studies himself." she asked.

"Not that he has said," answered Nanette, "I know he has the intelligence, especially in mathematics, but he was so bored with school that he was happy to be over with it."

"Well, maybe he will change his mind." replied Danielle, resuming her stride.

"Perhaps, but for now he is satisfied to work hard during the week and have parties on the weekends."

Which was the very thing on Julian's mind when he arrived home Friday evening. After the usual family meal, he relaxed beside Nanette and broached the subject.

"Nanette, tomorrow night Paul Moreau is having a party at his flat, and many of our friends have been invited. You will know most of them—Pierre, Lucien, Marie, Angie."

"And, of course, your Louise, I presume?"

"Yes", replied Julian with a smile. "Happily she will be home tomorrow and wants to be there. And, she would like you to come also. I think you should come. You work and study your magazines too much."

Nanette hit him with a pillow.

"I enjoy it," she said firmly. "You know how much the fashion world means to me: the dresses, the models, the excitement of a new line of clothing."

"And the shoes," remarked Julian.

"And the shoes," she said. "So, Papa has told you about my lovely new shoe line."

"Yes and he told me how they flew off the shelves last week, and how you took Monsieur Tarrand by storm when he visited the shop. Sounds as if he can't keep his eyes off you."

"Nonsense. He just likes beautiful things, and admires those with the good taste to by them."

They both laughed, and Julian asked again, "So, what do you say. Will you come with us tomorrow night?"

"Of course I will, so long as you don't introduce me to those I haven't met as your little sister."

"Agreed. Louise will be pleased. She has been wanting to see you in one of your high-fashion dresses for a long time. She likes nice clothing too, you know."

"So, it is a dressy party?"

"Oh yes," replied Julian. "Paul Moreau throws the fanciest parties of anyone, and he lets everyone know to wear their finest."

On the evening of the planned event, Julian drove Nanette in his dented, old Renault to pick up Louise at her home. Louise was a tall, lovely girl, very intelligent and just a bit shy. Her dress was in a fashionable style, and her long, dark hair was piled high, surrounded by a ring of flowers. She wore several rings and bracelets, and long, dangling earrings. This was to be her first party given by Moreau.

The women's anticipation grew as they neared Moreau's house. Nanette had been out with groups of friends before, but never to something as lavish as Julian had suggested this might be. Since most of those expected to be there were of Julian's age, and older, she worried about her ability to keep up with the conversation.

Paul Moreau always had ample money to spend. As an only child of a French father and an Austrian mother, both wealthy in their own right, he usually got what he wanted. He stood a few inches under six feet, with close-cropped dark hair, and a heavy build. He was known to be quick tempered and shrewd. His flat was on the second floor of a building on the left bank of the Loire, a few miles outside Nantes. It was quite spacious and had a large balcony overlooking the river. Lights from homes across way sparkled on the dark, fast flowing water, and an occasional barge floated silently past the property. The moon hung like a half-eaten pie, surrounded by thousands of smaller, jealous stars which no-one cared to name. A warm breeze made it a perfect night for being either inside or out, and the party-goers did both.

The trio arrived at the same time as several others, allowing some introductions to be made before entering the flat. Once inside, they joined a dozen earlier arrivals who were enjoying the music, the conversation, and the wide variety of drinks Moreau provided. Nanette noticed immediately how well the guests were dressed. On their way to the party, Julian had told Nanette about one of Moreau's parties to which a young woman arrived whom Moreau had met and invited just the day before. Unfortunately for her, he uncharacteristically failed to mention anything about the mode of dress, and the poor girl arrived in something quite casual. She was very embarrassed, but Paul, who hoped to seduce her, explained that she had just come from Mass, and hadn't had time to change.

On this night, no one made that faux pas. The young women wore stylish, and in some cases, very revealing, dresses, their hair newly coiffed, their necks and wrists adorned with jewelry. Nanette recognized one or two of the designs, and knew the houses from which they came. She wore one of her own creations, which made her look elegant and very desirable.

More than a few heads turned and watched her through the evening.

Moreau's spacious flat was decorated with flowers and dozens of candles. On the walls were a few very good paintings by contemporary artists, and in one corner stood a large marble of a nude woman, which could have been the centerpiece of a garden. He had arranged his furniture so as to open a large space for dancing. One of the guests who had come alone, was serving as an ad hoc bar-tender. He chose some phonograph records and began to play music, receiving as many jeers as he did cheers for his selections.

No-one invited to his parties ever complained about Paul Moreau's generosity as a host. Now, as always, his table was weighed-down with a wide sampling of hors d'oeuvres: smoked salmon, marinated herring, steak tartare, pates, and cheeses. There was a selection of good wines and champagne, of course, but also whisky, gin and vodka.

By the time everyone arrived, the guest count was more than thirty, mostly singles, but a few steady couples. As was the case throughout Europe, nearly everyone smoked cigarettes, filling the room with a blue haze.

Nanette, had circulated widely throughout the night, greeting those she knew and learning the names of those newly met. She danced with several partners, some agile, and others quite awkward, Nanette uncertain whether from the alcohol or by their nature. She wandered about the room, seeing here and there small groups of people discussing subjects which interested them. In one corner a cluster of mostly men argued over which cyclists had the greatest chance for victory in the summer Tour. In another, several friends were having a serious discussion about Germany's political situation.

Nanette recognized the man leading the discussion. He was Robert Talon, an economist a few years older than she, who had recently made headlines in the newspaper criticizing the government for not taking a more firm stance against Germany's weapons buildup. He used the word 'appeasement', and warned that Hitler was following the same path as the Kaiser in 1914.

"I spent three months in Berlin last fall," he told them, "and you would be surprised at the kinds of things the newspapers there are calling for. The German leadership—meaning the Nazi Party, of course, consider the Versailles Treaty a piece of paper to wipe your ass with. They know our 'great men' in Paris are scared shitless at the sight of a jack-boot. Look, when a German brigade marched across the Seine into neutral territory last year, our leaders were so paralyzed that nothing happened."

His listeners seemed struck by his words. A few more of the guests drew close to hear him.

"Do you honestly believe Hitler would risk another war after the beating they took in 1914?" someone asked. "He knows what it cost them and how the population suffered. Can you expect the people to support him if he calls for war again?"

"That's the point," replied Tolan, "Hitler has convinced them that they were too severely punished by our allies after the war. He blames us, and the Brits. And, he has another angle to win him support."

"The Jews!" someone put in.

"Precisely," continued Tolan. "Nothing rallies people around a cause better than naming a common enemy to blame for the woes of the nation. Hitler's two objectives appeal to many Germans: rid the country of the Jews, and win back the lands that rightfully belong to Germany."

"But he won't stop at that, will he?" asked someone.

"You're damn right he won't", said Tolan with energy. "Do you stop gambling when you're on a winning streak and have money on table? Believe me, my friends, we have lost our chance to stop them, and there will be hell to pay."

Nanette, shaken by that conversation, glanced across the room to see Julian, with an inquiring look on his face. He waved and gave her a gesture which asked if she were all right. She smiled and nodded affirmatively. Nevertheless, the recent conversation and the now choking smoke led her to move outside onto the balcony, for fresh air and time to digest what she had just heard from Robert Tolan.

She wondered to herself if things were really as bad as Tolan made them out to be. Of course she had read of Germany's arms buildup, but accepted the argument of many that it was necessary to provide a defense against Bolshevism coming out of Russia.

"God knows we have enough problems with Communists here in France," she thought.

Beginning to shiver despite the warmth of the air, she found a stool and sat, breathing in the fresh air, and resting her tired legs. A few minutes later, sensing that someone was standing behind her, she turned her head to find Paul Moreau.

"Getting damn stuffy in there," he said, slurring his words.

"Yes, and I needed to sit out a few dances.' she replied.

He moved closer, his body touching hers, and she could smell the strong odor of alcohol, and feel his breath on her neck.

"Well, it always gets like that. Shows that my friends are having a good time," he said.

"It seems to me that your guests are enjoying themselves," offered Nanette.

"How about you, are you having a good time?" he asked, now with his hands on her shoulders.

"I am," she answered, swiveling off the stool and stepping back against the railing, facing him. "But I think we will be leaving soon. I've had a busy day."

"Oh, come on. The night is still young. You're a big girl now. Why leave when things are just starting to get, friendly."

He said the last word with a wink and a sly smile, then stepped forward and tried to kiss her. She turned her face aside, and he grabbed her by the shoulders trying to force her to look at him.

"Paul, stop. I don't like this, and you're hurting me." she whispered insistently.

Suddenly, he turned her around and pressed himself against her from behind, at the same time placing his arms around her, cupping her breasts in his hands. His breath came fast, and felt hot in her hair.

"Stop it, Paul, I mean it. You're drunk and out of control," she said more loudly, but without effect.

Then his hands tore away from her body and she heard a crash. She turned to see Julian standing over Paul, who rose and took a swing at Julian. Julian blocked the punch and sent a fist into Paul's face, bloodying his nose.

A crowd of guests gathered at the doors, hardly believing what they were seeing. Nanette tried to rearrange her dress and pushed through the throng, crying. Paul was spurting blood on the balcony until someone came with a towel. They led him into the flat and helped him to a sofa. Unable for the moment to speak, he pointed a figure a Julian, then made an obscene gesture, and another, meaning for Julian to leave.

Julian gathered up Louise and Nanette and said good-bye to the astonished and somewhat outraged guests.

One of them, a close friend of Julian, went to the door with them and asked: "What the hell happened out there?"

"Moreau got a bit frisky, is all," he answered. "When he wakes up sober, he'll forget the whole thing."

When they got to Julian's car, Nanette climbed inside and began to sob.

"Oh Julian, I am so sorry. I ruined the party and now I'm worried that Paul will take this out on you."

Louise put her arm around Nanette and said, "Nanette, you have nothing to apologize for. That pompous jackass is the one who should apologize, to you and to all his guests."

Julian agreed. "Louise is right. You don't invite someone to your party and assault them. His actions are inexcusable. You have nothing to be sorry for."

"But it may mean your job." exclaimed Nanette.

"Most likely, yes. But working around Paul has not been a pleasure, believe me. He struts around the offices like he is the most important person alive, when in reality, he does very little. I accidently overheard an argument one day when his father accused him of laziness, and threatened to cut his salary. Paul went on a three-day buying trip the next day."

Nanette began to calm down, grateful for both him and Louise.

"Thank you, Julian, for what you did. And, despite that nastiness, I had a wonderful time tonight. Your friends are interesting and delightful people. It's just too bad that things ended the way they did. But thank you both."

Julian's off-handed comment to his friend, that Paul, when he became sober would forget the whole affair, was wishful thinking. There was too much pride at stake for Paul. And so, on Monday morning, Paul's father called Julian into his office and apologetically told him that a slow-down in business made it necessary to make some cuts. Julian was terminated immediately.

To show his good will, the boss, who had always liked Julian and appreciated his accurate accounting, gave him a sum of money equal to a month's wages. Julian said he understood, thanked the man for his generosity, and left, wondering where he would find a new job.

He remained in Nantes for the day, visiting two businesses where he had contacts, hoping to find employment, but without success. He began to notice what he hadn't observed before: drab men loitering on street corners, numerous shops boarded up, the city and its citizens seemingly without verve or spirit. It matched his own mood, for despite his words to the contrary, he was troubled by his firing. He had liked working with the old man, and would miss their frequent conversations. Paul's version of what happened at the party must have been quite sensational for his father to agree to Julian's dismissal. What made matters worse, were the poor economic conditions all across France. Recovery from the world-wide depression had been slow. Businesses were lucky just to hang on, and very few were hiring.

Feeling depressed, Julian entered a café for lunch, brightening a bit as he saw Robert Tolan sitting at a table, gesturing for Julian to join him.

Tolan was the prototypical academic, with his thick glasses, unruly hair, and rumpled clothing. What attracted people to him were his bright eyes, easy smile, and sharp insights into politics.

"You were quite the hero Saturday night," Tolan said.

"Really? After breaking a man's nose and ruining the party?"

"Exactly. Everyone loves Paul's parties, but no-one loves Paul. He finally got what he deserved, we all thought. But I'm surprised to see you in the city. Thought you might get sacked . . ."

"I was," replied Julian miserably. "Right when I went in to work. The old man was generous, though."

"Always liked the old fellow," remarked Tolan. "I advised him on a number of ventures and he responded gratefully. How he got such a shit for a son, I'll never know. Probably takes after his Austrian mother. Ever meet her?"

Actually, I never did. Saw her once or twice, but was never introduced. Word is, she's a cold potato."

Julian, turning serious, lowered his voice. "Robert, I know what you write is an honest appraisal of what you've seen, but are things really as bad as they seem, or is there a way out for us?"

"Believe me, they are much worse than you can imagine. The Nazi death squads, the concentration camps, new laws limiting freedoms, the crackdowns on political opposition, and the crusade against the Jews and dissenters is all frighteningly real, and getting more serious every day."

Julian sat quietly for a few minutes, fingering his glass. He looked out of the window, at the people passing by, and wondered if what was happening in Germany could happen here.

"Do you honestly think they will attack us again?" he asked.

"Yes."

"But what about the Maginot Line. Won't it hold?"

"Consider this, Julian. Where did Germany's invasion come from in 1914?"

"Through Belgium."

"And where does the Maginot Line end today?"

"At the eastern edge of the Belgian frontier with France. Point well made," answered Julian grimly.

"But that's not the whole point," continued Tolan. "The Maginot Line, for all its sophistication and vaunted strength, is a relic. It might have served us in 1914, but not today."

"Why do you say that?" asked Julian, resting his chin on his hands, elbows on the table . . .

"Do you remember reading about Germany's part in the Spanish Civil War last year?"

Hitler used it as an excuse to carry our maneuvers with his own forces, helping Franco win. And the weapon which terrorized the Republican army the most was the Stuka dive bomber. Hitler has a whole arsenal of new aircraft. Even if our line completely encircled us, it might stop ground troops, but it can't stop bombers."

Julian sat quietly, sweating, looking off into space, dispirited anew. He looked up at Tolan's nodding head, his thick glasses, graying hair, pursed lips.

"What can we do?" Asked Julian, his mind in a turmoil.

"Fight! When the time comes, we must fight. Whether our leaders have the stomach for it or not, those of us who love France, must fight."

He paused, then rose from his chair.

"But for now, my friend, I must get back to work, and you must find a job. I'm sorry I am not in a position to offer you anything. In a poor economy, economists are not highly valued. When things turn around, we are heroes. Such is my life. Take care."

CHAPTER 3

NANETTE SAID NOTHING about Saturday night's row to her parents, but worried all week what the repercussions had been for Julian. Several times she phoned his flat with no answer. The one person in whom she did confide was Sister Danielle, whom she knew would understand her feelings. Danielle agreed that it was probably right not to alarm her parents, and to let Julian be the one to recount whatever the week might bring.

The occasion for that was Friday evening, when Julian made his usual family visit. Paulette had prepared a succulent roast of lamb, served with new potatoes and Brussels Sprouts.

The dining room, as always, brought a feeling of warmth and love. Its walls were hung with prints of paintings by Goya, the windows and chairs hung with Spanish lace brought by Paulette from her place of birth.

Geraud asked the question which was the standard each Friday at this time.

"Tell us, Julian, how were things this week?"

Nanette, who had kissed Julian and hugged him firmly when he arrived, had been fidgeting all through the meal. Now she waited with worrisome eyes at what Julian might say, knowing how much he must have dreaded this moment.

Julian cleared his throat, tried to put on a bright smile, and answered his father's innocent question.

"To be honest," he began, "it was not the best of weeks. For a while now, the books at Moreau's trading house have shown a serious down-turn in business. What I rather expected might happen did come about this week. Monsieur Moreau had to cut back on his staff, and let me go. He paid me a handsome gift, but now I am looking for new employment."

Paulette's hands dropped into her lap with a smack.

"Oh Julian," she cried, "My poor boy. You were such a faithful worker. How could he. What will you do now?"

Before he could reply, Nanette learned forward in her chair and added, "Dear Julian, I too, am so very sorry."

Paulette, her motherly instinct to soothe and protect asserting itself, said,

"Julian, you must come home. You will find something here in Cande. Those self-important city people have no feelings. Stay here until you find something."

Geraud, whom Julian thought might be the first to voice his outrage and disappointment, sat quietly while his wife and daughter continued to commiserate with his son. He cleared his throat, stood and raised his wine glass.

"To better days ahead," he shouted, to the bafflement of the others.

The three of them, not responding to his puzzling toast, looked at him as if he were drunk, or crazy.

"Papa, what are you saying? Are you all right?" asked Nanette, her arms outstretched in unbelief at what she was hearing.

"Better than all right." Geraud replied. "The best I have ever been. And now I will tell you why."

He took a long drink from his glass, set it down, and put his hands on the table, palms down. His eyes shone brightly and he had a mischievous smile on his face.

"I have been planning to have a talk with all of you for some time, waiting for the right moment to arrive. And now, with what has happened, is the time. First, Irene, my long-time book-keeper—with me for eighteen years—has given her notice. Believe it or not, at fifty years of age, she is getting married, to her dentist, whose wife died two years ago. He is retiring and wants to travel, and so, she said yes. She's leaving in two weeks. Therefore, I need a new book-keeper, and a helper with other things. Julian, I offer you the job for as long as you want it."

Julian raised his hands in the air, got out of his chair, and gave his father a hug.

"Thank you, Papa," he said, "To be honest, I have been looking all week for employment and there is nothing available."

Paulette sat in wonderment, her mouth agape, unable to find words to speak. She rose and went to stand beside Geraud, putting an arm around him kissing him on the forehead.

Nanette clapped her hands in joy and blew kisses to both men. "Papa, that's a wonderful offer," she said. "Julian will be an excellent accountant for us. And what fun it will be to work together. A true family business. But you said Julian would be helping with some other things. What did you mean?"

"That is the second thing. A very big thing that I have been waiting to discuss. It mostly concerns you; a big decision for you."

"You aren't trying to marry me off to someone, I hope," she asked in jest.

"Well," he replied with a turn of his head, "to be honest, old Pierre Durat has had his eyes on you for years. Think of what a beautiful honeymoon you could have riding on his handlebars."

Everyone broke out in laughter, then Geraud sat down and looked seriously at Nanette.

"Do you remember the visit we had from Emile Tarrand a few weeks ago—of course you do. Since then we have had several conversations on a subject concerning you."

"About me? Papa, how could that be?" asked Nanette, wondering how this could be true.

"Wait, and I'll explain myself," replied Geraud.

"Monsieur Tarrand has seen you and watched your work carefully, and has been quite impressed. When he was here I took the liberty of showing him some designs from your sketch-book, because that was an area of your talents about which he knew very little. He was amazed that such ideas could come from some-one so young. But I assured him that you have been a part of the fashion world for quite a while. The point is, he wants to make you an offer to come and work with him, in Paris, as his design associate. Not as his assistant, but as his associate, which means, you and he together in the selection process."

Nanette, overwhelmed beyond words, sat with her eyes wide, and heart pounding. Before she could think of what to say, Geraud continued.

"He also wants you to model some new lines."

"Model!" exclaimed Nanette, "He has a hundred women more beautiful than I to display his dresses. People would think him deranged."

"He certainly doesn't agree with that, nor do I. Some, really only a few, as beautiful as you, perhaps, but none with the combination of style, talent, and looks that you present. And those are his words, by the way, although I fully agree."

"As do I," remarked Julian, raising his glass.

"Oh, stop it. This is all too much," retorted Nanette. "I respect and admire M. Terrand, but why does he need me. Is there something else?" she asked warily.

Paulette, wondering the same thing, said, "Geraud, is he, do you think, wanting Nanette for something else?"

Geraud smiled and shook his head.

"If I thought so, I would never even agreed to speak about his offer. But, my dears, I thought you already knew. M. Terrand is of a, ah, different persuasion. I assure you, Nanette would be perfectly safe with him."

"And so, my sweet," he said, looking at Nanette, we don't want your answer now, but will you give his offer some thought? What do you think?"

"I'm completely stunned by all this. I would never in a million years have thought something like this would come my way. It's a great chance for me, I know this, and with Julian agreeing to be here with you, it makes it easier for me to leave. But I still don't know what to say. I would have to speak with M. Terrand, get more details, and learn what he expects of me."

"Of course," replied Geraud sympathetically, "And he has suggested just that. Whenever you are ready, he will bring you to Paris to meet with him. He'll see to your lodging, and you know it will be first-class. So, think about it, and talk to me."

Think about it was all that Nanette did in the hours and days which followed. It was in her dreams and in her musings, as she tried to envision what changes her life would experience. She weighed the positive and negative sides of the move, and, apart from missing the enjoyment of working with her family, could see no down-side to the proposal. She knew however, that before coming to a decision, she would have to lay out the whole scenario to Sister Danielle.

Danielle was out of town, so a few days passed before Nanette and she had a chance to meet. When they finally came together, and Nanette told her friend of the offer, the nun crossed her hands on the table where she sat and nodded her head, in understanding of the heavy decision facing Nanette.

"I see what a great opportunity this is for you, my dear. I know you are not foolish, but the idea of living in Paris must be a great attraction; one might even say, a great temptation."

She played with her wine glass as she thought of what to say next, then continued.

"I won't tell you that I know much about the ways of business and commerce. I only see them from afar. I suppose one could make a case for going to Paris with this popular person, as a way of advancing yourself. For, if you turn him down, such an offer is not likely to come your way again. And then, you will have to be content to be as you are, your father's assistant. Not a bad thing, of course, but you are a woman of many talents and skills, and perhaps Cande is too small for you."

"Yes, Danielle, that's what I struggle with. I'm not an ambitious person—I'm happy and contented here—but I wonder if I will still be five or ten years from now. And I wonder if I might look back with regrets if I refuse this offer."

"I have often heard the advice, 'Follow your heart'," said Danielle, "But I can't say it is always the best way. The heart can be a fickle thing, prone to emotions which don't last. Bring together your heart, your keen mind, and what your trust in God has to say to you. Weigh the alternatives, present and future, and then make your decision, and make it without regrets."

"I have been trying to do just that, but it is still difficult. One thing I tell myself, is that, if I go, and after one year find it not to my liking, I can always come home. Surely M. Terrand won't make me sign a long-term contract."

"Yes, I suppose you can look at it that way," said Danielle slowly, "It gives you and escape. But if you go into it that way, I think you will not be putting your whole self into the venture. If you say yes, do it with all your energy. And make it lead to something great and wonderful for yourself."

The meeting in Paris took place ten days later. In a prior telephone conversation with her, Terrand's secretary gave Nanette a briefing about what to expect, and the kind of clothing to pack.

The limo came for her on the day and time arranged. As she took her seat in the luxurious vehicle, she nearly shook with excitement. She had little idea of what to expect, but knew it would be one of the most important days of her young life. The limo delivered her to a lovely hotel not far from Terrand's offices and show rooms, in a fashionable district of Paris. Her afternoon arrival gave her time to bathe and dress for dinner at what Jerome said would be a fine restaurant.

"Look your very best," he said with a smile, "Emile wants to show you off tonight."

When Jerome left, Nanette looked around the brightly lit, large, and tastefully decorated suite. On the table was a bouquet of flowers and a note welcoming her to Paris, hoping she found the rooms comfortable, and reminding her to be ready at eight. She danced into the bed-room where there were more flowers, and a luxurious robe lying across the bed. She had to pinch herself to see if she was dreaming.

There was a knock on the outer door, which Nanette answered to find a bell-hop with her luggage, and a woman of her age dressed as a maid. Her luggage was placed in the bed-room, and the bell-hop, with a smile and a tip of his hat, left before Nanette could offer him a tip.

The maid stayed behind, and introduced herself.

"I am Renee. How may I help you?"

When Nanette was searching for something to say, Renee smiled and added:

"If you like, I will unpack your bags, prepare your bath, and help you dress."

"Oh, yes, thank you," answered Nanette, totally unprepared for such attention. "Please hang my dresses."

Not knowing quite what to do while Renee went about her tasks, Nanette went to a window and looked out on the busy avenue below. Traffic sounds rose to her ears, the flow of autos, and the honking of horns by those impatient to get home. It was such a contrast to Cande, where life moved at a slower pace and, people were more considerate of others. Lights were coming on in the shops across the way, and the walks were filled with pedestrians hurrying this way and that. There were many cyclists, and she smiled as she thought of Pierre Durat on his old bicycle, and how bewildered he would be trying to navigate such busy streets.

"Mademoiselle." Renee called from the other room. "Excuse me, but do you wish me to lay out a particular dress for this evening?"

Nanette walked into the room as the maid added:

"These are very beautiful dresses. You have excellent taste, and on you they must look magnificent."

"Thank you," replied Nanette, blushing. "I'll wear the red one, I think, and the matching shoes."

When Renee finished her tasks, Nanette thanked and dismissed her, then slipped gently into the warm bath, into which the maid had poured a fragrant oil. As she lay back, letting her tight muscles relax, she wondered if she could ever get used to such treatment.

At precisely eight o'clock Terrand's limo driver came to her door and escorted her to the car. Nanette was surprised to find the streets still crowded with vehicles. After a ten-minute drive, the car stopped at what looked more like a mansion than a restaurant. Only a very small plaque next to the entry identified it as "Maison Philippe". As the limo stopped, a valet opened the door for Nanette, while the driver came around and escorted her to the steps of the restaurant. The door swung open to reveal Emile Terrand and Jerome waiting. Terrand took her hand, and kissed it.

"Mlle. Lemond, welcome, welcome," said Emile effusively. "You look utterly ravishing. I hope you found your accommodations comfortable. Jerome, take her wrap. Isn't it a wonderful evening? There are some friends here I want you to meet, then we'll have some dinner and have a little talk afterward. Do you like salmon? I hope so. It is delicious here. The chef is quite superb, and the wines, oh my."

Emile went on like that as they crossed a room filled with diners, several of whom waved and blew him kisses. The three climbed a short flight of stairs, entering a smaller room with a single, long table, filled with gleaming silver and crystal. Nanette, believing that she and Emile would be dining together, or perhaps with one or two of his friends, was astonished to find eight other men and women around the table. She became very nervous as the men rose, their faces displaying obvious delight at having this gorgeous woman in their midst

She was indeed a picture of beauty. Her dress was made of red silk-taffeta, with matching bows on the top edge, a fitted bodice and waistline, the knee-length skirt covered with silk-tulle. Her shoes were red satin pumps, accentuating her long, curvaceous legs. She had taken special pains to apply her makeup just right, and her features glowed.

Nanette was introduced by Terrand as someone who might be joining his firm, which she was certain everyone there had been told beforehand. As the names of the guests were given to Nanette, she recognized two of them. One was a model, probably in her mid-twenties, whom Nanette had seen at showings several times. She wore a dress of diaphanous fabric, which covered but barely disguised her firm breasts. She had wide lips, heavily colored, and her hair was pinned up, holding a glittering tiara. She smiled cooly, offering a slight nod of her head.

Next to her stood a middle-aged gentleman whom Nanette knew was Emile's business partner. He smiled and welcomed her with a sweeping hand gesture. The others, an equal number of men and women, were new to Nanette by face, although one name stood out. He was Baptiste Chillon, an art-critic known throughout France.

Once seated, the waiters plied them with wines. Other, empty glasses, now being removed, indicated that the guests had already had cocktails while awaiting Nanette's arrival.

The several courses of the meal were artfully prepared, and the accompanying wines, refreshing, if heady. Conversation was light and easy, no-one asking Nanette about her background, but including her in the conversation. Baptiste told of a recent journey he had made to Munich for what was called the "German Day of Art", to view what artists were producing under the severe strictures of the Nazi regime.

"Probably paintings of fat women peeling potatoes." someone quipped, drawing laughter.

"You might think so," replied Baptiste. "Their models are certainly more fleshy than ours, and the subject matter more utilitarian, but I was amazed at the quality of the works and the amount of total nudity. One thing the Nazis haven't lost is an appreciation of the human figure."

As he ended the last sentence, he raised his glass and nodded to Nanette, turning her face to a scarlet.

Sensing that the mention of Nazis might turn the conversation to things political, Emile changed the subject, asking if anyone was planning to attend the symphony on the coming weekend. This led to a rash of comments and opinions as to the skill of the orchestra and the selections they had recently performed. The conversation lasted until it was nearly eleven, when Emile rose and thanked his guests for coming. The party followed his lead, moving toward the door, telling Nanette how pleased they were to meet her, and thanking Emile for the lovely evening.

When the eight had gone, Emile said, "Nanette, you were wonderful. These are my closest friends and associates. I wanted you to meet the people who surround me, and them to meet you. But I am sure that you are very tired. My driver will take you to your hotel. Why don't we meet tomorrow at ten. I'll send the car for you at 9:45. Is that good for you?"

"Certainly," answered Nanette. "And thank you for this evening. I was very nervous and didn't know what to expect, but everyone made me feel comfortable. I had an enjoyable time."

So many thoughts and emotions circuited through Nanette's mind as she prepared for sleep, that she found it difficult to relax. The conversation of the evening had been stimulating, and it was as clear as it was expected, that Emile's friends were well-read and intelligent. She wondered if such dinners were de rigeur for the group, or if this was a special occasion arranged for her, and their, benefit. If she did accept Emile's offer and move to Paris, she hoped she wouldn't be expected to eat so sumptuously very often, or to have to bear the cost of entertaining others in turn.

She also wondered what the cost was for renting a flat, and the cost of transportation if she had to travel very far to work. It was certain that she could not afford to live in a neighborhood such as this. She began to realize that she had many more questions to ask Emile than she had previously thought. She had been fortunate to live at home in Cande, sparing herself the cost of housing, but now that good fortune and innocence was coming to haunt her. Resolving to have as many of her questions as possible answered the next morning, she rolled over, said a prayer, and let sleep finally draw her in.

The offices of Emile Terrand were located on the top floor of a three-storied building on a busy avenue. The first floor contained his show-rooms and the gallery where his models strutted when buyers were brought together. Nanette and Geraud had been there several times. The second floor, brightly lit by large windows on the south, was divided into an area where Emile worked on designs, and a large cutting room. Nanette joined Emile, Jerome and his partner in one of the business offices, after touring the second floor and speaking with several of the employees. The impression she received was one of an industrious work-force who enjoyed their tasks and went about doing them with great satisfaction.

Emile's office was spacious, the walls covered photographs. Some showed models wearing his creations, others of Emile with notable female personalities for whom he had designed dresses.

They sat at a small table, coffee having been brought, with small pastries. Emile began.

"My dear, I have had my lawyer prepare a contract, to serve as a basis for our discussions. It is, of course, malleable, and I want you to speak forthrightly regarding any parts of it with which you disagree or wish to amend. Forgive me for speaking so formally, but in matters of this nature, I find it important to be precise, and to leave social convention for more appropriate occasions."

"Yes, I understand, and agree fully," replied Nanette.

"Good. Let us then go through the various points, dealing first with your role as my associate, and secondly, your role as a model. Please feel free to interrupt at any time. Jerome, if you please, one by one."

Jerome read through the first part of the agreement, pausing after each point to allow Nanette to ask for clarification, offer suggestions, or to reject it entirely.

In essence, the contract called for a three-year commitment from Nanette, during which time she would assume the position of design consultant, free to offer alternatives and/or additions to dress designs, including the choice of fabrics. She would also be expected to submit designs of her own. An annual monetary sum was stated for this work, which Nanette thought was quite generous. She asked questions several times, and was satisfied with the answers, a few of which came from Emile's partner.

The part of the contract dealing with modeling, called for her to appear as a model for just one year, in both the winter and summer shows, as well as at least five private showing for selected clients, of which her father had been one. It added an additional financial enticement.

When the reading of entire document was completed, and all Nanette's questions answered, she smiled and said,

"I have some practical concerns about which I need some information. I know little about the cost of living in Paris. Forgive me for asking about such mundane things, but can you give me some idea of the cost of renting an apartment, and how often I would be attending evening affairs in connection with my employment?"

"Ah, yes," replied Emile. "Jerome, I think you may have some ideas about rents."

Jerome did, from his own experience, and offered some broad ranges, depending upon the area of the city.

"If you decide to come here," he offered "I can put you in touch with an excellent agent, who will give you good advice."

"As to your social obligations," said Emile, "I will make few demands on your time. On the average, we entertain clients about once each week, not more, as a business expense. Apart from that, I hope that, in time, my friends will become yours, and that you will join us as we enjoy evenings together, such as the one last night. But be assured, that will be entirely your choice."

Nanette said she was pleased with what she had heard thus far, but was not ready to commit at this point.

"I would like to take a copy of the contract for my father and our solicitor to look at," she said, "And I should be able to let you know my answer in one week, if that is acceptable."

"Perfectly," answered Emile, his partner agreeing. "And if any questions arise, please contact me immediately. Now, let's have some lunch."

After they ate, Emile apologized for not inviting her for dinner that evening, explaining that he and Jerome were taking the train to Brussels for a meeting. Instead, he offered Nanette the service of his chauffeur for the afternoon, which she gladly accepted. Nanette met the chauffeur, whose name was Marcel, outside the building, and was asked where she wished to go. She told him she wanted a tour of the city and a few close suburbs.

As they drove, she thought to herself how interesting it was that she lived only a few hours from Paris, but had never really come to know the city. It seemed to her to be such a vibrant, exciting place, and she wondered if she could feel at home here. But, she asked herself, how could she know unless she tried. And three years isn't a lifetime.

Twilight was upon them as they drove back into the city from the west. Lights were coming on and the sight of the Eiffel Tower, bathed in light from top to bottom, took her breath away. The great arch was similarly lighted, and she understood why Paris was known as "The City Of Light".

She thought of how exciting it must be to live in such a city, where one could go somewhere different and see new sights every day of the year, never tiring of things to do.

Marcel asked what time Nanette would like to leave for home the next Morning. She told him nine o'clock would be fine. He delivered her to her hotel, and after receiving her thanks, saw her to her room and said good-night. Nanette dialed the hotel desk, asking for a table in the dining-room for eight o'clock. She then bathed, put on a modest evening dress, and went to the dining-room where her table was waiting. Heads turned as she crossed the floor and took her seat. The staff was very solicitous, informing her that M. Terrand had taken care of all arrangements, and bringing her a split of champagne with his compliments. All this attention was almost intoxicating.

She was seated with her back to a wall, which pleased her, since it was not only quite private, but allowed her a view of other guests, arriving and leaving. She had always enjoyed watching people, especially in new surroundings, trying to guess what topics couples might be discussing by noticing their body-language and facial expressions.

After giving a waiter her order, three men, dressed in dark suits, were shown to a table on her right. They seemed not to notice her as they passed and took their seats. One looked at his watch, said something to the others, and shook his head as if annoyed at someone's delay. Their language was German.

A sommelier arrived at their table, suggesting some wines, which they discussed among themselves before making a selection.

Nanette's salad arrived, and as she sampled it, another man, dressed similarly to the other three, approached their table. It was almost comical to see them jump to their feet as one, and stand erect, almost at attention. The newcomer nodded, shook each one's hand, and took his seat., the others following suit

This man seemed slightly younger than the others, perhaps in his early thirties. He was tall, rather good-looking, with brown, wavy hair, and a ruddy complexion.

As soon as they gave their dinner orders, the men leaned forward to listen to the late-comer. Nanette was just out of hearing, but she could tell that the conversation was of a serious nature. She had passed on the soup, but her salad was delicious, as was the filet of Dover Sole, one of her favorite dishes. She had coffee, some brandy, then rose to leave. As she passed the table of Germans, their conversation stopped. The tall man turned his head toward her as she passed, and nodded. She nodded in return and retired to her room, wondering what sort of plot those men might be planning. She laughed to think how naively suspicious she was, realizing that this was Paris, an international gathering place, and not Cande. She undressed, and got into bed, determined not to think about the contract, and found falling asleep much easier than the night before.

⚬≪⚬

They drove home in a rain storm, which lasted throughout the journey. The drabness of the day contrasted with her mood, which was cheerful and bright. She reflected on the meeting with Monsieur Tarrand and his associates, and on the questions she had asked. She felt a sense of confidence in her understanding of what was offered her, and satisfied that she had asked the right questions. While she still felt there was much to learn and discover, even the two days she spent in Paris seemed to mature her. She looked forward to sharing it all with her family.

"Its good to be home again," thought Nanette after saying good-bye to Marcel in Cande, and receiving a warm greeting from her parents. She unpacked her things, then went with her father to La Belle Femme, where she stayed until closing. After dinner she shared her experiences in Paris with Geraud and Paulette, and asked about Julian. She also produced a copy of the contract proposal, asking Geraud to look it over, and whether he thought it should be reviewed by a lawyer.

"Yes, my dear," he asserted. "In such matters I always rely on the advice and expertise of M. Pigan. If you like, I'll send it over to him in the morning, or perhaps you would like to do so yourself."

"I would, Papa, if you will call him beforehand."

Paulette, who had been fidgeting throughout Nanette's description of her visit, was worried about the whole affair. She liked having her daughter at work in the family business, where she was close and safe, and enjoyed the warmth of their weekend dinners. Like many people whose whole lives were lived in small towns, she was wary of large cities. So, sensing Nanette's positive attitude toward the offer, she wanted to know more precisely her daughter's feelings on the matter.

"I wish I could tell you that I have come to a decision," said Nanette, "but I haven't. Paris, as you might imagine, sweeps you off your feet. There are so many things to do, so much to see, and so many interesting people to meet. But I don't want those things, which are so appealing to the senses, to be my only criteria. I want to think seriously about the job itself, and whether I will be satisfied with my work. It is a bit frightening to think of working with Emile—that is, M. Terrand."

"Yes, my dear one," said Paulette tenderly, becoming more sympathetic, "but where will you live, and take your meals? Have you asked about those things also?"

"Jerome, who is M. Terrand's secretary, offered to put me in touch with a rental agent who will assist me in finding an apartment somewhere in a safe area, but not too far from the offices." replied Nanette. "And as for eating, I will take your recipes, Momma, and do my best."

The week moved much more swiftly than Nanette liked. She delivered the contract to Monsieur Pigan and arranged to meet with him Friday morning. In the meantime, she worked as usual in the dress-shop. But there was a difference. As she went about her normal duties of arranging dresses, dusting shelves, and listening to the petty gossip of the women customers, she felt a sense of boredom and discontent. When a particular elderly woman asked to try on a fourth dress, Nanette became impatient and said something unkind to her. The woman left in a huff, and, in that instant Nanette realized how inconsiderate she had been. She rushed after the woman and apologized profusely.

When she returned to the shop, she asked herself, "What is wrong with me? Two days in Paris and I am becoming a snob. Is that what I want? Oh, God, why did I let myself be drawn into this predicament?"

She decided to once again talk to Sister Danielle. The nun was in the church, changing paraments for the Feast of the Blessed Virgin Mary, coming the next day. She and Nanette hadn't been together since Nanette's return from Paris.

"Can I help you with those linens?" offered Nanette.

"Nanette," called Danielle happily. "It is so good to see you. So, you survived two whole days in Paris. Tell me all about it."

Nanette told her first about the lavish attention paid her by M. Terrand, then about the job offer, and finally her impressions of the city itself. She then had tears in her eyes as she revealed what had happened in the store, and her act of rudeness toward a customer.

Her friend listened and then said: "It was an unfortunate lapse of courtesy, but think of what then happened. You didn't just let it go and try to justify you words. No, immediately you realized what you did was wrong, and acted to correct it. The woman, if she has any sense of compassion, appreciated your apology, and thought you a better person for it."

"I truly hope so," responded Nanette.

"You are usually a very patient person," noted Danielle, "Why do you think you became so irritated at that woman?"

"I've asked myself that very question. For one, I think its because I'm edgy and upset with myself for not being able to make a decision about Monsieur Terrand's proposition. For another, and I'm almost afraid to say it, after my trip to Paris and seeing the work being done by Terrand, I feel bored and not challenged enough. Does that make sense."

"Oh yes. You may remember what I said about Paris—a temptation as well as an opportunity. You just got a small taste of it and now you hunger for more. And, if you believe deeply that it is what you want, then you must go, or be forever unhappy."

She smiled and took Nanette's hands in hers.

"Remember, angels will always be watching over you. Say your prayers, go to Mass, and stay in touch with your Danielle. Now I must complete my work. I will see you here tomorrow, yes?"

Nanette assured her that she would be there for Mass, thanked her for her advice, and left. She saw things clearer now, and felt a burden had been lifted from her shoulders. As she walked back to the shop, she did something she had not done for quite some time: she began again to sing.

Geraud's lawyer had read through Emile's contract offer, having only a few minor suggestions. He told Nanette he thought it was a generous and forthright offer. She felt relieved to hear this, one more obstacle out of the way to her final decision. That came on Friday evening, as the family gathered for its usual meal.

Nanette told her loved ones of her meeting with the lawyer, and her conversation with Sister Danielle . . .

"You all know how much I have agonized over this matter. I have finally made a decision. I am satisfied that Papa and Julian can take care of things here very well without me, and I believe that Monsieur Terrand's offer is a good one for me. It will test me in areas I don't know much about, and hopefully, I will take with me some new ideas to enrich his business. So, if I have your blessing, I will give him my answer tomorrow."

They all assured her of their good wishes and prayers, hoping that she would be safe, happy, and very successful. They also wanted her assurance, which she gave, that she would stay in touch and come home to visit often.

"One moment!" shouted Geraud, who left the room and returned with a bottle of expensive champagne, saved for a special occasion. Paulette went for glasses as Geraud undid the wires. The bottle opened with a pop, the wine was poured, and a toast proposed.

"To our dear, sweet, Nanette," offered Geraud. "May her beauty, kindness, and talents change Paris forever. God bless and keep you."

Two weeks later, she said her tearful farewells, and left, both excited at what lay ahead, and a bit sad to be leaving her home. Only now did she realize how very much her mother and father meant to her. As did most young people, she had always taken their love and care for granted. She prayed that her success in Paris would mean as much to them as to her, and that in some way, she could repay their love.

CHAPTER 4

AS PROMISED, NANETTE kept in touch with her family and Danielle, writing to each once a week. In late September—the year was 1937—she wrote to her friend.

> Well Danielle, it's certainly a whirlwind here. Today marks the end of month one for me. My mind is spinning with the names of people I've met, and with locations, fabrics, buyers and suppliers. My apartment has become more comfortable with the addition of new furnishings, and you wouldn't believe what great meals I have made for myself. So, am I happy? Yes, because M. Terrand continues to entrust me with new tasks each week, and compliments me on the job I am doing. Oh, I forgot to tell you; I have my first modeling assignment next month, with styles for spring. I am so excited, since two of them are my own designs.
>
> And now, a little secret. I have a date for Saturday with a friend of Emile, whom I met twice at parties. He seems quite nice, and has a government job, but I'll tell you more later. Be well!
>
> Nanette

Nanette's new friend was Lucien Salan, a tall man in his late twenties, with short, dark hair and a serious demeanor which belied his fun-loving nature. His position, which he didn't explain to Nanette, and the difficult times France was facing, occupied his mind most of the time. When Nanette met him at one of Emile's parties, she wondered if he was gay, but learned this was not the case when he asked if he might take her out. They agreed on a date and where to meet.

Lucien selected a nice restaurant for dinner, after which they walked along the banks of the Seine, enjoying the warm evening. When Nanette found the courage to ask him what his position was with the government, she was surprised to learn that he was one of four deputy directors of the Ministry of Finance.

"That sounds impressive," remarked Nanette, "but what exactly does a deputy director do? I'm sure you don't count francs all day."

"No," he said smiling, "but I do try to keep track of how many francs we have in the treasury. My main job is to monitor the income from taxes, and the outflow of the expenses for running the government."

"I see," said Nanette. "And how is the nation doing? With the number of unemployed, it must be difficult to bring in enough taxes."

Lucien, surprised and pleased that his date might have the slightest interest in government affairs, warmed to the subject.

"Stop me when I begin to sound boring," he said. "But yes, these last two years have been especially difficult. But I believe we are making the right changes to end this recession. It won't happen tomorrow, but surely in the new year. We have to find a way to cut the costs of production, so we can compete more effectively in world markets. Unfortunately, we will certainly see a rise in taxes for all of us."

"Are you saying France is in trouble?" asked Nanette.

"Our credit rating is at the bottom," answered Lucien, "and with the specter of Germany rattling its sabers again on the frontier, there is great concern that we couldn't finance another war if it came to that."

"Lucien, you're not boring me, but I am becoming frightened. Thank you, but let's talk about more pleasant things. Have you brothers and sisters?"

They talked and walked, and he kissed her lightly on the cheek when they said good-night, he expressing the hope that he might call on her again, to which she agreed.

———— ✆ ————

As the year wore on, Nanette immersed herself fully in her work. She hadn't realized how complicated a Europe-wide business could be, but was glad to learn. She modeled dresses at the fall show, wearing one on her own designs, which drew many positive reviews. Emile was asked repeatedly who this ravishing new model was, to which he gladly answered, "My associate, Nanette Lemond."

The Paris Exposition of 1937 brought hordes of people to the city, many of whom visited Emile's pavilion. The whole firm worked for weeks to put it together. First, they had an architect design the space. Next they had artists paint backdrops of gardens and fountains. Lastly, were the decisions about which models would display their fashions, how frequently, and in which dresses. The exhibit achieved great success, and enhancing Terrand's reputation alongside such names as Lanvin and Shiaperelli. Orders for Terrand's fashions soon arrived from many nearby countries.

Despite the overall popularity of the Exposition however, the nations economy continued to slide, until the Minister of Finance was replaced. His successor set into motion a series of reforms which revitalized the economy. Industrial production soared in the next year, employment improved greatly, and people began to once again have confidence in their government. The fashion business rode the roller-coaster better than many, proving again that the wealthy didn't allow distractions to keep them from enjoying the finer things in life.

Nanette came to know Paris in ways she never thought possible. Her wide-eyed early enthusiasm gave way to a savvy about areas to avoid, good places to eat and shop, and how to deal with those who sought to take advantage of the ingenue. She continued to see Lucien, but less frequently, as the change of leadership in his branch of the government required him to work overtime to keep up with new programs.

Emile was immensely pleased with Nanette's work, and, as 1938 came to a close, he gave a dinner in her honor, crediting her work with the fact that the company, despite what was happening all around it, was staying afloat and had the prospect of new international outlets.

A year-end bonus enabled her to lay aside some funds, which she used to plan a party of her own, in the spring, inviting those she had come to know well and whose company she enjoyed. Lucien was able to attend, which pleased her very much, as well as Emile, his business partner, and others.

Her visits home became less frequent, due both to the press of business and her desire not to miss the weekend social scene. She still wrote to Danielle, usually once a month, but the content of her letters were banal and lacking in particulars about her life. Danielle, noticing a change in her friend's attitude, worried about her, and decided to give her a call, which she did late one evening.

"Hello, Nanette here."

"Nanette, it is Danielle. I have wanted for so long to speak with you. Can we talk now?"

"Oh, Danielle, How are you, my dear? Yes we can talk. I'm afraid I haven't been very faithful in writing lately. We are so very busy. Time simply flies away."

"I'm sure you are busy, you have always been in such a rush. But tell me truthfully, how are you, how is your life?"

Nanette was somewhat annoyed at the tone of Danielle's question. She felt she had revealed as much as she wished to in her letters. Why did Danielle need to know more?

"I'm just fine, Danielle, really fine. I enjoy my work and have new friends, with whom I am quite happy."

"Ah yes, new friends," said Danielle. "Of course you always made friends easily, and in a large city it is important to have friends close at hand. Are they all people in the dress trade?"

"Not at all," replied Nanette, becoming impatient with the questions. "Emile has contacts with people in many areas, as do I. Artists, bankers, politicians, government officials, all these are our friends."

"And Lucien? You only mentioned him a few times in your letters. Are you still seeing him?"

Nanette, now irritated, felt she had answered enough questions, and wanted to end this conversation.

"I still see him, but not as often. He works long hours. And now Danielle, I really must ring off and get some sleep. Tomorrow I go to Brussels for a meeting. I promise to write more often."

"Ye, please do, when you can," said Danielle. "I worry about you, and pray for you every day. Stay safe. Good-night."

Nanette placed the phone on the receiver and began to cry. She didn't know why. Was it the sound of her friends's voice, so gentle and so kind? Was it that she felt herself losing touch with her roots. Was she becoming so sophisticated that the ordinary things of life held no meaning for her any more? Danielle said she prayed for her every day. Nanette couldn't remember the last time she prayed, or went to mass. Was she truly fine, as she told Danielle, or was it all on the surface? Was her high living a cover over a hole inside, an emptiness longing for something undefined?

She lay on her bed, pondering these things, recalling how content and happy she had been in Cande, and wondering if her life now was as well suited to her inner nature as she was putting on. Perhaps she needed some time away, time off from the mad scene which possessed her being, time to be with family and old friends. Just for a while. Just to put things into perspective. She would see to it as soon as she returned from Belgium.

Nanette entrained to Brussels in the company of the firms lawyer. A formerly successful dress shop in that city had gone bankrupt due to poor management, with thousands of francs owed to Terrand. His lawyer met with his Belgian counterpart, while Nanette surveyed the remaining merchandise, some of which would be returned to Emile.

The meetings took place over a period of three days. On the afternoon of the second day, someone interrupted the meeting to say that Mlle. Lemond had an urgent phone call. Thinking it was Emile, calling with some new information, Nanette excused herself and went to the phone. It was Sister Danielle.

"Nanette, it is Danielle. There is no easy way to tell you this, but your parents have been seriously injured. I won't go into details now. Can you come here immediately?"

Nanette was stunned. Her heart was racing, and she had to sit.

"Of course," she replied, in a shaky voice. "I will take the next train. What happened? How were they injured? How are they?"

"They are in St. Clair Hospital in Nantes. It was a fire, and . . ."

"A fire!" exclaimed Nanette, "Oh my God. Julian, is he all right?"

"Yes, but come quickly. There is a train leaving Brussels South in thirty minutes. Try to make it and I will meet you at the Nantes station."

"I'll make it. The station is not far from here. Oh, Danielle, pray for them."

Nanette rushed back into the meeting room and quickly explained the substance of the call and the need to get to the station as soon as possible. One of the men said he had a car outside and would take her. She thanked him and gave the key to her hotel room to their lawyer, asking him to recover her belongings and bring them to Paris when he returned.

She made it to the station and boarded the train, which left on time, as usual. It sped across the Belgian/French frontier with a minimum of fuss. Nanette sat facing a window, hardly seeing the scenes flash by, praying and hoping her parents would survive. She realized she hadn't asked where the fire occurred, assuming it was in their home, since both parents were involved. Did they lose their home as well? She wondered. So many thoughts flashed through her mind. She hadn't seen them in over a month. Why hadn't she paid more attention to their lives? Her visits home had been so infrequent and so short, that she couldn't even remember what they talked about during her last visit. They had done so much for her, and loved her so much. And she had let them down.

"Calm down", she told herself. But it was difficult to do. There was so much she didn't know.

The train arrived on schedule, with Danielle waiting. She took Nanette by the hand and rushed out of the station and into a waiting cab. Danielle put her arm around Nanette.

"My dear girl, I know what a shock this is to you, and to us all. Julian is at the hospital. He will be so comforted to see you."

"Tell me now Danielle, what happened, and how badly hurt my parents are."

"All that I know is this. Your father was home for his mid-day meal when the house somehow caught fire. Apparently the fire spread quickly, and before they could get out, they were overcome by smoke. Julian was on his way home when he saw the flames. The fire brigade had already been called by a neighbor, and together, they and Julian went in and brought your parents out. They were taken immediately to the hospital."

"How did you ever find me?" asked Nanette.

"Julian called from the hospital and asked that I contact M. Terrand's offices, which I did. A receptionist told me you were in Brussels for a meeting and gave me the listing for the place where it was taking place."

"Dear Danielle," said Nanette through her tears, "you are truly my friend, and I feel so sorry that I've neglected you, and neglected my family too."

"Just now you must be brave and strong," asserted Danielle. "What is past is over. Now we must deal with present and trust God to carry you and your family through these next hours and days."

The cab driver, told of the urgency of the drive, spared no time getting to the hospital. Inside, the air filled with the acrid smell of antiseptic, the two women asked directions, finding Julian standing outside the room of his mother. Nanette rushed to him, and they took hold of each other with a fierce embrace, tears flowing down their cheeks.

"Oh Julian," cried Nanette, "I am so sorry. How are Mama and Papa?"

Julian continued to hold her tightly. In a choked voice, he answered: "I must tell you the truth my dearest. Papa had too much smoke in his lungs. The doctors tried their best, but they couldn't save him."

Julian held on to Nanette as he felt her faint and begin to fall. Danielle moved in quickly and helped Julian move her to a chair, holding her head down to allow the blood to flow back more rapidly. A passing nurse, seeing what had happened, rushed to her desk, returning with smelling salts.

When Nanette revived, she looked wide-eyed at Julian. "Is it true? Is Papa really gone?"

"Yes, it is true," replied Julian, holding her hand.

Nanette, trying to compose herself, but with her mind in a turmoil, asked about their mother.

"She's still alive and getting treated. One of the doctors said she has not awakened since they brought her in, but they're using oxygen and some medicines to keep her stable."

Danielle placed her hand atop theirs. "Then we must pray hard." she said.

They entered her room together, Nanette gasping as she saw the dull pallor on her mother's face beneath the mask. Paulette had always been a steadying influence in Nanette's life. While her father was a dreamer, her mother was grounded in the practical matters of daily life. Nanette took one of Paulette's hands and reached out with the other to Julian. Danielle took his other hand, and Paulette's, completing the circle. Danielle offered a fervent prayer, than led them in saying the Rosary, all three feeling the intensity of the moment.

Chairs were brought into the room, allowing them to stay with Paulette through the change of nurses, deep into the night. Julian offered to go for some food, but no-one felt hungry. The earlier sounds of people in the halls were replaced by a silence which made even the ticking of the wall-clock seem loud. Paulette hadn't moved since they arrived, and their hopes that she might suddenly awaken and breathe on her own grew dimmer as the hours labored on.

At one point a nurse came and told them they could view the body of Monsieur Lemond if they wished. By that time the parish priest had arrived, and the quartet went to the morgue together. It was another overwhelming experience, made more so by Geraud's seemingly uninjured body, which gave the impression that he was only sleeping.

The priest offered the Prayers After Death, and together they prayed the Our Father. Nanette and Julian kissed Geraud's forehead, whispered that they loved him, and tearfully left.

In the early hours of the next morning, Paulette's fragile life slipped away, almost unnoticed, crushing Nanette and Julian in almost unbearable grief. They realized in that moment that their parents, their home, and all the mementos of past joys and happiness had suddenly been swept away. Now, they had only each other.

CHAPTER 5

THE LEMOND FAMILY was respected and loved by the citizens of Cande, and offers of temporary places to stay for both Nanette and Julian were immediate in coming, as news of the tragedy became known. Julian accepted the offer from Louise's parents, and Nanette from a close school friend. The double funeral and burial was held three days later, the church overflowing with people from a wide area. Emile Terrand had come to Cande the day after the deaths, and returned for the funeral. He told Julian that he was covering the costs of the funeral, and had sprays of flowers filling the chancel. He wanted Nanette to take as much time as she needed before returning to Paris, and offered to send his car for her when she was ready.

The day after the funeral the grieving brother and sister went to the site of their family home, the smell of destruction still permeating the air. Tears welled in their eyes as they realized that nothing had been saved of their life together.

The house had been nearly two-hundred-years old, in the Lemond family for six generations. Nanette closed her eyes, letting the charred skeleton whisper to her of all it had heard and seen. Crowds had flowed down this road, carrying the tri-color of the Revolution; the boots of thousands of soldiers trod the cobblestones in war after war. Horses gave way to automobiles; gas lights to electricity; out-houses to indoor plumbing. Dozens of Lemonds uttered their first cries in the rooms of the old house, and more than one took their last breath there. Now it was gone.

Julian saw something metallic laying on the ground near the former entry. He picked it up, wiping off what soot he could with some blades of grass. It was the brass plaque which had always told those arriving what to expect. It read, "Peace to all who enter here".

From there they went to LaBelle Femme, the monument to Geraud's life work. The floor inside the mail-slot was littered with scores of cards and letters, sent by friends and customers. The pair worked together to gather them and sort business mail from the condolences.

"They were loved by so many," remarked Nanette.

"And deservedly so," replied Julian. "No-one could have asked for more honest and hard-working citizens or more loving parents. What wonderful memories we have to console us."

"Julian," said Nanette, "Do you want me to come back and help you run the business? I truly would do so, if you would like it."

He took a deep breath, shaking his head from side to side.

"Nanette, I know Papa was planning to tell you this sometime soon, and I must tell you now. Since you left—and believe me, not because you left—sales have steadily declined. We asked ourselves why again and again, and finally discovered that people are terribly worried about the rising tide of unemployment, and what the next year will bring. They are simply saving their francs for what they believe will be hard times ahead. Haven't you sensed that in Paris?"

"Oh Julian, I have been so out of touch with ordinary people, that I don't know. We had a very profitable last year, and most of the people I know are having as good a time as ever. We still have parties and the cabarets seem to be filled. Maybe it's a distraction from reality, or perhaps its just that the wealthy will always find ways to enjoy themselves."

"Well, there are no distractions here," said Julian. "People are worried, and when they worry they draw into themselves and their families. They go to fewer parties, have fewer occasions to dress-up, and buy fewer clothes."

"How bad is business?" asked Nanette.

"Bad enough that Papa was closing the little gift shop and finding a cheaper line of clothing to carry. He already told Emile. Didn't he mention it to you?"

Nanette furrowed her brow in consternation.

"Are you certain he told Emile?" she asked. "He has said nothing to me. When did Papa tell him these things?"

"At least two weeks ago. I heard part of the conversation on the phone. It was just after we took an inventory and realized how much of Emile's merchandise had been unsold for months. Emile seemed to take the news well, according to Papa."

Nanette was quite puzzled. She and Emile had a great working relationship, and, while she was out of the loop on the financial side of things, everything she saw and heard led her to believe that business was moving along well. She couldn't understand why Emile had kept this from her, especially since it involved her own family. Was he trying to spare her from the reality of the situation? She resolved to confront him about it as soon as she returned to Paris.

"What will you do now?" she asked Julian, setting other thoughts aside.

"I'm not sure. Everything has happened so quickly. Papa was the heart and soul of this place. He was on a first-name basis with all our suppliers and most of our customers. Everyone trusted him, and he trusted others. Believe it or not, many of the agreements with our suppliers were done with a simple hand-shake. It drove me crazy trying to keep the accounts, but in the end the promises were kept. I don't know if I could go on that way."

"Do you think it would help if I came back?" Nanette asked again.

"I honestly don't know. I knew you would offer to do that, you sweet girl, but I'm not sure there is a future here. We would both have to find places to live, and the income is not so great. You know well that our niche was in the high-fashion trade. Once we lose that and begin carrying an every-day line, our best customers no longer have a reason to travel the distance to get here. They have their own city shops. So please, go back to your job, and when I come to some decisions I promise to let you know. I suppose you will have to come back here anyway in a short while to settle the legal matters, then we can go from there."

———⊗⊗⊗———

Nanette left on the morning train, too upset with Emile to ask for his driver. She was torn between her love and gratitude for him, and his secretiveness about her father's revelations to him. He was in his office when she arrived, and he greeted her with a warm embrace. The blood was throbbing in her temples as she tried to think of how to confront her boss and friend.

"Dear Nanette, you look so tired from your long ordeal. We have missed you and we think of you every day. Please sit and tell me how things are going."

"We are coping," she replied, but it is still hard to believe what happened."

She looked him in the eyes and continued.

"And poor Julian, he has so much to contend with, especially with a failing business. Oh, Emile, why didn't you tell me."

Emile, who had taken a seat behind his desk, now rose again and crouched beside her chair.

"I can see you are upset, my dear, I sensed it when you came in, and I understand why. So let me tell you. Your wonderful father has been one of our best customers for years. But you know that. And I considered him a friend as well. Lately, say for the past six months, he has bought almost nothing beyond one or two single dresses for a special order. I initiated the telephone conversation we had a few weeks ago, and that's when he told me his business had fallen off.

He was apologetic, owing to his excellent character, but I told him I understood and hoped that things would improve with time."

"I know all that," said Nanette, impatiently. "But why didn't you say something to me. After all, I'm not a disinterested party, you know."

"Dear girl, please," remonstrated Emile, troubled by her accusative tone. "The reason is because I made a promise to your father not to tell you. He was quite insistent that he wanted you to learn it from him. In fact, he was quite worried that you might find it out at one of our board meetings, and I assured him that I would prevent that from happening. Fortunately, or unfortunately, our board did not meet before, ah, before last week's tragic events."

Nanette reached out a hand to Emile, who took it and kissed it.

"Forgive me, Emile," she whispered, "I am ashamed at myself for thinking ill of you. You have never been anything but kind and considerate of me. It was just that . . ."

He squeezed her hand as he broke in.

"No, no, there is nothing to apologize for. Of course you would think as you did. But it is over, and we are back as before, not so?"

"Yes, we are back as before," she replied with a smile. Now let me see the rest of the financial picture. How are we doing? In January you told us we had a successful last year. Have things changed so much?"

"Sadly they have, and very quickly. The bankruptcy in Brussels was one sign, and there were others. After speaking with your father, I made some phone-calls to other shops in the Loire Valley.

Your father had mentioned a sense of fear among people as to what was to come, and this was confirmed in my conversations with others."

"How much has business dropped?" she wanted to know.

"Ten to fifteen per-cent, and I expect it to get worse once the mood here catches up with the countryside. Its strange, isn't it? Usually it is Paris which leads the national sentiment. Now, it is the other way around. Here we worry some about Germany, but the attitude seems to be "se la vie", and our life goes on. And just to prove that, I will let you in on another secret. A new cabaret has just opened, and Edith Piaf will be performing, wearing a dress I designed for her. I think you need some cheering up, so we will go to dinner together, then to her show, and I will have you meet her afterward. Will you come?"

"Of course I'll come, you dear man. You do have a way of making me feel better."

"Then, go back to your apartment, get fancied up, and I'll let Marcel know to come for you at eight. Welcome home!"

Nanette called for a cab. On the way to her apartment she thought of Emile's last words,

"Welcome home". She had not wanted to think of Paris as home. That word was reserved in her mind for the warm house in Cande where everything she loved in life had dwelt. She worried about Julian, whether he would keep the shop, or, if not, where he would find employment. The economy now wasn't any better than when she left. Perhaps the insurance money from the house, and whatever inheritance was left, might help him for a while, but what then. Only time would tell.

———— ∞ ————

It was nearly a month before Nanette returned to Cande for a meeting with Julian and their lawyer, M. Pigan. They found to their sad disappointment that Geraud, despite his good business sense, had not made a will, and had undervalued the house. The result was a meager inheritance. Leaving the ownership of La Belle Femme in limbo. They looked to Pigan for advice.

"There is no fear of losing the shop," he said, "It will stay in the family, but now under whose name? You must decide that. Julian is named as beneficiary on the insurance policy on the house, and again, what you agree to do with those funds is up to you."

Nanette and Julian looked at each other questioningly, he feeling embarrassed and she more concerned than upset.

"Julian," she said, "I have income enough from my job and some savings. The insurance money ought to be yours, and I am glad it will come to you. As for La Belle Femme, everything depends on what you finally decide to do with it. And I want that to be your decision entirely."

"We really need time to think this through," Julian said to M. Pigan. "Can we meet again in a few weeks, after we sort things out?"

"Certainly. As long as the accounts payable are kept up, there is no reason to rush, but we shouldn't let it go longer than another month."

After a date was set for the next meeting, the two left Pigan's office and went for lunch. The day was dreary and overcast, the streets nearly empty of shoppers. They were both astonished to see an old man sitting in front of one of the shops, holding his hat out, begging for money. Nanette had seen men doing this in Paris, but in Cande! It was a shock, especially when, as they walked by, the man replaced a small sign which had fallen. It read "Ancien combattant". Julian, who always had a soft place in his heart for veterans, dropped a few coins in the hat and, with tears in his eyes, shook the man's hand. Nanette took Julian's hand and squeezed it.

When they found a table in a small café, Julian, looking glum and tired, said:

"That was kind of you to say what you did about the insurance, Nanette. Truth is, I can really use the money. What small income the shop has been bringing in has all gone to pay bills. I was down to only one other employee, and I had to let her go last week. The trade just isn't there anymore. I don't know what to do."

Nanette reached across the table and took his hand.

"I know business is bad Julian. I spoke with Emile last week and he told me the same thing.

I hadn't realized it until I confronted him about what you told me. Emile likes to keep a brave front, but I'm afraid he can't do it for long."

"Is your job in jeopardy?" asked Julian.

"Oh, I don't think so. I have a contract, so the firm would have to nearly close before he would let me go, and that surely won't happen. Emile is too shrewd for that. He'll find a way through this. But about our shop. What are your thoughts."

"I'm so glad you said "our shop", because it truly belongs to us both. The thought of closing makes me feel like a failure, as if I'm letting Papa down. Yet, I see no future there as long as conditions in the country remain as they are."

"Julian, don't do this to yourself," she said sternly. "If Papa were alive, he would have to face the same problems, so don't blame any of this on yourself."

Julian took a deep breath and exhaled. A couple he knew greeted them as they passed, and former neighbor came over to tell Nanette how much they missed her. Then the two sat quietly for a while, having deep thoughts as they ate.

Julian broke the silence. "I have been thinking about joining the army."

Nanette dropped her fork midway to her mouth and looked at him in astonishment.

"The army! Julian, you're not that kind of person. I mean, can you imagine yourself shooting at someone? That's not your nature. You've never had a gun in your hand as far as I know. Of course you're strong and masculine, but to go into battle against other men. I don't understand your thinking."

"Wait." he said. "Its not the nature of many men, but they still do it to defend their country. Look at that old man out there. Who knows what he was; a teacher, a farmer, a butcher? But he did his part and France was victorious. Robert Tolan, you remember him I'm sure, is certain another war with Germany is inevitable. And he knows a lot. If that happens, I'll probably have to serve anyway, with little training. If I join now, I'll be properly trained, and perhaps will be able to choose an assignment where I don't have to be on the front lines."

Nanette shook her head, angry and frustrated at such an idea.

"Julian, please think this through more carefully. Surely there are other alternatives. I beg you, do not even consider it anymore until we see what we can do about the shop. In the meantime, I will make some inquiries among people I know in Paris. Maybe something will open up there for you."

Julian nodded, in a real defeatist mood.

Nanette continued, "I'm going to give you some francs—no, don't protest—enough to carry you through the next month. You can repay me from what you get from the insurance. Agreed?"

"Thank you, dear sister. You have always been the one with good solutions. I'm sorry I feel so badly. Yes, let's do as you proposed. Maybe a miracle will happen and sales will pick up."

Nanette returned to Paris and to her job, throwing herself into her work with vigor. Even Emile, who knew she was a working dynamo, was impressed with her renewed enthusiasm. It was clear that she wanted to do all she could to keep the business afloat, especially when she questioned Emile about a party he was planning for clients at a very expensive venue. At first he bristled at what seemed to him to be an unwanted intrusion, but realized quickly that she had the best interests of the company in mind. The party was still held, but at a more modest restaurant. Nanette called her friend Lucien, hoping he might be her escort. He told her his work had become so intense because of the poor economy that he hadn't had a day off in weeks. She went ahead with the planning, arranging for a comedian, whom she had met in one of the cabarets, to entertain after dinner. He was a tremendous hit with everyone. When the evening ended and the guests had gone, Emile gave Nanette a kiss.

"Thank you, my dear, you are so cunning," he said. "I think we could have held this affair in a barn and still made it a success. I have never had so many favorable comments. Our clients will be talking about this for a long time."

As she had promised Julian, Nanette asked among her friends and acquaintances about possible employment for her brother. No-one seemed to be hiring, not even for manual labor. One of the problems, she learned, was that the influx of refugees from Germany, including many Jewish families, had grown rapidly since the Nazis came to power. The increase in unemployment set the people's teeth on edge. Riots broke out in Paris and other large cities, demanding the exclusion of foreign elements from the country. While Jews made up only a small portion of the refugee population, they received the most harsh ridicule and treatment. Rumors abounded, fueled by anti-Semitic publications and organizations. Jews were accused of being Communists, of sapping the economy, and fomenting war against Germany.

A few weeks later Julian telephoned to tell his sister that he had come to a decision regarding the shop, and to ask her to come to Cande for a meeting. She took the train, wondering as she rode, if this would be her final trip to her home town. She felt intensely sad, both for Julian, and because Emile's business was on the verge of collapse. As the train passed the many small towns and villages, she wondered how average families were able to cope, and if they felt that sense of futility which seemed so pervasive.

Julian, carrying a brief-case, met her at the station, hugged her warmly and took her to a nearby café.

"Dear Nanette, you look so tired," he said, "and I know it is not just from traveling here. I hope what I have to tell you will not bee overly upsetting. Some news is good, some sad."

"At this point, I am ready for anything," she replied.

"Good. First, maybe the sad news. We have an offer from someone who wants to buy the shop. Not the business, because there were no buyers. But he location of the shop is, as you know, very prominent. I don't know what the man intends to do with the building, but his offer seems generous."

He told Nanette the amount that was offered, and she agreed that, under the circumstance it was a solid one.

"As for the merchandise," Julian continued, "We will have to clear it out, and for that I would need your help."

"Of course," she said, "Let me know when you are ready to do that. Oh, Julian, if that is what you call the sad news, please think otherwise. I knew we couldn't continue to keep the shop open, so I think this is good news, despite our emotional attachment to La Belle Femme. But tell me what you say is the good news."

"I have a job," he said smiling. "In fact, I'm already working. There is a small factory in Angers whose accountant died suddenly, and who needed someone with experience immediately.

A friend heard about it, gave them my name, and I started last week. I have a small flat in Angers and will move tomorrow."

Nanette clapped her hands in delight, her face lighting up with a smile Julian hadn't see in a long time.

"Tell M. Pigan to draw up the papers for the sale," said Nanette.

"I already have", Julian replied, "They need only our signatures."

He opened the briefcase, withdrew some papers, and while she read the contract, excused himself to go to the washroom. When he returned, she noticed the redness around his eyes and realized he had been crying.

"Its all right, Julian. It had to be done. This is not your fault, nor mine. Its an ending, but also a beginning. Think how fortunate we are. We have memories of wonderful parents, we both have jobs, and we're young and healthy. Now, add your name to mine, and let's put sadness behind us and celebrate with some good wine."

As it happened, it wasn't necessary for Nanette to return for the clearance of the shop's merchandise. A shop owner in Nantes, learning of the sale of the property, made an offer for all the clothing. Julian called Nanette to ask if she agreed, which she did. A month later, La Belle Femme was put to rest.

———⌘———

All other problems around the world took a back-seat to the events of September, 1938, with the German invasion of Czechoslovakia. Britain's Prime Minister, Neville Chamberlain, flew to Germany for a meeting with Adolf Hitler. Of utmost importance, was the avoidance of another great war. The two leaders agree to a meeting with other European powers in Munich later that month. There, France, Britain, and Italy reached an agreement which gave Germany a portion of Czechoslovakia in return for a guarantee that there would be no further aggression.

Parisians, many of whom had left the city in fear of a German invasion, returned to their homes and gave their lives back to normalcy. In the eyes of many, however, France should have stood firm against the Nazis, and come to the aid of the Czechs. They believed appeasement was a futile gesture, especially the Jewish population of France, who had experienced Nazi fanaticism first hand. They were right. Six months later. Hitler entered Prague and occupied the remainder of Czechoslovakia. Dark clouds hung over Europe again, as they had twenty-four years before.

Chapter 6

LIKE MOST OF their countrymen, Nanette and Emile watched helplessly as events unfolded around them. They were in a conference with other staff when Emile was called to the phone. He returned quickly and ended the meeting. Nanette caught up with him as he was preparing to leave the building.

"Emile, what is it," she asked anxiously.

"Get you wrap and come with me if you like," he answered. "I'll explain as we drive."

A cab was summoned, and once seated, Emile shared what he had just heard.

"Isaac Gluck has been arrested.' he told her.

Gluck was a political journalist whose writings excoriated the French leadership for Munich. He was a long-time friend of Emile's, and Nanette had met him on several occasions.

"Arrested!" exclaimed Nanette. "Oh Emile, what can we do?"

"I don't know. He has been taken to the Prefecture of Police for arraignment. I called my lawyer to meet us there. Perhaps we can arrange something."

"It's his attacks on the government, isn't it?" Asked Nanette.

"Yes, but it has less to do with that than the fact that he is a Jew. You know how people feel, believing the Jews are pressing us to go to was against Hitler. He's being accused of incitement."

"Well, someone needs to incite us," state Nanette forcefully. "I hate the thought of another war, but the longer Hitler is allowed to have a free hand in Europe, the stronger and more confident he becomes."

"You're right, of course," agreed Emile, surprised at her fervor. "But I fear that few of our leaders have the stomach to stand up to him."

They arrived at the Prefecture, where the politically accused were taken rather than to a local police station. Emile's lawyer was already there, having been informed that, due to matters of state security, Gluck was being temporarily held incommunicado. The lawyer had fumed to no avail, as did Emile and Nanette when given the news. They were told to check back in a few days, after formal charges were filed.

The two rode back to their offices in a depressed mood. Emile was unusually quiet as the minutes passed.

Nanette took one of his hands in hers.

"Dear Emile, I know how you must feel. Isaac is such a good person. He doesn't deserve this."

"None of us do," he said grimly. "Our once proud nation has become a whimpering pup. We are weak, and in that weakness we turn against each other rather than confront the real foe. It can only end horribly for us all."

Two weeks later, despite the please of his lawyer, Gluck was found guilty of incitement and sent to prison.

⬦

Events in Europe moved swiftly and cruelly in the next dangerous months. In a move which both surprised and alarmed the French and British, Germany, in August, signed a non-aggression pact with the Soviet Union, lessening the threat on its eastern border. Then on September first, 1939, Hitler ordered the invasion of Poland with a strike so fierce and rapid, that the Polish army was destroyed in less than a month. Two days later, France and Britain declared war on Germany.

France sent reinforcements to the fortresses along the Maginot Line, and the British landed an expeditionary force of 80,000 to deploy along the frontier with Belgium. Now France's laissez faire attitude toward German military preparations began to show clearly. The absence of a government Ministry of Munitions resulted in a dire shortage of armaments of all kind. Debates had gone on for years over the question of supplying the French army with planes, tanks and other motorized vehicles, and the opponents won out. Horses were more reliable, they argued, and did not rely on a supply of foreign oil. In the opinion of the French General Staff, the surest way to defeat an invading German army was to be on the defensive. Belief in the Maginot Line to stop a German attack was so great, that the declaration of war had only a moderate effect on life in Paris. During the next eight months of this "phony war", lights across Paris, rather than blacked out, were dimmed blue. Some families fled again to the countryside, but for most, life went on, overcast by a dread of what might lie ahead. There was still a lively night life in the city. On the Rue de Clichy, lining the street like so many monuments to hedonism, were the artistic cabarets. Drawing in the young, the rich, the famous and the voyeur, they offered an escape from the drab atmosphere which permeated daily life.

For Emile, business continued to drop, but at a slower pace. He also began spending a good deal of time away from his office, which he did not explain to Nanette, but which she was certain was an attempt to find new outlets. That explanation was confirmed, she believed, when Emile told her he had several trips to London planned, after speaking with the managers of some prominent department stores in that city. However, when she asked if he thought her input might be helpful, he told her it was too early to tell if things would work out. Such an equivocal answer concerned her, but she decided to let it go and see what developed. And so, the months came and went.

While the combined British and French forces waited for the anticipated strike, Germany realigned its forces from the east and continued to prepare materially for a great push westward. It came in April, 1940, with the invasion of Norway and Denmark, and in May when Belgium, Holland and Luxembourg were occupied. Additional allied troops were rushed to the Belgian frontier, with little effect. Breaking through near the city of Sedan, the German army pushed the allies into a small pocket at Dunkirk. While the Germans mysteriously halted their assaults, allied soldiers were frantically herded onto an armada of small ships and private vessels from England, ending all resistance in the north. The real war had come to France.

The day after "Dunkirk", Emile called Nanette into his office, where a troubled face greeted her.

"Emile, the new is bad, isn't it?" She exclaimed, her pulse racing.

"Horribly so. We held our breath for so long, and now must exhale the air of freedom and breathe in the rancid air of defeat. Please, sit, I'm afraid to end has come for us."

Nanette looked at him questioningly, hesitant to ask what she must, fearing what she might hear.

"For us? You mean for the business?"

"Yes, for the business. Let me explain."

He sat back in his chair, looking at the ceiling, as if deciding how much to tell her. The street sounds seemed unusually loud in the silence. Finally he spoke.

"Forgive me, but I have been weighing how much to tell you, my dear. Not because you don't deserve to know, but because too much knowledge may endanger you."

"Emile, please, don't treat me like a child," she said, "Tell me what is going on."

"We are all children, Nanette," he said resignedly, "I am a son and you are a daughter of France, but in the terrible hours which I am sure are coming, we are all children of darkness."

Tears formed in Nanette's eyes as she realized how deep and sorrowful Emile was affected by the invasion. But she was hardly prepared to learn what she would hear next.

"You asked me what I was planning during my trips to London, now I will tell you. Several years ago, when the Nazis came to power in Germany, and began persecuting and killing Jews, a group was formed to rescue Jewish artists, and musicians. As a person of means, and with many contacts and friends in the art world, I was approached and asked to join the group. Of course I agreed. Over the past five years we have secretly brought dozens of artists to France, from where most moved on to other friendly countries. For me, it has been a most gratifying venture."

He lowered his head and cleared his throat, Nanette sensing how emotional he was, and how difficult it must be for him to reveal this to her.

"Just yesterday," he continued, "word came through my contact that one of our operatives in Germany had been betrayed, caught, and tortured. In his terrible pain, he named the person who directed the rescues. He too was arrested, and in his office was found a list of contacts here in France. The names are all in code, of course, but knowing the effectiveness of the Gestapo, it is only a matter of time until we are all exposed."

Nanette was stunned. One part of her wanted to go to Emile and kiss him as the hero he was. The other part sat in fear of where all this was leading.

"Was London where you met with the others in the group," she asked.

"No. We never met each other, and I know only one other by a code name. My London visits really were to establish a new base for the business, as I told you, in case France should fall. And I expect that to happen within a few weeks."

"Oh my God," exclaimed Nanette. "How tragic this is. Tell me, what can I do to help?"

"I want you to help me pack what inventory we have and ship it to England as quickly as possible while the southern ports are still ours. And, my dear one, I have already been making some inquiries about a new position for you. Nothing yet, but the word is out. I have also instructed our accountant to remove the names of all our employees, including yours, and insert fictitious names. In this way, hopefully, you won't be accused of being part of my escapade. So, let's gather the staff, tell them the sad news, and get right to work."

Adolf Hitler took with him to his grave the reason why he stopped the advance of his forces and allowed the 345,000 French and British soldiers to escape from Dunkirk. But escape they did, and lived to fight another day. As the German Panzers moved toward Paris, hindered by a heroic but vastly undermanned French forces, the evacuation of Paris began in earnest.

It took Emile and Nanette a week to pack everything they wanted to save, watching daily for the news that the ports were still open. Each day, evacuations increased, and some parts of the city were left nearly empty. Nanette watched sadly as families on her street packed their belongings onto wagons and carts, to join the bewildered river of the fearful flowing interminably into the countryside. Shops were shuttered and traffic, once unbearable, became so reduced that the streets became playgrounds for the remaining children. When the Germans crossed the River Somme, even the French army began leaving Paris. The government moved its headquarters to Bordeaux, on the south-west coast. The city of lights had become a city of despair.

While they worked, Emile repeatedly urged Nanette to come with him to London, each time receiving the same response.

"It's truly kind of you to offer," she replied, "as I knew you would. But I simply can't go. For one, there is no guarantee that things will work out for you there, and I refuse to live off your generosity. But more importantly, the only family I have left, my dear Julian, is here, and I could never leave him. Your life is in danger, so you must leave, but, as you have said, I am a daughter of France, so I'll live as France lives. This madness has to end some day, and then we'll meet again."

Nanette phoned Julian as soon as she learned of his planned flight to England.

"What rotten luck," bemoaned Julian. "And what of your job? What will you do?"

"Emile has put out some feelers for me, and I'm sure I'll find something," she said, not very convincingly.

"Did he ask you to go with him?"

"Yes, you know he would, but I can't leave France. I don't even speak English, and frankly, I don't much like the British!"

"You're not staying because of me, I hope," he said.

"Well, you are my only brother, but there's more to it than that. This is our home, for better or worse. If there are tough times ahead, we'll simply have to become tough ourselves. Living in Paris has already taught me that. How are things with you?"

"Business is surprisingly good. Our company has changed from making plumbing fixtures to producing parts for tanks. I'm not involved in that end of the business, but we have hired more men, and even some women. Maybe I could get you a job here."

"No thanks," replied Nanette with a laugh, "I'll stick to other kinds of designs. I love you, brother dear. I'll ring you again soon."

<hr />

Emile left for England on June 12th. Along with many kisses, he gave Nanette a substantial sum of money to provide support until she found something. She learned later that he had also paid the rent on her apartment for the next six months. The day after he left, German tanks rolled into Paris. In Bordeaux, the leader of the government resigned, replaced by the 84 year old Marshall Petain, hero of the Great War. Petain believed the only chance France had to avoid total destruction was capitulation. His cabinet agreed. On June 22nd, 1940, in the same rail car where France had dictated the terms of the armistice in 1918, Hitler now made his demands.

Those demands stunned the nation. France was to be divided in occupied and unoccupied zones. The former consisted of the northern one-third of the country, plus the entire coast from Belgium to Spain. This zone would be manned and ruled by Nazis, while the unoccupied zone would be administered by a new government, situated in the small town of Vichy. The French army was disbanded and the French economy was to pay the costs of the occupying army.

Nanette sobbed for hours as German soldiers, tanks, and weapons stomped and rumbled down the street one block from where her apartment was located. She was disgusted to see flags with the hated Swastika appear from the windows of several houses, and to witness the joyful mood of the German soldiers as they roamed the streets. It was no secret that the Gestapo and the S.S. accompanied the army, on the lookout for any signs of resistance.

What resistance existed, was at first scattered and un-coordinated. The citizenry was stunned and dispirited. Thousands of French army troops were in England, while millions were captives of the Nazis, sent to camps in Germany. When Petain surrendered the Third Republic to Hitler, those who still held out hope for their beloved nation wondered from where new leadership would arise.

They found it in a little-known officer who had fled to England after making a valiant stand against the invaders. Charles de Gaulle, newly promoted to the rank of General, called for the nation to resist the occupation by whatever means possible. He moved with his staff to North Africa, establishing a Free French government in exile.

The resistance movement grew slowly. While most government officials, bankers, and business leaders chose to cooperate with the Nazi regime, some refused, and were imprisoned, tortured, or deported. The Germans found many French men willing to serve in a new French army, under Nazi control; some to occupy positions in government and the judiciary; and others to maintain a police force. Those wanting to resist, went underground, forming networks in the provinces, planning strategies. This movement enlisted thousands of operatives, men and women from all occupations and classes. It was dangerous work, and for those who were caught, imprisonment, or death.

Nanette missed Emile terribly, feeling suddenly quite alone and afraid. Even Lucien Salan, whom she hadn't seen for a long time, had left Paris, when the government moved to Bordeaux. She tried calling Danielle on several occasions but always found her out. Now, she phoned again and learned to her dismay that her friend was no longer assigned to the Cande parish, and no information as to her whereabouts was available. It saddened her greatly, making her wonder why the person who answered the phone couldn't tell her where Danielle had gone. Nanette was falling into a state of depression. Her natural disposition to keep busy was stymied by a lack of meaningful tasks. Day by day she sat by her apartment window, or took long walks, trying to fill her vacant hours, but not knowing where to turn.

She was just entering her apartment door when the phone began to ring. It was Baptiste Chillon, the art critic whom Nanette had met several times at Emile's parties, asking for a meeting with her. She agreed to have lunch with him the following day. They met at a nice restaurant, and Chillon was both surprised and concerned when he saw how thin she had become. He had intended to eat lightly, but ordered a hearty menu selection for them both.

"Thank you for meeting with me on such short notice," he began. "I spoke with Emile shortly before he left and he asked me to contact you occasionally, to see how you are. I intended to do so this very week, when another friend of mine asked for my assistance. This man, Jean Barras, is the owner of one of the better—no, the very best—artistic cabarets on the Rue de Clichy. His clientele is drawn from the highest echelons of society, and for that reason I have exhibited some of my art in his establishment."

Nanette was interested in what Chillon was saying, and the name of Jean Barras sounded mildly familiar, but she wondered what all this had to do with her. She sipped some wine as he proceeded.

"I'm not certain how often you have been to an artistic cabaret, and I am aware that some of them are quite rude places. But Jean's is a calm and beautiful place for people to relax and enjoy serenity, I assure you."

Nanette could wait no longer.

"Monsieur Chillon, this is all very interesting, and yes, I have been to several artistic cabarets, both rough and sophisticated. But what are you proposing?"

"Just this. Jean is looking for someone—someone as beautiful and talented as you—to sing in his club."

Nanette could hardly believe what she was hearing. A singer? A performer? Surely he was joking, or very desperate. Her amazed expression betrayed her astonishment.

"You are amazed at the offer, that I can see," remarked Chillon.

"More than amazed; unbelieving," she replied. "I have never sung on the stage. I like to sing, but I'm not a professional."

"I understand," he admitted," But I know you sing well, Emile has told me so, and just your lovely presence is a delight."

"I don't know what to say," she said, fumbling with her words.

"Of course not. It's so sudden, and I don't expect an immediate answer. But please at least consider having a talk with M. Barras. If you have the slightest interest, let me set up a time for you and Jean to meet. If you feel comfortable speaking with him, you might sing a song or two and see what happens. If nothing comes of it, you haven't lost anything but time. Will you do that?"

Nanette breathed deeply, wondering why she was so hesitant, when she was out of work and running out of money. Of course it was something so very different from any kind of work she had ever imagined, but it was an honest job, among people of the kind she had come to know in Paris. If—and it was a big if—M. Barras offered her the position, and she accepted—she certainly had the wardrobe to match her role.

"Why not." she said suddenly, nearly causing Baptiste to spill his wine. "Please arrange a meeting. I'm in limbo now, so any time will do. Just be certain that M. Barras knows I am an amateur."

The meeting took place late one afternoon, before the door of the cabaret opened. M. Barras was a pleasant-looking man, well dressed and spoken, with a moderate build, dark hair and a thin moustache. Nanette judged him to be in his mid-50s.

After introducing himself, he invited Nanette to have a seat, thanked her for coming, offered her something to drink, and got down to the business at hand.

"Let me tell you something about my cabaret," he began, "and then please ask whatever you wish. I opened four years ago, after a career as a dance instructor."

That rang a bell with Nanette, upsetting her that she hadn't remembered this man who was quite well-known. He had been the head choreographer and teacher at the respected Paris School of Dance. Little wonder that his clientele was drawn from the society pages.

"It may surprise you," he went on, "but I have always yearned to operate a cabaret. I find it exciting, refreshing, and a wonderfully creative opportunity. So, with my good friend Baptiste's urging, I started "La Splendeur", and it has been a success. I still teach a few hours at the school, but here is where my heart is now."

He smiled, and Nanette smiled back, intrigued by his story, and taken by his obvious joy in what he was doing.

"Now, you want to know why Baptiste asked you to meet with me. Our former singer, who was a beautiful woman, like yourself, became ill, and was no longer able to work. Baptiste and I agonized over someone to replace her, for our clients demand both beauty and talent. Then Baptiste remembered he had made a promise to M. Terrand to look in on you, and voila!, he thought you would be perfect for the position. Now, you want to know what would be expected of you. We begin and end each evening with a pianist and lead singer. Early, to satisfy those who come in for a few drinks and can't decide whether to stay or leave, and late in the evening, after the show, for those who want a quiet, romantic end to their day. The show I mention varies, with comedians, the most beautiful and artistic dancers, sometimes a special guest."

"It does sound exciting," remarked Nanette, finding herself drawn to everything Barras described.

"Then will you sing a few numbers for me?" he asked.

When she assented, he called off-stage to a young man who was introduced as Robert, the pianist. Nanette, rather nervous, looked through a pile of sheet music, selected two familiar pieces, and handed them to Robert. He looked at the titles, smiled, and handed them back with a nod, obviously knowing them by heart.

He played and she began to sing. Her voice was lovely, causing Barras to close his eyes, and smile with delight. Half-way through the song, her voice broke, and, turning away, she began to cry.

"My dear, what's wrong?" asked Barras anxiously. "You were doing wonderfully."

"It's nothing," she replied, regaining her composure. "I have sung this song often, and it reminds me of happier days. Let me have a glass of water and a few minutes, then we can go on."

But Barras didn't need her to go on. He recognized immediately the fine quality of her voice, and knew that, in a short while, she would be ready to perform. He told her that, but she insisted that she continue, asking where she would be standing and if a microphone was necessary.

Barras had the stage lights turned on, and those over the tables dimmed as for an evening. He pointed to a microphone, signaled for it to be turned on, and asked her to continue with the second number.

Nanette blew softly into the mike, nodded to the pianist, and began. She closed her eyes, trying to imagine how it would feel to sing before an audience. As the sound flowed through the speakers, filling the room, she felt her pulse quicken. It was a tender love song, which she sang with emotion and grace.

When she finished and opened her eyes, she saw that several other employees, drawn by her voice, had come from other parts of the building to see whose voice created such beauty. Following M. Barras' lead, they all applauded.

"My dear young lady," called Barras, "If you refuse my offer, you will break my heart. That was nothing but pure loveliness."

Nanette smiled widely, lowering her head in embarrassment.

"I've always enjoyed singing," she said, feeling a sense of relief that she had been able to finish the song without becoming emotional again.

"Then, why not allow others to enjoy it as well?" asked Barras. "I'm certain we can come to an agreement on salary, and you can begin as soon as you wish."

"I do have an important question," said Nanette. "What about the Germans? Surely the occupation will impact your business?"

"Ah yes, the Germans. They have already visited us. I was given to understand that we will be allowed to go on as usual, with one requirement. It's not something I approve of or like in any way. But it allows me to keep my cabaret, and my employees their jobs. So, I must agree."

When he paused, Nanette became puzzled.

"What is it?, she asked.

"I must post a sign which reads, "No Jews or homosexuals allowed."

Nanette returned to her apartment, feeling a mixture of hatred and resentment toward the Nazi invaders, but also a sense of relief that employment could be her's if she wanted it. She told herself that, with the Germans in control, things would be same wherever she went. She supposed Barras was fortunate to even be allowed to remain in business. She opened a drawer in her desk and counted what was left of the money that Emile had given her. With luck, it would buy groceries for another week or two, but not longer.

She went to a cabinet where she kept a few bottles of liquor, poured a small glass of brandy, and sat o the sofa. She was not desperate yet, she told herself, but must soon become so. She wanted to act as the adult she was, and come to a decision on her own, but still felt the need to talk it over with someone. It wasn't very late, so she phoned Julian, telling him what had been offered her.

His first reaction was excitement.

"Nanette, this is wonderful. What a break. I know it's not what you would ever seek, but it has come to you, and you can do it."

"I know I can do it, it's just so, so different. I loved my job, with its challenges, the chance to create, my partnership with Emile. I don't know if I will have the same sense of satisfaction if I do this."

"I understand," he said caringly, "But what satisfaction is there sitting in your apartment all day, wondering if something will come along? Sometimes our prayers are answered in ways we hadn't imagined."

The line was quiet for a moment, then Nanette said,

"I feel so much better already, Julian. Thank you for listening to my doubts, and helping me think more clearly. You're right. This is a break for me, and maybe it will lead to greater things."

Nanette rehearsed with Robert for five days of the next week They worked wonderfully well together, and Robert's continual appreciation and encouragement gave her a sense of confidence. She began to perform that Friday and Saturday night. The crowds not only loved her, they adored her. Jean Barras introduced her the second night with such ebullience, one might have thought he was in love with her. She appeared in a sparkling, emerald-green dress, off one shoulder, fitting her figure like skin. She sang as if she had been on stage a hundred times, filling each song with emotion. He voice, flowing so richly out of such a alluring body, melted every man's heart.

She was glad for the Sunday and Monday respite, never realizing how fatiguing show business could be. She called Julian to tell him of her early success, receiving his congratulations.

The cabaret opened again on Tuesday, which Jean—and he asked her to call him by his first name—which Jean warned her was usually the slowest night of the week. Instead, the place was filled with patrons, and a waiting line formed outside. Jean was giddy with delight.

"I've never seen anything like this," he exclaimed. "You are a sensation!"

Nanette sang two of her five opening numbers, then, feeling relaxed and self assured, left her mike behind and moved through the crowded room, singing as she went from table to table. The male customers applauded, and even their women companions smiled and nodded their heads in approval of her talent. When the set was completed, she went to her dressing room to rest as the showgirls came on stage. There was a knock on her door, and when she responded a waiter, holding a bottle of champagne, stood there.

"A gentleman in the hall asked me to deliver this with his compliments, and to ask if you might join him at his table," the young man said.

"Please tell the gentleman I appreciate his gesture," she told him, "But I must rest before my closing songs."

What she said was true, but her curiosity was piqued. When she returned to the stage some time later, she glanced around the room, to see if anyone made a movement which might indicate that he was the one who sent the wine. No one did, as far as she could see, but the air was a bit hazy with smoke, and some parts of the room were darker than others.

As each night passed, an increasing number of German officers began to attend, always given the best seats and catered to eagerly. They had money to spend, ordering the best wines, and German beers which Jean began to import for their enjoyment—via the Black Market—of course. Rationing had begun all across France, with much of the food requisitioned for the occupying army, or sent to Germany, but Barras had the contacts necessary to provide for his customer's wants. This puzzled Nanette, although she knew she was in no position to question or protest. Life had become a matter of survival, but she was nevertheless disgusted at the way many of the show-girls threw themselves at the officers. She vowed to do nothing to encourage the Nazis. She would do her job, and no more.

Nanette continued to sing five nights each week to nearly full houses, although the number of French men began to decline as the economy worsened. They were replaced with a growing number of German officers in the company of French women, some of whom she recognized from the society pages. The mystery-man didn't send her champagne for a two week period, then appeared again, and was again refused. But, after this third invitation, Nanette couldn't contain her curiosity any more, and she asked the waiter to note where he was sitting the next time he came in, so she could see him.

"Well, Mademoiselle, he is here for your opening songs, but each time you refuse him he immediately leaves."

"Is he a German officer? She asked.

"No, not at all. He is a French man, perhaps thirty-five, well dressed, but not friendly—not to me. He just asks me to deliver the wine and the invitation."

Nanette knew the only way to solve the mystery was to accept the invitation one time, thank the man, and ask him to stop.

On the next Tuesday evening she sang her opening set, and went to her dressing room. As she half expected, the waiter arrived with the usual offer.

"Tell the gentleman," she said, "That I will join him at his table shortly, but only for a few minutes. Please come back in ten minutes and take me to his table."

She fussed nervously with her hair, checked the seams in her stockings, and applied some cologne. Then she sat, looking into her dressing-table mirror, and whispered to the image in the glass:

"Why am I so nervous? I sent the message that this would be nothing more than a brief hello, and I meant it. Or do I mean it? Why do I have this detached attitude toward men? Since Emile left I haven't been to a party or even to dinner with others. Don't I want to have a social life again?"

The knock on her door ended her one-way conversation, and she went with the waiter. Men rose as she passed their table, eyes following her as she moved to the last table in the back. The man got up, nodded to the waiter, and gave a slight bow.

"Hello Nanette. I'm so happy we can meet again."

Nanette's eyes blazed in anger and unbelief as she looked into the smiling face of Paul Moreau.

"Paul, what are you doing here? I have nothing to say to you. Had I known it was you sending me those messages, I would have told you from the beginning that I don't want to see you. After what you did to Julian and me, you have a lot of nerve even coming here."

"Now, now, don't be so rash," he whispered. "With conditions as they are, I might be able to do you some good."

"You must be joking," she exclaimed. "I wouldn't take anything from you if I were down to my last sou."

"Bold words from a cabaret singer," Moreau said with a laugh and a sneer. "You don't have Emile Terrand to provide for you any more."

"Emile never "provided" for me," she asserted quickly. "I earned my own way, and continue to do so."

She said those words a bit loudly, causing heads to turn from nearby tables. She knew she had either to leave or to sit. She sat, many questions to be answered.

"What are you doing here in Paris," she asked angrily

"Business, my dear. Very good business. In fact, since the occupation, things have never been better."

"You disgust me," she said, shaking her head, trying to keep control of her emotions. "You work for the Nazis, lining your pockets with stolen money. How low can you sink?"

"Tsk, tsk, tsk," he murmured, "One does what one must do. But you have learned that. My business ventures are the same as before, but with new customers. Just as it is here. Do you think this place could remain open and be profitable, or that you would even have a job, if it weren't for the Germans? Look around you and face the facts. You need them as much as I . . . So don't think you're better than me."

Tears formed in Nanette's eyes as she realized the truth of what Moreau said, and the enormity of that bitter reality.

"What do you really want, Paul?"

"Only a little companionship. I come to Paris for meetings with a particular officer each Tuesday, and he tells me what he needs. I would like to come earlier, on Monday, and spend an evening with you."

"That's out of the question. For one, I have a policy not to date any customer of the cabaret. And for another, I simply don't like you. No, to be perfectly frank, I despise you. These are reasons enough to tell you no, and good night. Now, stop bothering me."

She got up and walked away, moving more quickly than she would have liked, trying to hold back the tears until she reached her dressing room. Barras caught up with her as she arrived back-stage, and stopped her.

"Nanette, what is it. You look so upset. I saw you at someone's table. Shall I deal with him?"

"No, no, thank you, Jean. It was someone from the past, and he brought up some sad memories. But I'll be fine. I just need some time alone."

When Jean left her, she entered her room, closed the door, and began to cry. Damn him, she thought, why did he have to come back into her life.? She sat, putting her head in her hands, recalling his bitter words about catering to the Nazis. She felt trapped, as she realized so many of her countrymen were. What could one do? Regardless of what Paul said, or how right he was, she still hated him for what he did in Nantes. She hoped this would be the end of it, and that she would never see his face again.

She had enough time to rest, to calm herself, and to get the red-ness out of her eyes, before her next set was scheduled to begin. She determined to sing as well as ever, and to not allow that nasty encounter affect or blemish her performance.

CHAPTER 7

THE FIRST YEAR of German occupation was one of great adjustment for the French people, especially in the northern, occupied areas. Shortages of food and fuel made life difficult, as they faced a winter more severe than usual. Interaction with the German military varied throughout the region. In some villages, citizens never saw a German. In others, soldiers were billeted in private homes for weeks and months.

The German High Command had given instructions to the officers of the occupation to maintain a rigid discipline among their troops—to practice polite domination. Looting and forceful attempts upon French women were dealt with severely. The Nazis knew that cooperation from the French people would come more easily if they were treated with respect. Such respect, however, had its limits. German demands had to be met. The choices which French government officials and businessmen faced were difficult and complex. To cooperate with the enemy was abhorrent to most, and refusal to do so resulted in a loss of one's business or job, and the prospect of imprisonment or deportation. The overarching emotion felt by most everyone, was fear.

There were others, however, for whom the occupation brought new opportunities for profit and pleasure. Some befriended the Germans and associated with them freely. Thousands of French men joined the German army. Some took positions in the police force or the hated Militia, actively seeking out Jews, communists and resisters. The pursuit of self-interest led others to devise ways to ingratiate themselves with occupiers.

One such person was Paul Moreau. Using his contacts with suppliers, both surface and black market, he made it known to high-ranking officers that he could provide for all their special needs. In his frequent trips to Paris, he had met with a number of Nazis in the military central administration. The word spread: if you need anything, call Moreau.

Countering such practices—and Moreau certainly was not alone in his kind of dealings—were those determined to frustrate German policies and aims. A resistance movement grew slowly, members gathering in local groups called the "maquis". The resistance gained force after October 1940, when laws were enacted prohibiting Jews from holding public office in government, schools, and medicine, and surging even more when Germany went to war with the Soviet Union. French Communists now joined forces in an uneasy alliance with other resistance groups. Over time, France was the object of four contending forces: the Nazis, the Militia, the Resistance, and the Free French Forces, building up in Algeria.

In response, the work of the Gestapo increased, with an increase in arrests and deportations.

Especially targeted, and roughly treated, were known Communists and German Jews who had taken refuge in France.

For Nanette's brother Julian, both the occupation and the way many Frenchmen accommodated it, was a source of disgust. He had despaired when he heard the news of Petain's surrender of the nation, and vowed to do what he could to resist Nazi influence and authority. His opportunity came in a chance encounter with Robert Tolan in a café in Nantes.

"My God, Robert," exclaimed Julian, "I would have thought the Gestapo had put you behind bars long ago. How are you?"

"I am well, my friend—as well as one can be under the circumstances. Simply trying to keep body and soul together. Actually, I work for them—the Germans, that is. Not the Gestapo, but for the newspaper the Nazis publish."

When Julian's face betrayed astonishment, and then disgust, Tolan went on.

"Easy, my friend. I'm a reporter, so I report the news. I don't make it, and I don't like it, but I tell it. And so, I stay alive."

Julian rose and prepared to leave.

"Take care, Robert. I'll pretend we didn't meet, and try to remember what you once stood for."

"Sit down, Julian," whispered Tolan, grabbing Julian by the arm. "It's not what you think."

"How the hell do you know what I think", replied Julian harshly. "It seems we don't think alike any more, and I need to leave before what I have to say becomes the subject of one of you articles."

Tolan continued to grip Julian's arm tightly.

"Sit down." he said through his teeth, glancing around to see if anyone was noticing their conflict.

"What do you want of me?" asked Julian angrily.

"I can't tell you now," replied Tolan in a very soft voice, but if you happen to stop in at the Coq Rouge in Champoteaux around ten tonight, you might learn something."

Letting go of Julian's arm, he said in a normal voice,

"Good to see you again, my friend. Let's keep in touch."

Julian straightened himself, nodded and went out, somewhat angry, but mostly puzzled about Tolan, and what he had hinted about the coming night.

The Coq Rouge was a small bar at the edge of Champoteaux, on the south bank of the Loire. The town itself was unremarkable, the bar even less. It was an ancient structure, with a low roof, windows in the front, and a single door at the top of a short flight of stairs. Julian entered the bar-room, which was filled with smoke and the noise of many conversations. The place appeared to be a hangout for fishermen, and an assortment of old men, who lamented the sorry state of the nation, and recounted their heroic stand against the Boche in the Great War.

Julian was unnoticed by everyone except a middle-aged man, who sat by the door, eyeing him cautiously. Julian went to the bar, ordered a brandy, and wondered if Tolan would comd to meet him.

The conversations continued, mindful of him, an occasional shout of disagreement rising above the din. An unkept hag, seemingly as old as the building itself, came in from a back room with a plate of pomme frites, the aroma contrasting pleasantly with the smell of stale smoke.

Julian sipped his brandy, wondering why he had come here, not knowing what to expect or if Robert would even show, as he intimated. Another man of Julian's age came in through the front door, spoke a few words to the one seated nearby, then went passed the bar into the doorway out of which the old woman had come. Two minutes later the scenario repeated itself, but this time the man at the door abandoned his post, and went with the other to the rear. The bar-tender asked Julian if he wanted another brandy. He looked at his watch and was ready to reply when Robert Tolan appeared in the door-way and beckoned to him to follow.

They went through a small kitchen, smelling of cooking oil and cheese. The man from the front door—Julian now thought of him as a look-out—was there, waiting.

"This is Julian Lemond, from Cande, and now from Nantes," Tolan said.

"The one you spoke of?" asked the lookout.

"The same. We have known each other for years."

"You trust him?"

"I trust him completely."

"Tell me your views of the occupation," prodded the lookout.

"How can a loyal French man have any view other than complete and disgust for our government, and hatred for the

Nazis. And, loathing for those who support them." Julian replied forcefully, knowing he was taking a risk, but feeling strangely comfortable with this man.

"Come with us," the man ordered, nodding to Tolan.

They went outside, and Tolan, apologizing for the inconvenience, placed a blindfold around Julian's head. They got into a car and began to drive, Julian aware that another car followed. Some minutes later, the car left the roadway and bounced along a track, coming to a stop. Tolan led Julian down a path toward the river, where they entered a boat-house which smelled of fish, and rotting wood. Julian was seated at a table, on which he rested his arms. He sensed the presence of others, besides those who brought him here.

"This is a friend of Turtle," the man he thought of as lookout said, referring to Tolan by his code-name. "I believe he might be willing to join our fishing club. Ask him whatever questions you have."

For the next thirty minutes the men—it seemed as if there were six or seven total—grilled Julian about his background, his political views, his job, and his willingness to risk his life for France. He believed that his responses would be acceptable to them, but had questions of his own.

"It's obvious that you are part of the Resistance," he said, "and I both admire and envy your efforts. I know that even a meeting like this is incredibly dangerous. But before I consider joining you, I need to know what would be expected of me"

There was a pause, as if the men were deciding who would speak for them. Finally, one of them spoke.

"As to the specifics of what we do, or plan to do, that is something you may learn in time. If you join us, you will be given assignments as they arise in our planning. You will not see us or know us by other than a code-name, and one will be given to you, once you prove yourself trustworthy. Do you understand?"

"I do," answered Julian, wet with sweat from his grilling.

"Then, if you agree to join us, I will leave it to Turtle to arrange a drop-point for us to contact you. In the meantime, be aware that you have already stepped into dangerous waters. Any attempt to betray us will be met with the most dire consequences. We are no less ruthless than our enemies."

Julian was relieved beyond measure when the meeting ended and he was taken back to the Coq Rouge. His mind was swimming with the things he heard and the enormity of the decision which faced him. But there was also an inner excitement as well. He hadn't joined the army as he once considered he might, and thanked God that mistake wasn't made. For all he knew, if he had enlisted, he might already be in a German prisoner of war camp. So, if he couldn't fight the Nazis one way, he could do it another. Even before being dropped off at his car, his decision was made.

He told Tolan. "Robert, if the "Fishing Club" will have me, I mean to join."

"I thought you might. The way you reacted to me in the café, convinced me you would want to help. Don't change your daily routine. When I need to contact you, this is what I'll do."

He then suggested a means of contact, and said goodnight.

Nanette's life followed a routine to which she had become accustomed. When she first started her singing job, the late nights were difficult getting used to. Now, she enjoyed the luxury of sleeping late in the morning, and using the afternoon for long walks. She thought once of taking a train to Nantes to see Julian, but decided she would phone him instead. She didn't find him at home the evening she called, and hoped he had found a new girl, since Louise had graduated from the university and moved away. Julian's mind, however, was on other things.

His first assignment came in less than two weeks. A note at his pre-arranged pick-up point told him to walk down a certain street two evenings later, and to assist a woman pedestrian. She would drop a folder containing some sheets of paper. As he helped her retrieve them she would point to a particular sheet, which he was to take and deliver to a drop point so marked. It was a simple courier task, but Julian took it very seriously and carried it out without trouble. The same type of task was given to him in succeeding weeks, followed through successfully. He was pleased with himself and with the fact that he was becoming a trusted member of the maquis.

On his next courier run, Julian made the pick-up and was about to leave, when a large, dark sedan drove up beside him. Two men leaped out, took Julian by the arms, and forced him into the back seat of the car. He tried to protest, but was ordered not to speak. They rode for a while, Julian in a state of panic. The car stopped and he was roughly pulled out and taken into a large house, and down a flight of steps to a basement room. Two chairs stood there, facing each other. Julian was made to sit in one. In the other was an officer of the S.S.. Julian shook with fright. The room was dimly lit, until a bright beam was focused on Julian's face, causing him to squint.

"So, this is our little trouble-maker, Julian Lemond," the officer said. "A courier for the pathetic little resistance cell in Nantes. We have been watching you work. Very much the amateur.

No creativity, no mystery. A pity you won't be around to learn to do it better."

Julian was fearful beyond belief. His pulse raced, his hands were wet, his whole body feeling weak. Who betrayed him, he wondered.? Had he been right in his first reaction to Toland? He wasn't given much time to think. The officer began to interrogate him. Where did he come from? Did he have siblings? What of his parents? What business was he in?

Then began the specifics. Who was the leader of his maquis? Where did his group meet? What plans did he know of? And so on.

Julian answered the personal questions truthfully, aware that the S.S. likely knew the answers anyway. As to those related to the resistance, he pleaded total ignorance, protesting that they had obviously mistaken him for someone else. He claimed that his courier duties were a way of making extra money, in addition to his regular job. He swore that he never read any of the papers he delivered, and therefore had no knowledge of their content, which he assumed had to do with business activity.

The questioning lasted over an hour. When it ended, the S.S. officer rose and smiled. He glanced toward a doorway and nodded. Robert Tolan entered, also with a smile.

Julian hated with vehemence the sight of the man, until Tolan spoke.

"Forgive us, Julian, but this was quite necessary. You held up wonderfully. Congratulations!"

Only then did Julian realize what this had been, a mock interrogation to see how well he would do under questioning. Doubtless, the Nazis would be more severe, and use more forceful methods, but at least he passed this test.

"I nearly pissed my pants, Robert," he said. "You guys are quite convincing. Did I really do all right?"

"Yes you did," replied Tolan, becoming serious. "We needed to do this now, because we have plans that include you, and we had to be certain you wouldn't fail us."

"I'm glad it's over," said Julian, now able to smile. "Maybe my pulse will return to normal in a month!"

I'll be in touch in a week or two," said Tolan, putting a hand on Julian's shoulder.

———— ∞∞∞ ————

The week which followed was filled with terror and turmoil for Julian and his employer. Arriving at work Monday morning he was alarmed to see several black sedans of the type used by the Gestapo parked at the factory entrance. Once inside, he was instructed to go to a certain room, where he found the factory owner and several managers, looking gloomy and anxious. The door closed behind him.

"Gentlemen," began a severe-looking German agent, "It has been determined that, in the public interest, this shop should be operated for the production of materiel necessary for the good of the people. Therefore, beginning in two weeks, your machinery will be converted for the manufacture of artillery shells. To assist you in reaching monthly production quotas, we will provide you with managers who will oversee your work."

When the factory owner opened his mouth to protest, the agent pointed a finger at him and said sternly,

"Any effort to hinder the carrying out of this order will be met with severe consequences. If you want to continue to employ your workforce, you will comply with this order without question. Do I make myself clear?"

The owner, his shoulders sagging, nodded his head.

"Good. Then we are understood. Tomorrow our engineers will arrive to direct the changes. You are dismissed."

Julian's stomach was churning. This order meant he would be working for the Nazis, an idea which sickened him. He wondered what his new tasks would be, since the usual business of accounts payable and receivable would end, leaving only the payroll.

As he was about to leave the room, the agent who had just spoken to the owner told Julian to remain. The officer was about

Julian's age, doubtless someone who had been indoctrinated as a Hitler Youth. His bright-red Nazi armband looked crisp and new, as did the whole uniform, indicating that he was likely new to his rank. His tine of voice was imperious.

"You keep the company books, is that correct?" he asked tersely.

Julian nodded.

"Then in these two weeks you must settle accounts with your suppliers and customers. After that, we will have someone here to assist you as to the kind of records we want kept. I have been told that you are very accurate in your work. We will accept nothing less as you continue to work under new management."

Julian left the room with a feeling of deep despair. He saw it all so clearly—Nazi bosses, Nazi methods, Nazi production, and finally, Nazi slaughter with the arms they produce. He hated the very thought of coming to work under these conditions, but knew he had little choice. If he quit, he would become homeless, and without the means to support himself. He might even be hunted and sent away.

In that woeful hour, he joined the tens of thousands of his countrymen faced with the same bleak future. At the same time, however, it reinforced his determination to work with the Resistance in every way possible.

CHAPTER 8

NANETTE BECAME WORRIED when she hadn't heard from Julian for several weeks. He usually called to ask how she was, exercising his big-brother prerogative of watching over her. She phoned him four times before finally finding him in.

"Julian, I've been worried. It has been difficult to reach you. Is everything all right?"

He vacillated between being completely truthful, and not worrying her further. He tried to be vague.

"Just some re-adjustments at the factory. We're making some new products, but my job is essentially the same. I'm doing well, really. But tell me about the cabaret."

Nanette decided also to be vague as she answered.

"The cabaret is still going strong. It's amazing, given the repressive climate here, that the ones with money to spend, are here night after night. I suppose we provide an escape from reality."

"And the Germans?" Julian asked.

"Yes, they come too. I didn't like it at all, at first, and I guess I still don't, but they act like all our other patrons, and are polite and appreciative. Sometimes I have to remind myself that they are the enemy."

"Please, Nanette," he said forcefully, "Always remember who they represent. Politeness is not cover for cruelty. Anyone who crosses them finds that out soon enough."

"Julian," she replied quickly, and with concern, "Are you in some kind of trouble?"

"No, of course not. But I've seen what they can do, and it makes me both sick and angry, especially knowing there is little we can do about it."

"Tell me, what have you seen?" she asked.

"Well, you know there are people who try to profit from the occupation, and those who detest it, and resent the collaborators. Some of the latter have formed groups to resist the Nazis, and the Gestapo has been working hard to stop them. There have been arrests and, ah, well, many arrests."

Julian stopped, aware that he had already said enough, and angry with himself for giving Nanette more cause for worry.

"Julian, you're not mixed up with them, are you?" she asked anxiously.

"I admire them," he answered "but I have enough to handle at my workplace."

"Promise me you'll be careful."

"Of course, dear sister. I'll continue to do my job, and be the obedient boy I have always been. I'm so glad you called. I promise to call in two weeks. And you too, exercise care."

The flippancy of Julian's remarks troubled Nanette. She read between the lines about his company's "readjustment", quite sure it meant that the Germans had taken control. She also sensed that Julian was under a lot of pressure, but wasn't willing to tell her why. She knew she had to stay in touch, and hoped he felt the same.

When the call ended, Nanette prepared for her evening performances. As she looked through her wardrobe, she thought how fortunate she was to have such a variety of lovely dresses. Many women in Paris had adapted to a new style of daytime dress, referred to as "Mode Martiale", short skirts, which saved on cloth. It was one indication of how difficult life was becoming for the average citizen. There were others. Taxis became fewer in number due to a shortage of fuel. Many more bicycles were used for transportation. Grocery shelves held few items, and many families joined together to cycle out into the countryside to find provisions. She was one of the fortunate few.

She almost cried at that thought, but caught herself. She didn't need reddened eyes again. Her makeup and hair finished, she left for the cabaret, carrying the two dresses she would wear that evening. Along the way, she bought a newspaper from a vendor, not being choosy. They were now all propaganda sheets for the Nazis anyway, but she hoped there might be come indication of how the war was going outside France. In the two years of occupation so far, there had been news only of German successes. She had read of the bombing of London, and remembered hearing the sound when masses of bombers flew overhead with their murderous cargo. She wondered what Paris might look like now, if France hadn't surrendered. Would the bombs have also been falling here?

An article on the second page caught her eye, because it had a mention of Varades in large print. Varades was a small village, like Cande, and some ten kilometers to the south. The article told of a man who had been shot by the Gestapo two days before for subversive activity. The nature of his crime wasn't mentioned, only that he was a danger to public safety. Nanette knew that was a phrase used by the Gestapo and S.S. to excuse themselves from any recrimination. She also believed that this shooting represented only a fraction of the killings taking place, and that it was reported to frighten people into thinking twice before trying anything rash.

She shook her head, uttering a small prayer that Julian would not take foolish risks, and walked on. When she arrived at La Splendeur, she entered her dressing room hung her dresses, and further prepared herself. Attendance had been down that week, but now it was Friday and both she and Jean hoped for a full house. She wasn't disappointed. As she came on stage, to a loud ovation, she noticed that most of the tables were occupied, with the German officers sitting near the stage, as usual.

She sang two songs, meandering around the room, moving her arms and body to match the mood of the music, and was about to begin the third, when Jean Barras signaled to the pianist from the rear to hold the next number. Nanette was puzzled, and returned to the stage . . . In that instant, there was a movement of chairs as everyone in the cabaret rose to their feet and stood at attention. An elderly officer, accompanied by two aides, entered, smiled, and shouted, "Heil Hitler". The response was an immediate echo of his salute. He seated himself near the rear of the room, while the others remained standing.

Jean rushed to the microphone to make an announcement.

"My friends, we are honored to have as our distinguished guest, General Hans von Boineburg-Lengofeld."

Applause filled the room, after which the audience returned to their seats.

"We are at your service, Herr General. Please make your wishes known," said Jean.

He left the stage to attend to the General, while the pianist played again, and Nanette continued her set, using the mike. As she left the stage, Jean, acting as excited as a school-boy on his first date, asked Nanette to come with him to the General's table, so he could introduce her. Understandably, she became excited herself, for this man was the commanding officer of the Paris garrison of 20,000 troops, one of the most desirable posts in Europe.

As she approached the table, all three men, including the General, rose, amazing her.

She was introduced first to the General, who kissed her hand, then to his aides, who smiled and nodded. One of them looked vaguely familiar, but Nanette had no recollection of where she might have seen him before. As they all took their seats, Nanette noticed two cruel scars on the old General's face, the result, she learned later, of Soviet artillery fire at Stalingrad. He had, nevertheless, a kind, almost grand-fatherly look, which helped overcome her nervousness.

The two aides were both S.S. officers, the larger, dark and heavily built man, a Lieutenant, and the other, whom Nanette still couldn't place, a Hauptmann, or Captain. As they carried on a light conversation, the General admitted that his command of the French language was limited, echoed by the Lieutenant. The Captain, however, who had been introduced as Manfried Zeller, spoke the language clearly and correctly.

"You speak so well, Captain," remarked Nanette.

"Why not," he replied. "Before the war, I was attached to the embassy here, for two years. I love Paris, the language, the music, the food, and the beauty."

He accompanied the last word with a gesture toward Nanette, causing her to blush. But when she heard him speak of the food, she suddenly remembered when she seen him before. It was in the dining room of the hotel where she stayed after her interviews with Emile. He was the one for whom the three other German-speaking men at the next table were waiting. She was certain of it.

"And you, Mademoiselle,." he asked. "Are you Parisian? I think not, only by because of a slight accent. The Loire Valley, perhaps?"

"Very good," she said, laughing. "You are a good guesser. I'm from Cande, actually, not so far from Nantes."

"I don't know it," he confessed, "but it must be a small town, and there are so many."

"Very many," she agreed. "My father had a dress-shop where I worked before coming here, to work for a designer."

"And now you fill the air with such lovely music, and our eyes with such a feast of beauty."

Nanette smiled and inclined her head. What a charmer this handsome man was. With his looks, his tone of voice, and his wavy hair, he bore a slight resemblance to Julian.

Zeller signaled to the waiter who was hovering nearby, and turned to the General.

"Champagne, my General?" he asked.

"Yes, the best they have."

"Mademoiselle, you will have a glass with us.?" Zeller asked.

"Yes, thank you. Just one. Champagne makes me feel dizzy, and I have more work to do."

The wine arrived while the other performers went through their routines. The General entered some of the conversation, but seemed content to listen to Nanette and Zeller for most of the hour. The Lieutenant uttered not a word, but was happy to watch the exotic dancers.

When the General gave a slight nod to Zeller, the Captain rose and said:

"I believe we must leave. We have had a delightful evening, and General Boineburg wishes to thank you for gracing our table with your presence. I hope we will have the pleasure of seeing you again, soon."

Nanette said good-bye, thanked them for coming, and headed for her dressing-room.

As she walked, past the tables amid the admiring glances of the patrons, she realized what had just happened. She had spent a hour with the enemies of France; with the one German who held Paris in his grasp. She had smiled, and joked, and drank with a man who, with a stroke of a pen could have a hundred men shot, a house burned, a family sent to a camp, the entire city destroyed.

She recoiled with Julian's words thundering in her ears, "Politeness is no cover for cruelty".

She believed that, and yet, these were men who might just as well have been businessmen, lawyers, doctors, or any other occupation. Maybe they didn't even want to be here. They too, even as important as they were, answered to a higher authority in Berlin. Perhaps they were as much caught in a web as she and her countrymen.

"You must stop thinking like that," she told herself. "Don't be duped like that again".

In the meantime, Jean, seeing the General's party readying to leave, rushed to their table to thank them for coming, and told them the champagne was gratis. After shaking their hands and wishing them well, he went to Nanette's room.

"Nanette, you were wonderful. When General Boineburg is happy, everyone is happy. I was told that he seldom goes to a cabaret. He came here especially because he heard of you, and he handed me this to give to you."

Nanette took a folded napkin from Jean, and opened it. On the cloth was written "Merci!", along with a 1,000 franc banknote.

It was more than she made in a month. Jean saw her look of amazement and smiled.

"Not bad for a few songs and a little conversation, don't you agree?"

"Jean," she said wearily, "I appreciate the money, and the attention, but I simply cannot do this again."

He looked stunned.

"What? Do What? Have a drink with one of the most important persons in Paris? Have a nice conversation with one of our guests?"

He became a bit angry as he went on.

"Don't forget, Nanette, entertaining people is our business. Your business. At this time we don't have the luxury to choose whom we serve. So we swallow our pride, set aside our politics, and give the customer what he wants. Or else, we will all be in the bread line!"

Nanette walked the city the following day, wishing she had done more of it before the invasion, when Paris was a breathing, bustling place. Now there was a dreariness about it, even the buildings seeming to emote resignation and sadness. Many shops had closed, and those which remained open had few wares to display, and fewer customers looking to purchase. She crossed the Seine on the Pont de Grenelle, passed the replica of the Statue of Liberty, and down the Rue Lenois to the Church of St. Jean Baptiste. She felt suddenly guilty for not having been to Mass for over a year. She wondered what dear Danielle would think of her, reminded again of her apparent disappearance, and the heart-break she felt in not hearing from her.

She entered the small nave, genuflected, crossed herself, and knelt in a pew near the back. The church was nearly deserted save for an elderly woman, who now rose from her seat and walked toward the entrance, her wooden-soled shoes clicking on the stone floor. As she passed, Nanette noticed the thread-bare condition of her dress and shawl, contrasting almost sinfully with the fine clothing Nanette wore. Stopping at the door, the old woman turned and shouted, "God help you if you are one of them!", and climbed slowly down the steps.

The woman's words sent Nanette nearly into a faint. She had to hold onto the edge of the pew in front of her to keep from collapsing. Her pulse pounded and she breathed with difficulty. Why would the woman accuse her of something, she asked herself? She wanted to run after the woman and say to her, that she wasn't the only young woman in Paris who dressed well. But something surged deep inside her breast, a realization of how close she was to becoming 'one of them'. Whether the old woman suspected that she was a whore or a collaborator didn't matter. The appearance she gave to others did, and it both saddened and horrified her.

She waited for a few minutes until her head cleared, then rose to leave. But as she looked at the large crucifix over the altar, she sat down and began to cry.

She prayed, "O god, what is happening to me? Where has my simple, happy life gone? Where are my friends to console me?"

She saw a small psalm-book in a pew-rack and flipped it open. On the well-worn page before her eyes was Psalm 137. She read the words, written so long ago, but also the outpouring of her own soul.

> By the waters of Babylon we sat and wept, when we remembered Zion.
>
> On the willows there we hung our harps.
>
> For there our captors called for songs, and our taskmasters music, saying: "Sing us one of the songs of Zion."
>
> How shall we sing the Lord's song in a foreign land?

She stopped there, identifying with this ancient man. He had been taken from his homeland; her homeland had been taken from her. She would sing the songs of Zion—the songs of France, from an earlier blessed time—but she would sing them for herself, not for her enemies. She would sing them proudly, as a tribute to the land she loved, and hoped to one day see restored to freedom.

She closed the book gently, kissed it, and replaced it in the rack. Closing her eyes, she said simply and earnestly, "Yes God, help me".

The weeks which followed brought her no consolation or peace. General Boineburg didn't return to the club, but his aide, Manfried Zeller did, every Friday night. Each time he came, Nanette was invited to join him at his table, which she politely refused to do. It was Paul Moreau all over again. After three such visits and invitations, Jean Barras spoke to her about it.

"You are being quite rude to an important and big-spending guest," he said.

"I'm sorry, Jean," she explained. "I simply am not comfortable being intimate with German officers. Plenty of our girls like it. Please talk to one of them. Collette is a beauty, ask her to go to him. He'll soon forget me."

"No-one forgets you." Jean responded, perturbed by her attitude, but being careful not to press his star performer too much. He tried to be persuasive.

"He'll keep coming for a while, but if we lose him as a patron, others may leave as well."

"Jean, please," she said wearily, "The man wants someone to take home and sleep with. They all do. Let Collette try with him. She likes that. In fact, she would love to have an officer to look after her. Besides, she has bigger breasts than I."

The remark amused Jean, but he wasn't convinced.

Seeing his hesitation, she said, "Try her, Jean. Ask her to pay special attention to him. You'll see that's what he wants. And we'll all be happier."

There was no question at all about Collette's attractiveness. A bit shorter than Nanette, but with natural blond hair, ample breasts and a broad, sexy, smile, she did turn heads. She was one of the exotic dancers, not a singer, and not the best conversationalist, but these were traits about which most men didn't care anyway. Realizing Nanette would not budge, Jean decided to talk to his dancer.

The following Friday, Collette, eager to please her boss, and equally excited at the prospect of being with the Captain, went to his table as soon as her routine concluded. She had felt aroused as she danced, acting especially provocative, electing cheers from the patrons and a long applause when she finished.

She noticed that Zeller had joined in the applause, and leaving the stage, moved toward his table. Along the way, another officer, mildly drunk, grabbed her by the arm and spun her into his lap. He said something to her, but when she whispered something back, he released her and apologized, looking worriedly in the direction of the Captain's table. Zeller, of course, had no idea what was going on, but when she approached his table and asked if he would buy her some refreshment, he invited her to join him, and called for a waiter.

They talked together for a few minutes, but when they had exhausted such subjects as the weather, the quality of the other acts, and the makeup of the crowd, things turned silent. They smiled at each other frequently, but Collette, despite her flirting, realized that Zeller wasn't looking for a warm body. After an uncomfortable half-hour, she thanked him for the drink, and excused herself.

As he had done the three times before, Zeller signaled for a waiter and ordered a bottle of champagne to be sent to Nanette's room, along with a note inviting her again to join him. Nanette decided to be honest with him and lay her cards on the table. Instead of her simple refusal, she wrote a note to Zeller, which she sent via the waiter.

Dear Captain Zeller:

You have been so very kind during the past month, and I am truly grateful for your generosity. I enjoyed the conversation with you at the General's table. However, I must ask you to please stop sending me gifts, and invitations which I cannot accept. It has been, and continues to be my policy, not to become familiar with a single guest. To do so would only provoke jealousy among our other guests, many of whom are as frequent in attendance as you.

I hope, despite this refusal, that you will continue to patronize our Cabaret to enjoy our entertainment.

Sincerely, Nanette.

The note had the desired effect. Zeller stopped sending invitations and gifts, and, to Nanette's relief, continued to come each Friday. Now, acknowledged to be one of the regular Friday guests, his table always awaited him, with a bottle of his favorite champagne on ice.

The dilemma seemed to have ended amicably.

CHAPTER 9

THE SITUATION FOR the citizens of the Loire Valley was not as satisfactory. As the activity of the Resistance increased, so did the arrests and shootings. Realizing the danger the stepped-up Gestapo investigations posed, Robert Tolan and his cell decided to postpone any actions until things settled down. They met less frequently, the interim giving the leaders to plan their next moves more carefully.

The Gestapo and the French police—now working hand in hand—relied a great deal on informers, and rewarded those who betrayed their neighbors or fellow citizens. Some of the more unscrupulous ones saw these times an opportunity to settle old scores. Others collaborated for financial gain or promised access to more food and fuel, both in dwindling supply.

No-one was better at manipulating the system for his own benefit than Paul Moreau, and his influence with the Nazis grew as the months passed. He continued his weekly visits to Paris, where he was well known among the German brass. After several unsuccessful attempts, he was finally able to arrange a meeting with the one man whom he thought would bring him greater influence and wealth. The man was an aide to General Boineburg. His name was Manfried Zeller.

Zeller, who read people well, took an instant dislike to Moreau, but realized he might prove useful. He asked the man to sit, and explained why he had agreed to this meeting.

"The General," he said, "has a fondness—no, a passion—for fine champagne. In fact, he is accumulating quite a collection of rare vintages. But some particular ones have eluded him. He would be quite grateful to the person who might find some of them for him. If I gave you a list, do you think it might be possible?"

Moreau, wanted to sound important, but also attempted to make the request seem difficult.

"Some years of certain vintages are indeed virtually unobtainable," he said. "I say 'virtually', but not impossible, because someone with the right connections may be able to locate even them."

"And you," said Zeller, "are the someone with right connections."

"I can only promise you I would do my best. Do you have the list from the General?"

Zeller opened a folder on his desk and produced a page with a half-dozen typed lines. He glanced at it briefly, then handed it to Moreau, who also gave it a quick look.

"I'll return in two weeks," said Moreau. "I hope to have good news for you then, and the cost of whatever I am able to find."

Zeller rose and showed Moreau to the door. When he was gone, Zeller thought to himself, "What a weasel".

Moreau returned to Nantes, having looked at the list Zeller gave him. He was impressed by the choices made by the General. He knew immediately a few of the selections would really be impossible to find. For the others, he knew exactly where to go. He grinned as he thought to himself how important he was becoming to the Germans, and how bright his future seemed.

The Loire Valley was home to many splendid chateaux, some over 300 years old, belonging to families which had somehow survived the Revolution. Moreau knew that a number of them contained wine-cellars, kept up to date by their owners. One man in particular, Henri de Coursey, was a well-known collector. Moreau decided to try him first, if he could arrange an appointment. De Coursey seldom associated with commoners, his thick Gallic blood going back to the Crusaders. But Moreau was shrewd. He would find a way.

The solution to his problem presented itself only a few days later. A merchant in the village of Ancenis, on the Loire, was caught hiding a family of Jews he hoped to smuggle to England. He was arrested, and his property confiscated by the Nazis. In his warehouse they found stocks of food-stuffs, furs, appliances, and cases of wine. The Gestapo chief for the region, having previously had dealings with Moreau, called on him to help identify and place a value on the items.

Moreau was more than pleased to assist, and in perusing the store of wines, found several he believed would interest de

Coursey, and provide the means of obtaining an appointment with the man.

He telephoned the chateau and gave the person who answered the reason why he sought a meeting with the master. They would get back to him. Which they did within the hour, setting up an appointment for the next day.

Moreau took with him two lists, the one from the General and the other containing the names and quantities of the wines in the warehouse. De Coursey was impressed when he looked at the names on the first list. The General was obviously a connoisseur like himself, something he admired in the man, despite his being a Nazi. But then, he thought, true culture has no frontiers.

"Your General," he remarked, "has superb tastes in champagne. Of course I have most of these in my cellar. But why would I wish to part with them?"

"Perhaps as a trade," suggested Moreau. "I have access to a very large quantity of fine wines, which I could make available to you."

He handed the second list to de Coursey, which the man read through.

"Hmm, very interesting," said de Coursey. "I don't suppose you would like to tell me where these wines are located?"

"Only that I have total access to them and am authorized to use them for the purpose of fulfilling the General's desires," replied Moreau, lying with impunity.

"You realize, of course, that your wines, which are certainly above the ordinary, are in a much lower class than those you seek. There is no question of a case for case exchange," said de Coursey.

"I understand fully," said Moreau, smiling. "I am in a position to offer you a five to one exchange for the first three on the General's list, and an eight to one exchange for the others, in whichever vintages you choose."

"Numbers five and six are not in my collection, and you will not find them available anywhere in Europe. I know, I have tried. Numbers six and seven I have, but in such limited quantity, that I will release only one bottle of each, in the ratio you offer. As for the others, yes, I can meet your terms. When will you have them here?"

"In one week," replied Moreau, aware of the fact that obtaining the General's authority to get the wines from the warehouse would take another trip to Paris.

"Very well. I agree."

"Agreed," said Moreau, shaking de Coursey's hand, and excited beyond belief.

Moreau made an unscheduled trip to Paris, after phoning Captain Zeller and explaining the circumstances. When he arrived, Zeller gave him a sheet of paper with orders from General Boineburg, authorizing Moreau to have access to a specified quantity of wine from the warehouse.

Moreau returned home, elated that things were going his way. Then the tide turned.

When word got out of the arrest of the Ancenis merchant, and people learned what he had been hoarding, they were furious. A large crowd gathered outside the warehouse. Citizens, cold and hungry, clamored for a share of the food that was inside. The small police-force tried to restore order, but found the crowd hard to manage. One of the doors was smashed open and people rushed inside, grabbing bags of wheat, flour, and whatever they could carry out. The chief of police called the German commandant at his office, asking for assistance, and troops were quickly sent. In order to avoid unnecessary bloodshed, the mayor of Ancenis asked for a meeting with the Commandant, which was held within the hour. After some negotiation, the Nazi officer agreed to ration out half the food supply to the citizens, with the other half saved for his troops. Items other than food were not to be disturbed.

The mayor rushed to the warehouse, still the scene of struggle with both the police and the small force of soldiers. People were screaming, while some threw rocks at the soldiers. Several people had been injured, and some arrested, while others had run off, their arms filled with sacks of food and bottles of wine. The situation was clearly out of hand, but when the mayor appeared, assuring the crowd of a fair share of the food, things began to calm . . .

Moreau, learning of the near riot in the newspaper the following day, hurried to Ancenis to assess his losses. He found that, once the police had gained control, most of the merchandise was spared. Showing the authorization he had received from Paris, he had men help him load as many cases of wine as his small van could handle, setting aside those he would come back for the next day.

All day long, the citizens of the small village stood in line for the food promised by the mayor. By day's end, the townspeople's share of the food was exhausted, and the warehouse locked and guarded by three German soldiers.

Julian, warned the previous day that an action was imminent, got a call late that night, with the code 'Rouge', which signaled immediate action. A second word told him where to meet the others.

At two in the morning, four men, one in a policeman's uniform, crept quietly up to the Ancenis warehouse. The single guard outside was quickly subdued, and the four used a key provided to them months before to enter. The two guards inside, half drunk on the wine they pilfered from the cases, were also disarmed without a struggle. The uniformed man then went outside and lit two matches. A van moved out of the shadows and into a large door on the side of the building. The door closed as Tolan stepped out of the vehicle.

"We must hurry," he exclaimed, which was unnecessary, but made him feel better saying it. There was always the possibility of an army patrol coming along to check on things.

Tolan led the men to the bathroom at the rear of the building. Inside was a urinal, and a toilet with a board across it which read "Out of order". In reality, it had never been in order. The men lifted the stool with the floor-boards attached, revealing a cavity packed with boxes. The men hauled the boxes out, loading them into the van. Julian, taken completely by surprise, and sweating nervously, did his share, wondering how long these boxes had been there, and what they contained.

When the loading was completed, the stool was replaced, and the truck, now driven by someone other than Tolan, exited the warehouse and drove off.

"What do we do with the guards?" asked Julian.

"They come with us," replied Tolan.

The bound and gagged soldiers were herded together and taken down a steep path to a wooded area nearby. A pile of recently emptied bottles lay there. Their hands still tied, the guards were forced to drink even more wine and brandy, until they passed out. They were then untied, and left laying there in a drunken stupor.

Inside the warehouse, one of the other invaders overturned an oil stove, letting the fuel flow freely toward a large bundle of clothing. He checked outside, was given the go-ahead, and set the fuel alight. He ran out the front door, which was left open, to indicate additional laxness on the part of the guards.

The raiding party was well out of the village when the fire brigade was summoned. Looking back, Julian could see flames lighting the sky. Tolan smiled at him.

"Good work," Tolan said. "Your first taste of resistance work. There'll be hell to pay in Anceris today, but we had to get these arms out, which may save the owner's life. Do you feel all right?"

"Yes, I feel terrific!"

———⊸⊗⊗⊘⊶———

When Paul Moreau learned what happened, he screamed in anger and went directly to the warehouse. Half his trading supply was gone. Livid with rage in seeing that much of his profit had slipped away, he was nevertheless determined to give de Coursey what he had, and salvage what he could of the deal. He made the exchange the following day, Moreau obtaining only two of the champagnes the General wanted, while having to give up everything he had taken from the warehouse. He was disappointed, but could at least report some success. And it had cost him nothing.

He called Captain Zeller, telling him of his partial success, and asking where to make the delivery.

When Moreau arrived in Paris three days later, he was met at the arranged site by both Zeller and General Boineburg. The latter was ecstatic when he saw what Moreau had been able to find.

"Excellent, absolutely, excellent," he exclaimed. "To be honest, I did not think you could find any of my missing wines. And you have brought two. Wonderful! Zeller will settle with you. Thank you, thank you."

He turned to leave, cradling one of the bottles in his arms, then turned and exclaimed,

"Zeller, this calls for a celebration. That cabaret where we went together, with that ravishing woman, make reservations for tonight. Moreau, will you be my guest?"

Paul agreed, and when the General left, he said:

"I have seemed to make your General happy. Now, what can I do for you? Coffee, chocolate, jewelry? Or perhaps a lovely woman? Or do you already have a companion?"

Zeller bristled at the question.

"M. Moreau, my personal life is none of your damn business."

Moreau became instantly apologetic, and a bit alarmed.

"I am so sorry, Captain. I didn't mean to pry, not at all. I have introduced many officers to fine women, and only wanted to help, if I could. Please forgive me."

"Yes, of course," replied Zeller. "Now let me see the bill for your services and I will arrange payment. Perhaps at another time I will ask something of you for myself."

Zeller returned to his office, uncomfortable at the thought of going to La Splendeur to spend an evening with Moreau, but not knowing how to avoid it. The answer came ten minutes after he got to his desk.

A courier arrived with a communique from OKW West, headquarters of the commander in chief of the Wehrmacht—the German Army. It asked for an immediate report on preparations for the defense of Paris. Zeller knew that such a report had been asked for a month before, but Boineburg had dragged his feet, and Zeller knew he would have to find a way to make things look better than they were.

He went to the General's office and told him of the demand. The General seemed unperturbed.

"I don't know why those people won't leave us alone," he exclaimed. "All is good here, why stir the pot? You can put something together to mollify them, can't you Zeller?"

He told the General he would get to it immediately and tried to appear disappointed that the task would make it impossible for him to join the General for dinner. Then he lied and said,

"I understand that La Splendeur is quite full. Some kind of party. May I get you a reservation at La Chat Noire?"

"Such a worker, you are," replied the General with a smile, "I know you would be restless the whole evening, so you stay and work, and we will have fun. And yes, La Chat Noire will be fine. Helmut can accompany me. Tell him to make the arrangements and to contact Moreau. Now give me Moreau's charges and I will pay him myself."

Zeller knew the task facing him wasn't an easy one, but was relieved to be excused from an evening with Moreau, and especially at La Splendeur. With regard to the report that was demanded from OKW West, he would have to be careful, for his neck was on the line as well as Boineburgs. He would fill the report with progress already made, avoid areas which had been neglected, and hope for the best. The one thing in their favor was the relative calm the city had been experiencing in recent months. He sat down at his desk and went to work.

Nanette made her usual Friday night appearance before a full house. The crowd was noisy, but quieted when she took the stage, and gave her another loud applause when she finished her set. She was relieved that Zeller wasn't there, or was she? She hadn't wanted to have to refuse him again, but was sorry that he was not there as a customer. Perhaps he was out of the city, or busy working, or——-?.

"Stop it, Nanette", she told herself. "You wanted him to stop bothering you, and apparently he has decided to do so. You can't have it both ways."

During the first act which followed Nanette, a German officer stormed into the room, much out of breath. He called for attention, and read an order received from headquarters. All the officers in the cabaret rose, excused themselves to their companions, and hurried out.

Nanette, in her dressing room, heard the sound of tables and chairs being shuffled, and the boots stomping out, but had no idea what was happening. She went out in time to see the last of the men make their exit, leaving behind scores of women and a few French men. Jean Barras saw her and came to her side.

"What's happening, Jean?," she asked.

"I don't know for sure. It seems to be something big, but not about Paris itself, from what little I heard."

He went to the table where the wife of one of the officers was sitting, and asked if she had any information she could share. He could see she was crying.

"All I know is this," she replied anxiously, "There has been a massive bomb attack on Nantes and St. Nazaire. All our men are on the alert. I know nothing else."

Both cities, especially St. Nazaire, had been repeatedly bombed by the allies, seeking to destroy the oil refinery, the submarine pens, and shipyards. But this attack, in February of 1943, was the most disastrous, as Nanette and Jean would soon learn. Three-fourths of St. Nazaire was burned, sending thousands of residents fleeing east to other towns and villages.

Nanette thought immediately of Julian, praying that he was safe. Jean asked the remaining women if they needed transportation to their residences, and assigned his wait staff and band-members to accompany those who did.

Nanette went to the telephone, finding all the lines blocked. Jean told her to wait while he closed and would take her home. She was grateful for that, hoping that Julian might attempt to get through to her at her apartment.

It was the next morning before he called, from Cande, to tell her that he was safe, and that his work-place had sustained only minor damage. His apartment, on the edge of Nantes, had been spared.

"Oh, Julian, I am so relieved," she said. "It must have been terrible."

"Both terrible and wonderful," he replied. "Bad for the people who lost homes, but great for our cause. Some important Nazi installations were destroyed."

"I'm just glad you are not hurt. What about your job, is it still secure?

"Well, you probably surmised from our last discussion, that the Germans took control of our plant. I thought it would put me out work. But since I knew the accounting system so well, they consider me an essential worker. That's very lucky for me, believe me. Many men of my age have been taken away, to God knows where."

"Julian, you will be careful, won't you? I mean, not to do anything to get you in trouble."

"Of course. I know how to stay in line."

Paul Moreau felt himself very lucky. The bomb raid on Nantes had caused only minor damage to his father's warehouse, and most of the merchandise was salvageable. He was on his way back to Paris now again, making stops at several German posts along the way with items requested by the officers. He had increasingly ingratiated himself with the Nazis, who knew he dealt in some illegal trade, but who overlooked it in favor of satisfying their desires for things otherwise unobtainable. He therefore had access to people the average Frenchman had only heard about.

Once in Paris, he phoned the General's headquarters, asking to speak with Captain Zeller. After a short wait, Zeller came on and agreed to see Moreau briefly in an hour.

"Captain, thank you for making time to see me," said Moreau, once inside Zeller's office. "I wanted to deliver this small gift to you, and to ask if the General had any requests for my next visit."

He handed Zeller a box of Swiss chocolates.

"Thank you," the Captain replied,. "As you may understand, all of us have been rather occupied lately, so the General has not spoken of any needs. Perhaps, when things calm down some, he will make his wishes known to me. You will be back again in a few weeks?"

"I plan to, yes."

"Then inquire of us again," said Zeller, rising to indicate the meeting was over.

But as Moreau was about to leave the room, Zeller called him back, and told him to sit again.

"It's, ah, about a young woman," Zeller said, sheepishly. "I would like very much to see her, but on the several occasions that I asked, she has refused me. I suppose I should give up trying, but I don't know much about French women. Perhaps there is something I am not doing correctly.

Maybe you could make some suggestions."

"This woman," asked Moreau, "is she single?"

"But of course. It is nothing like that," replied Zeller quickly. "She sings in a cabaret."

Moreau became instantly alert. He slid forward in his chair, then stopped, not wanting to show too much interest. He tried to resume a casual demeanor.

"In a cabaret," he echoed. "So, she must have many admirers. Perhaps she is very choosy.

Or maybe she doesn't go out with customers."

"She said the same," said Zeller. "And I thought of not going to the cabaret anymore, but then I would have no way of contacting her. You can see it is somewhat of a dilemma."

"This cabaret. Is it a reputable one? I mean, high class?"

"Naturally. Many of our officers go there. It is not a crude place, as I hear many are."

Moreau was convinced Zeller was speaking of La Splendeur. Could the woman be Nanette?

He risked asking the question, his instincts telling him it was her.

"I could try speaking to her, Frenchman to Frenchman, and try to convince her it would be all right, but of course, I can guarantee nothing," said Moreau. "What is her name?"

"Nanette Lemond," replied Zeller, almost in a whisper.

"Nanette," said Moreau, pretending to be memorizing the name. "I will give it a try."

"You will let me know if you have success in a few weeks?"

"I will," promised Moreau, who then shook hands with the Captain, and left. He was not at all surprised that Zeller was attracted to Nanette, nor that she had given him the same brush-off he received. He did feel a pang of jealousy to think of them together, but knew the rewards to him personally would be great if he could somehow get Nanette to agree to a date. After that, it was totally up to Zeller. His mind was filled with nothing else on his drive back to Nantes, after a late start.

——— ⣿ ———

That same evening Julian received another call for immediate action. He met the others of his cell at the appointed location, listening while Tolan described their plans. A butcher in the city of Angers had become exceedingly friendly with the German Commandant of the region, and had fed him the names of suspected Resistance members in the area. Two of them had been captured and imprisoned, and now faced a firing squad. The leader of the cell in Angers, himself being watched closely by the Gestapo, had called Tolan, asking for his assistance.

"This will be a first for us," said Robert, "and I hope none of you will become squeamish.

The man is our enemy, worse than a Nazi because he betrays his own people. He will be eliminated to serve as an example for others."

Julian was amazed at the vehemence in Tolan's voice. He wondered how the plan would be carried out, and what his role in it would be. Robert clarified that quickly as he described the plan.

"We will go to the butcher's home, and two of us will enter. Julian, you will stay with the car, at the end of the alley behind the house. We will bind his wife and bring the man out by the rear door. At our sign, you will bring the car to us, we will put him inside and drive to the old bridge south of the city. We'll wait to be certain no traffic is in sight, then drop his body into the Loire. A note will be left in his home, saying this is the reward for informers and betrayers."

Julian felt numb. He didn't know if he was ready to participate in a killing. Tolan sensed his hesitation.

"Julian," he said, "you don't have to do this. I can call someone else. There is still time."

"No, I'll do it," answered Julian firmly. "I'll drive, but I don't think I can be the one who—you know."

"And you won't be," Robert assured him. "Marcel has the garotte and knows how to use it. So, are we ready? Let's go."

They drove the main highway from Nantes to Angers, the hour nearing midnight. The pavement was wet from a passing shower. Everyone in the car was tense, and became more so when they saw flashing lights ahead. They were relieved to find it was an accident, just being cleared away. Traffic coming from the other direction slowed to see what had happened. In one of the cars was Paul Moreau. As he passed the line of stopped vehicles, he glanced over and was surprised to see Julian in the driver's seat of one of the cars, speaking to another man in the passenger seat. He drove on, wondering what would bring Julian to Angers this late on a week night.

Tolan's plan was carried out with precision. The butcher, of course, pleaded his innocence, but to no avail. The men bound and blindfolded him, then drove to a bridge in a commercial district where they killed him and dropped his body into the river. They drove immediately back to Nantes, leaving Julian off at his apartment along the way. Inside, he fixed himself a drink to steady his nerves and sat on his bed. He was sweating heavily, his hands still shaking as he realized that although he didn't actually kill the man, he was an accomplice in his death. It was a sobering thought, making him wonder if he would ever be able to get out of his mind the picture of the body being pushed over the railing, into the river. Maybe Nanette was right: he wasn't cut out for this.

———— ⚬⚬⚬ ————

The local, Nazi controlled, newspaper published the story a day later. It described the butcher's death as a revenge killing by someone jealous of the man's job, or by a customer angry about not getting a proper ration of meat. Naturally, nothing was mentioned about the man's role as an informant.

When Paul Moreau read the newspaper article, images began to resurface in his mind. He Hadn't see Julian Lemond for years. Why, suddenly, would he appear in the dead of night, far from home, driving a vehicle? It was possible, even probable that he was connected in some way to the butcher's death. If so, he might be working with the Resistance, which held real promise for Moreau. If he could bring the Commandant in Angers information which might help solve this murder, it would enhance his reputation even more.

He drove to Angers the same afternoon, asking to see the officer, whom he had met once before. He shared his suspicions with the officer, who took notes, and asked:

"This Julian Lemond, you know the man?"

"I've known him for many years."

"As a friend?"

"No, more as an acquaintance. He once worked for my father, but he had to let him go. He was quite unreliable."

"Could this perhaps be a revenge on your part for something he did to you?" Asked the officer, familiar many with such accusations.

"Not at all," replied Moreau, acting hurt. "I hardly knew the man."

"You say that he and another person were on their way to Angers. About what time?"

"Close to midnight. I was on my way home from Paris, after a meeting with General Boineburg's aide."

The commandant's eyebrows lifted slightly.

"So, you know Zeller?" he asked.

"Yes. I think he will vouch for my honesty."

"Very well, we will look into this matter, although the evidence is quite slim. I suppose you expect a reward, if your man is found to have had a part in this?"

"Not at all," replied Moreau. "I'm just doing my duty as a citizen."

Julian was working at his desk when two men, wearing long, black leather coats and obviously Gestapo, approached and ordered him to come with them. He turned pale, but tried to conceal his anxiety.

"Can you tell me why?" he asked.

"You will find out soon enough, if you don't already know," one of the men answered.

Julian was taken out, past the worried glances of the shop workers, placed in a dark car, and driven away. At Gestapo headquarters, the men took him to a windowless room, telling him to sit and wait. He knew this was not a rehearsal as before. He was in trouble, and filled with fear about what was to come.

A middle-aged man, dressed in a business suit, entered the room and introduced himself with a smile.

"I am Dietrich Platt, and you, I believe, are Julian Lemond."

Julian only nodded.

"I hope we can make this as pleasant as possible," said Platt. "I have a dossier on your background and present work, so I won't waste time with such questions. What I want is your response to the accusation that you were in Angers on the night of June 20th."

"Angers?," replied Julian questioningly, "No, I was not there. Why would you ask me that?"

"Already I see that you are lying. You were identified as the driver of a dark-colored Peugot on the main road, near an accident site. Do also deny that?"

"Of course I deny it. I was nowhere near Angers. I work hard at my job and need my rest. The 20th was a Thursday, I believe, and I never, ever, go out when I have to work the following day. Wherever you got this information, it's wrong. Who said they saw me there?"

"The 20th was a Wednesday, but that's of no matter," said Platt. "You don't need to know our source, but it is someone quite reliable."

Julian tried to act relaxed, but his insides were churning, and he couldn't keep from squirming in his chair.

"Well, your informant was not so reliable this time, because I was at home every night of that week. As I said, I—."

"Yes, yes, you already said it. But for now, until we can look into the matter more closely, you will be held in detention in the local jail."

"Wait, a minute. I categorically deny being in Angers that night. But what does it matter. What happened there to bring about my arrest?"

Platt hesitated for a moment, then shrugging his shoulders, said:

"As you know, I'm sure, a local butcher met an untimely death that night. And we believe you were involved."

"What," shouted Julian, suddenly getting to his feet, "A murder! I have never hurt anyone in my life. It's impossible, unthinkable."

"Sit down," ordered Platt, "and be quiet. I simply want you to know that what we are dealing with is very serious, and, until we conclude our investigation, you will remain in our custody."

"But what about my job," pleaded Julian, "I work for your people. The work that I do is important. I'm not going anywhere. Where would I go? Please, let me continue to work while you do more investigating. I'm sure you'll discover your information is wrong anyway. And I won't lose my job."

Platt stood and looked at Julian.

"We don't make deals," he said, and left the room.

Julian was devastated. Who in the world had seen and betrayed him, he wondered, and how long would this investigation take? He felt totally disarmed and, knowing the way the Nazis operated, feared for his life.

Julian spent a restless, fearful night in his cell, thinking of the best and worst scenarios facing him. Perhaps they would believe his story and release him. Perhaps other evidence would be found implicating him, and he would be shot. He passed the bleak hours praying, berating himself for getting involved in such dangerous work, and worrying what would happen to Nanette if he was imprisoned or killed. How he wished he could talk to her, hear her voice, reassure her that things would be all right. Finally, sleep found him.

He was awakened by a shout and the rattle of keys as a guard brought him some bread and a cup of weak tea. Ten minutes later two guards arrived, taking him to a small room with a desk and two chairs, one occupied by Platt. He ordered Julian to sit, while the guards remained.

"Again, I will not waste time, Monsieur Lemond. A person in the household of the butcher, a niece who lives upstairs, has confirmed that the car used to abduct her uncle was a Peugot of the kind our witness said you were driving. Another witness has come forth, telling us that the same car was seen waiting a short distance from the bridge where the butcher's body was dumped into the river. Finally, a neighbor in your apartment block, who got up to let his dog out, saw you arriving home very late that night, dropped off by the same car. So you see, we have you. Now, if you wish to save your life, you will tell us who else was involved."

As he heard th evidence against him, Julian began to panic. His heart was racing, his hands sweaty, his throat dry.

"You're wrong," he declared. "Someone is setting me up. I am not—."

"Not part of the Resistance? Is that what you were going to say?" sneered Platt. We know this was an act planned by one of the cells, so it must have been yours. You can tell me now or tell me later, after we use a little coercion.

Julian tried to show a brave face.

"Coercion will be a waste of your time. It's all lies, no matter what others say."

"Time will tell," remarked Platt. "Take him back to his cell."

Starting at two that afternoon, and lasting all through the long and torturous night, Julian experienced what no decent mind could imagine, and what only the strongest and bravest could endure. The techniques of interrogation the Gestapo used exceeded the outer limits of brutality.

First, they beat him with a lash for fifteen minutes, then left him bleeding, in his cell. A half-hour later two men returned and asked if he was ready to cooperate. When he told them he had no information, they took him to another room, strapping him to a chair. A rubber-hood was placed tightly over his head' allowing him no way to breathe. When he struggled and gasped, his feet kicking, the hood was removed for just a few seconds, then replaced. Julian fainted after the third time. When he was revived, he again refused to answer their questions.

He was transferred to yet another room, which contained a deep sink, filled with water. He knew immediately what was coming and braced himself for the ordeal. His head was plunged into the water until his breath was gone, then pulled out, chocking and coughing. The men did this to him twice more, questioned him again, then returned him to his cell.

An hour later, Platt visited him in his cell.

"Your little adventures of the past few hours are only a beginning," he said. "If you wish to tell me about the others in your group, this will all end. If not, our real efforts will begin."

"You can't get anything out of an empty shell," replied Julian, barely able to whisper. "So I have no names to give you."

"Very well, but I don't believe you. So, we'll just keep trying. I think soon you will see the mistake you are making."

The two guards returned, moving Julian to one of the rooms he previously was in. A table was there, on which sat a large box. Julian was strapped in a chair, his trousers and underpants removed, and his legs also strapped. Julian squirmed in his seat, but was unable to move, as one of the men attached wires to his penis. The man nodded to the other, who turned a dial on the instrument on the table.

The pain was unimaginable. Julian's body thrashed and jerked, his eyes wide and his voice screaming. He felt his bowels let go. After five seconds, which seemed an eternity, the current was turned off. Julian breath came in pants. He felt humiliated, sitting in his own excrement. When he was asked and again refused to reveal others names, the pain came on again, deeper and longer, so excruciating that he lost consciousness. Cold water splashed on his face. He suddenly became aware of his surrounding, feeling the pain in his groin. His head slumped forward on his chest. He saw the wires, still attached, and prayed for this to end. But it didn't. Another jolt of electricity surged through him, his body fighting against the assault, powerless to allay the agony, which went on and on.

He awoke sometime later, he didn't know the time, his head throbbing, his whole being demolished. He lay in the filth of his excrement and vomit, hardly able to believe he was still alive, and half wishing he wasn't. His only consolation was that he had resisted giving them what they wanted, at least for now. Whether they would use other methods on him or not, he didn't know, but he would hold out no matter what. His fatigue overcame his pain, and he slept.

The following morning a guard brought Julian a plate of food and some tea. A bit later he was taken for a shower, and given some clean clothing.

Platt came to his cell and looked him over.

"It is such a shame," he said. "You seemed like a fine young man. But you are a stubborn and foolish one, and my patience has run out. This is your last opportunity to tell us what you know before you are shot. It is really worth your life? If you cooperate, I promise you, you will live."

"Go to hell, you inhuman bastard," replied Julian, with all the might his sore throat could muster.

Nanette was becoming panicky. Not only had she not received a telephone call from Julian as promised, but despite repeated attempts, was unable to reach him. She had a strange feeling, almost an intuition, that Julian was in trouble. She called the Cande parish priest, who told her he had not seen Julian for years, and had not heard or read anything to pass on to her. The priest took her number and agreed to call if he had some news. Nanette didn't know where else to turn. Then, she thought of one other person who might help her. She asked the information operator for the number of Robert Tolan, and was further dismayed to learn that his number had been disconnected.

There was only one solution: if she hadn't heard from Julian in another week, she would journey to Nantes and find him.

CHAPTER 10

WHEN MOREAU LEARNED of Julian's arrest, he was quite pleased with himself, because he felt he could use it to good advantage. He was eager to get back to Paris to meet with Zeller and outline his fiendish plan. Whether the man would agree to it or not depended on how desperate he was to be with Nanette. He placed a call to Zeller, asking the Captain to return it as soon as possible, stressing the urgency of the matter.

Zeller was inspecting fortifications all day, and went directly home, rather than to his office. He found Moreau's message early the next morning and made the call immediately. Moreau said he had a plan, but wanted to discuss it personally, saying time was of the essence. Zeller agreed to meet him the same afternoon.

Moreau was nervous as he entered Zeller's office, hoping the Captain would not be angry with the idea of the scheme he was about to present.

"You asked me to think of something that might convince Mademoiselle Lemond to agree to a date with you." he said. "Certain events in the Loire Valley offer a possible solution."

"What events," asked Zeller suspiciously.

"There was a murder. A well-known butcher, one of your informers, was killed, most likely by members of an area

Resistance cell. A man from outside the area was seen in the vicinity of the crime, and is being questioned by the Gestapo in Angers. The man's name is Julian Lemond.

Zeller gave a look of astonishment, and leaned slightly forward.

"He's related to Nanette?" he asked.

"Her brother. Her only sibling, and their parents are dead," answered Moreau, trying to sound sympathetic. "I knew the man years ago when he worked for my father. He's a good man, certainly not part of the Resistance, and I can't imagine his being involved in something like this. But I know, or have heard, that the Gestapo can be quite rough when they interrogate someone."

"What are you leading to?" asked Zeller.

Moreau knew he had to be extremely careful here, and not sound mercenary.

"From what I read in the local papers, the evidence against him seems very flimsy. I believe, given your authority, you could have the man released. You would be a hero to Nanette.

So, I suggest that you ask for a meeting with Nanette, telling her it concerns her brother. She'll come, I am certain of it. See how she reacts, then make her an offer."

Zeller leaned his head in his hands, thinking deeply. What if she thought it was all planned by him to break her down? Then she would hate him and be gone forever. He looked up at Moreau.

"Does she know? Has she been informed of her brother's arrest?"

"I don't know how she could. From what I have heard, he isn't allowed outside contact. I only know this from the newspapers, of course."

Zeller was thoughtful for a moment, then said:

"Good. I will call the commandant in Angers, inquire about Julian, and have him send me a list of recent arrests. I can tell Nanette that I saw the name, knew the man was from the same area as she, and wondered if he is related. I'll feign surprise and offer to help."

Moreau smacked his hands together.

"Wonderful. And of course, nothing will be said to her of my involvement."

"Naturally," replied Zeller.

"There is one other thing," Moreau said cautiously. "If Julian Lemond learns why he is being released, he will certainly try to dissuade Nanette from going through with it."

"And you suggest?" asked Zeller.

"Tell him that a friend with close connections appealed for his release."

"And that would be you," stated the Captain.

"It's an idea", suggested Moreau, shrugging his shoulders.

"Well, before we go any further, let me find out with the situation is with this Julian. Wait outside while I make a call."

Zeller knew the Commandant of Angers, a personal friend who served with him on the eastern front. He asked about Julian Lemond and was shocked to learn how far things had developed. He was told in no uncertain terms that Julian could not be released. The evidence against him was strong."

When Zeller told him Julian was the brother of a very close friend, and asked what could be done, the Commandant told him he might be able to save him from being shot, but nothing more.

Zeller asked him to postpone the execution until he got back to him, and hung up. He called Moreau back into the room.

'This is far more serious than you know," he told Moreau. "Lemond is scheduled to be shot very soon. There is quite a bit of evidence against him, and they are certain he was acting with the Resistance. The Gestapo was unable to break him, and so, he is to be killed."

Moreau paled and his mouth dropped open in disbelief. As wicked as he was, he hadn't expected this. He wanted to scare Julian, have him arrested for a few days, and act as his rescuer.

He squirmed in his seat and asked anxiously:

"Can you help him? Can you at least save him from being shot? My God, he doesn't deserve that, I'm sure of it."

"What you or I think is of no consequence," asserted Zeller. "But, I think I can save him from being executed, no more."

Moreau was silent for a time, obviously troubled.

"And Nanette, will you tell her?" he asked.

"Yes, and I must act quickly. Angers wants to make an example of Lemond, and they will unless I plead with them This is a mess, but hopefully I can make it happen. Then I will owe someone a lot."

Moreau left, leaving Zeller to find Nanette. He called Barras at the Cabaret, asking if he knew that Nanette had a brother, then asking for her telephone number, stressing the extreme nature of his request. Barras complied, Nanette answering the call on the second ring.

"Mademoiselle Lemond," he said, his voice trying to hide his emotion in hearing her voice, "This is Captain Zeller. I have some news to share with you about your brother Julian. Can you please come to my office as soon as possible, perhaps within the hour?"

At the mention of her brother's name, Nanette stiffened and became instantly alarmed.

"What sort of news?" she asked, her own voice shaky.

"Please, I would rather share it with you in person. Can you come now? I'll send a car."

Nanette agreed, gave Zeller her address, and hurriedly dressed and put on makeup. Her heart was pounding, knowing there must be trouble with the Nazis, or Zeller wouldn't have been involved. She said a prayer for Julian's safety, then went to the door to wait for the car, which arrived in five minutes.

Manfried Zeller was as nervous as Nanette, as he sat across the desk from the woman he cared for so deeply, thinking how terrified must be, and praying that they would both get past the new few minutes without breaking.

Mademoiselle Lemond, I an truly sorry to meet under these circumstances. I get reports each week from our offices in Angers and elsewhere. This morning I was looking at one of the reports, and came across the name Julian Lemond on a list of persons arrested. I was curious as to whether this man was related to you, and called Jean Barrras, who said you had a brother of that name."

"A prisoner?" exclaimed Nanette excitedly. "Of what has he been accused."

Zeller felt his heart melting for this dear girl, and nearly gave up on his plan.

"Please Captain," she said, "Tell me if he is all right."

"They say he was involved in, ah, the abduction of a butcher in Angers. They think he is a member of the Resistance."

"Oh my God," said Nanette, now visibly crying. "I know my Julian. He wouldn't do that. Where is he now? Can I go to see him?"

Zeller came around his desk, offering her a handkerchief. He had all he could do to keep from putting his arms around her to comfort her.

"I'm afraid he can have no visitors," he replied gently.

"Well, how long will they hold him?" she inquired.

Zeller hesitated, knowing what he had to tell her would be devastating to her. He blinked, fighting back tears in his own eyes.

"Tell me, what is it?" asked Nanette, sensing his hesitation.

Zeller took a deep breath, and replied. "I don't know how to say this—but, he is sentenced to be—to be shot."

Nanette gasped, and had to hold on to the arms of the chair to keep from falling off.

"O God, no. Please not Julian. No, no, it can't be. There has to be a mistake. I spoke with him just last week. He told me he wasn't doing anything risky. I asked him myself. They must be wrong, it can't be him."

Her breath coming hard, she looked at Zeller and asked: "Is there anything you can do, Captain Zeller? I will do anything to save him. Can't you just give an order and tell them to spare him?

She was sobbing now, almost ready to faint. Zeller laid his ace-card gently and hesitatingly on the table of her life and his.

"Nanette," he said. "I don't mean this to sound harsh or cruel, or selfish, but sometimes officers who have intimate companions are able to appeal for members of their families. I have seen it done."

"What do you want me to do?" she asked, her body shaking as she spoke through her sobs.

"If I could tell the commandant in Angers that Julian is the brother of my companion, I believe he would show clemency," he said softly and hesitatingly, almost hating himself for it.

Nanette continued to cry, and Zeller couldn't tell if she was still reacting to the news about Julian, or about his offer. He let her compose herself, saying nothing more until she spoke. He went to a side table, bringing her a glass of brandy.

"You want me to come and live with you," she stated.

"Please don't hate me for it, dear girl," he said politely, "it's the way things work. If you agree, I promise I will make no demands on you except for you to live with me in my apartment and be my consort when I go out socially. Nothing more. That is a solemn promise."

Nanette sensed the sincerity in his voice, and hoped she was right. She knew what Zeller said about "the way things work", was correct, which gave little choice. When it came to helping their own, the Nazis were quick to act. With others, they were merciless. She loved her brother above all else, and if this is what it took to save him, it was worth it.

"If I agree right now, will you assure me that he will be saved?" she asked. "How can I know your request will be granted"

"Let me make a phone call," he replied. "Please wait outside for just a few minutes."

When he called her back into the room, he walked over and stood beside her.

"The order for your brother's execution has been rescinded," he said. "He's to be transferred to the camp at Choisel, where he will remain a prisoner. It was the best I could do. I'm sorry I couldn't do more."

Tears ran down Nanette's cheeks.

"He must never know why," she said anxiously. "I don't want him ever, ever to know."

"He will be told that the evidence against him was not strong enough to warrant death.

When his transfer is completed, he will be allowed to write to you. Is that acceptable?"

"Yes, thank you," she said, feeling relieved but still extremely anxious, both for Julian and for herself. "When do you want our arrangement to begin?"

He looked at her with admiration and pity, but most of all with a deep-felt emotion that wanted to do nothing but protect her and care for her.

"I must make arrangements for a different flat. I have only one bedroom. I will find something with two. It may take a few days. May I contact you when I have things in place?"

She nodded. He took her arm and led her to the door, the closeness of her body and the thought of his becoming her protector filling him with comfort and joy. She turned, gave him a wan smile, and left.

When Julian was informed that his death sentence had been revoked, and that he would be going to a prison camp, a sense of relief flooded over him. He knew the life of a prisoner wasn't an easy one, but he would be alive, and hopefully would live to see the Nazis defeated.

After a week at Choisel, he was allowed to write to Nanette. He tried to explain what happened in words which conveyed his innocence, certain that his letter would be read, and possibly censored. Above all, he asked her not to worry over much and told her how much he loved her. Someday soon, he promised, they would be together again.

CHAPTER 11

MANFRIED ZELLER CONTACTED Nanette after a week, giving her the address and details of their new apartment. Since she had some of her own furniture, he sent a van to help her move her things.

He had found the flat after only two days, but it had taken several days more to move his belongings. In addition to his clothing—mostly uniforms which he was required to wear at all times in public—were furnishings and art. The art had been given as gifts, Nanette learned later. Several of the paintings were quite valuable, as were two fine, oriental rugs. There was little doubt in Nanette's mind that they had been taken from the homes of wealthy Parisians.

The van with her things stopped in front of a stately old building on rue Grenville. It was near les Invalides, with its Church of the Dome, where the body of Napoleon rested. The apartment building had a large glass window over the entry, opening a view to an immense chandelier hanging from the ceiling.

The apartment, on one end of the fourth floor, running from front to back, was high ceilinged and bright. The rooms were spacious and beautifully arranged, making her feel, for a moment, like a queen. It was obvious from the way the flat was furnished that Zeller had excellent taste. From the foyer, she walked through a sitting room into a dining room, and then a small but well-furnished kitchen. Doubling back, a hallway took her to one bedroom, and then another. She enjoyed the tour, but her delight was met by a feeling of unease, causing her to wonder again what she was getting into, and how much she could trust Zeller to keep his word.

Zeller stepped out of the first bedroom, smiled and said, a bit nervously:

"Forgive me for not meeting you at the door, Nanette. I was on an important phone call."

He took her hand and kissed it.

"Your room is the next one down the hall," he continued, "I have left space for your own furniture if you wish to use it. Otherwise, we can see what you need. You also have your own bath, and a splendid view from you window. I hope you like it and will be comfortable here."

It was an extremely awkward time for both, Zeller standing rather stiffly, and Nanette wringing her hands. She nodded and went into her room. It was quite large, with a double bed, a mirrored dressing table, and a large armoire.

"It's very nice, thank you," she said, turning to Zeller. "I—I think, I'll begin to unpack as soon as your men bring my things up."

"Yes, of course," he replied, "I must go back to my office. Please be ready to go for dinner at seven. It's a small restaurant that I like, not fancy, but good food and service."

He was about to stand at attention, then relaxed, smiled and said good-bye.

It took an hour for her things to be brought up to the apartment, and a few pieces of her furniture placed where she chose. Other pieces did not match the decor, and she suggested to the van driver that he do with them as he saw fit.

When the men left, she sat on the edge of her bed, and was about to cry. Suddenly she sat up straight and said to herself, "Nanette, you will not cry over this, not now or ever. You will not feel sorry for yourself. You made a decision—the correct one—the only decent and loving one—and now you must live with it."

She shook herself, stood, and began to unpack. She had a wide selection of dresses, mostly formal and elegant, which filled the armoire. On the dressing table she found a tin-box, the size of a large book, but deeper. Opening the lid, she found a note and a quantity of money. The note read:

Dear Nanette:

Since I have not been married, I asked some trusted friends how they handle finances in their household. I was told that the kindest way Is to give you an allowance each month to spend as you like. So I have enclosed what is in this box as a starting point, for you to buy clothing, or whatever essentials you need, without having to come to me for money. You can tell me if it is enough after one month.

I hope this is satisfactory.

Your Manfried.

Nanette smiled despite herself. The poor man was trying very hard to be kind. She looked at the wad of francs he had left, thinking it was much more than she would ever spend, unless she updated her wardrobe, which she probably should. She folded the note, replaced it in the box, and closed it.

They went to dinner that evening, the maitre de at small restaurant friendly and solicitous. Manfried introduced Nanette, then took her to the table reserved for them. He asked if she would like wine, but she preferred mineral water, which he ordered for them both.

Conversation was strained at first, but when Nanette asked about his family, Manfried became animated, and they both began to relax. He told her he was born in Bavaria, in the small town of Freising, near Munich. He attended the University of Heidelberg, completing a degree in engineering, and working for two years before going into the army. His parents were still living, his father a retired engineer, and his mother a home-maker, after an injury ended her career as a pianist. He had an older sister, Barbara, married to a farmer, and a younger brother, Horst, a lieutenant in the Luftwaffe.

Nanette asked if Barbara and her husband had children, and if so, did he have photos. He was quick to open his wallet and show her Barbara's family, of whom he was very proud. The photo showed a nice-looking couple, with three children, two boys and a girl.

"Euwe, Barbara's husband," he said, "is very happy to have the boys to help with the work on the farm. They really have a very good living. I worked for them one summer when I was at the university. I can still smell the scent of the sweet hay in the barn, and the taste of milk from the cooler at the end of a hard day."

He looked at Nanette with a bit of embarrassment, as if he were getting too personal.

"And Horst," she asked, "does he fly a plane?"

"Unfortunately, yes. He flies fighter planes, a dangerous job. He earned his wings just last month, and has already been in the fighting. I worry about him, as we are very close. I pray each day for his safety."

He prays! Thought Nanette. But why not? He is our enemy, but he trusts God to keep his brother safe, just as I do.

"Well, you know about my poor Julian," she said. "He is the only one I have left. My parents died together in a fire a few years ago. My two older uncles were killed in the Great War, and their wives died a few years ago. So it is only me."

And now you have also me," remarked Manfried.

Not knowing how to respond, Nanette simply smiled, and said nothing.

Thus began a routine which they followed each Monday for the next month, until Manfried asked Nanette if she would consider leaving her job at La Splendeur, so they would be free to go to other events and parties, and have more times together in the evenings.

"Since I work each day, and you work nearly every night, it is difficult for us to know each other better," he said. "I am not suggesting that you must leave the cabaret. I promised you I would not make such demands. But it would make our lives as a couple more complete. But only if you wanted to."

Nanette realized what he said was true. They had spent very little time together, which, at first pleased her. But as she came to know him better, she began to enjoy his company, especially since she had virtually no contact with her former acquaintances. She told him she would discuss it with Jean Barras and see if something could be worked out.

Jean, who knew by now the arrangements between Nanette and Manfried, said he was willing to offer her more evenings off, if that would keep her with him for a while longer. They discussed various options, agreeing that she would work Thursday through Saturday of each week, which were the busiest nights. She agreed and told him she thought Manfried would be pleased, which he was.

On Friday through Sunday mornings she slept, but on the other days, she woke early enough to prepare breakfast for Manfried, who was an early riser, and who usually left for the office by seven. He would call at least once each day to ask how she was feeling, and arrived back at their apartment by 6:30 each evening. Nanette often wondered what he did that consumed so much time, and often required him to work all day on Saturdays.

For her part, Nanette realized she had to find something to occupy her time on her free days. Manfried, sensing her need to keep busy, suggested that she visit some of the places in the region around Paris, such as Versailles. She did so on several occasions, finding most of the usual tourist sites nearly empty. Train schedules were hardly adhered to anymore however, so travel became more difficult. On one journey, to Reims, to see its Notre Dam cathedral, the train simply stopped running, and she had to call to Manfried for help. He gladly sent a car for her, and although he was worried for her safety, they were able to laugh about it over dinner.

A church nearby their apartment had a Saturday evening Mass, which Nanette began attending. She learned there of an organization recently formed, to assist prisoners of war interned in German-run camps. The Nazis did not prohibit such help, in fact welcomed it, since it took some of the burden for providing food and clothing off their shoulders. Nanette was amazed to learn that many Parisians, though poor and needy themselves, were willing to share their meager resources. Nanette was directed by the priest of the parish to the woman in charge, and Nanette became a volunteer, She sorted used clothing and a variety of items which were taken each month to a camp just outside the city. She hoped and prayed that people near the camp where Julian was interned had such a program, and that he might benefit from such generosity. She learned soon that he did not.

One evening, as she arrived at la Splendeur and entered her dressing room, she saw an envelope from the post lying on the table. It was addressed to her, in care of the cabaret. Closing her eyes in a brief prayer, she opened it to find that it was from Julian, as she had prayed it might be. It read:

Dear Nanette:

I am allowed this one letter, to tell you I am in a camp somewhere in France. I am treated well, but have no contact outside the fences. I am not permitted to receive mail, but I know you think of me, and you are with *me in my thoughts and prayers. Keep holding onto the hope that some day soon, we will be together again.*

Your loving brother, Julian

Nanette, crying as she read her brother's words, held the letter close to her face and kissed it. It was a relief to know he was still alive and relatively safe for now. She uttered a prayer of thanks, put the letter in her bag, and prepared for performance.

The weeks came and went, Manfried keeping his promise to not press Nanette into an intimacy she was not ready to accept. They learned to relax, and laugh together, sharing events from their past. When walking to and from a restaurant, he would hold her arm. She finally grew tired of eating out every evening, and suggested that she prepare dinner on the nights when she was off, to which he readily agreed. Shopping then became one of her tasks, and not an easy one. Food-stuffs became shorter in supply as each month passed, and their cost rose astronomically, making her wonder how the average citizen was able to eke out a living. Her days were less boring, however, and shopping and preparing meals made her feel as if she were contributing something to the otherwise one-sided relationship.

As winter arrived, and Christmas neared, Nanette thought about home, and what a special, joyful time it had always been. Every Christmas eve her family joined with others to sing carols in the town center, then went to midnight Mass, where she often sang the

Magnificat. The haunting, opening words of the verses now echoed in her mind:

> My soul magnifies the Lord, and my spirit rejoices in God my Savior; for he has regarded the low estate of his handmaiden.

He eyes filled with tears. What happy times they had been, and how low her present estate had become. But she knew a loving God was still her refuge, and would not let her be forsaken. She would do what she could to bring a semblance of joy into this dreary time. She had taken care every year, in choosing just the right gifts for her parents and brother, and decided she would surprise Manfried with a gift. She thought about it carefully, deciding on a warm scarf to match his overcoat.

Two weeks before Christmas, on a Thursday afternoon, Nanette arrived home after a day of volunteer work. As she entered the apartment, she saw Manfried's overcoat and tunic lying over a chair, and heard sounds coming from his room. It sounded like crying. She knocked on the closed door, and heard him say to enter. He was sitting on his bed, his eyes red, all semblance of his normal control gone, his cheeks wet with tears.

She walked to his side.

"Manfried, what is it," she asked in a tender voice.

"It's Horst, my brother," he said. "I just received word. His plane was shot-down, and before he could escape the wreckage, it burned. He died a horrible death."

Manfried put his head in his hands, shaking it from side to side. He seemed so weak and vulnerable, that Nanette could not keep from putting her arms around him, and holding onto him tightly. Her tears now also began, and she laid her cheek on his and kissed him. They stayed like that until he became calm.

"I'm so sorry, dear Manfried," she whispered, and in that instant realized how much she had come to like—she couldn't say love—this kind and gentle man. And she knew why. It was as she had once told Danielle: the only man who could win her heart must be like Julian, and here he was. Yes, here he was, wearing the hated uniform of the enemy, an intruder into the life of her nation, a figure of authority. But beneath it all was a man who knew pain, kindness, tenderness, and above all, patience. He could have been a tyrant, but in all these weeks he had asked nothing from her except to be by his side. And now, he needed her, more than ever.

That night, she went gently to his bed, and the two became one flesh.

The days which followed became easier for them both, although Nanette pondered what had happened and tried to understand. She found that in her mind she could use that four-letter "L" word, but not in their conversations. Sundays became the day they looked forward to with a happiness she hadn't felt in a long while. They took long walks, bundled against the cold, always ending up at their favorite fountain in the Luxemburg Gardens. They would sit until nearly chilled, then return to their apartment and enjoy each other's warmth.

Just a few days before Christmas, Nanette went to La Splendeur, and was met at the entrance by Jean, who was looking very discouraged. He informed her that the cabaret would close within a week.

"Jean," replied Nanette, "I had no idea things were going so badly. There has been some drop-off of customers, but has it been enough to make closing necessary?"

"It's not just that, Nanette. For several months I have had to bargain very hard for the wines and champagnes we serve, and finding whiskeys has been nearly impossible. One night last week, a night you were off, of our best local patrons had a small party here, and ordered his favorite champagne. When I told him we were out of stock, he became angry and left, taking three other couples with him. I have tried every supplier I know, including black-market sources, and have no luck. What can I do? Anyway, I am tired of all this. It will be good to relax for a bit, while I still have money enough to get along. But I feel very sorry for you and the other girls."

"Please, Jean, don't worry about me. I'll be all right, and I think most of the girls will too.

Will you stay open for Christmas eve?"

"Yes, and for New Year's eve. That will be the last. We'll have a big party. I wanted to know if you would sing a few last songs."

"Of course I will."

On Christmas eve, Manfried and Nanette went to an early mass, then to a party, given by General Boineburg. It was Nanette's first officers' party, and she felt uncomfortable at first among so much German brass. Manfried beamed as he introduced her, clearly the most beautiful woman there. A couple of his fellow officers joked with him, comparing him to a monk who suddenly discovers beauty. He took the ribbing well, and laughed at the jokes. Nanette recognized several of the women, and even noticed that one of them was wearing a gown she had designed for Emile. She was pleased that it still held its style.

The party seemed to belie the scarcity all around them. Tables were filled with meats, cheeses, and breads, and there was wine in abundance. Obviously, the Nazis had better connections than Monsieur Barras. A small orchestra softly played throughout the dinner, then more lustily as the tables were cleared and couples began to dance. It was the first try at dancing together for Nanette and Manfried, but after stumbling a bit, they found each other's rhythm and steps and whirled around the floor like old timers. It was very late when the party ran its course, the only discordant note to an otherwise pleasant evening, the singing of the German national anthem.

"Did you enjoy the party," Manfried asked, as they were driven home.

"I did. I really did," she replied. "At first, I felt out of place. Most of the people knew each other, and I was new. But they seemed so happy to see me with you, that I began to feel welcome, and very special. I could tell, by the way the men joked with you, that you are a very popular man."

"Oh, I don't know," he said shyly, "I try to be fair with them. But you were indeed welcome. Those jokes about my being a monk: I hesitate to tell you this, but you are the first woman I have ever been with. Some began to think I was, you know, different. But I never found anyone I was truly attracted to, until I met you."

"So you saved it all for me," responded Nanette with a chuckle, squeezing is arm.

"All for you, and you deserve so much more. You have two kinds of beauty, inside and out. It's a rare combination. How lucky I feel."

He became very quiet then, and in the darkness of the car, she could hear only his breathing. As they passed another vehicle, a beam of light fell on his face, and she saw tears on his cheeks.

"What is, Manfried? Is something wrong?" she asked with concern.

"All this joy I feel, all the love you have given me," he breathed deeply, and turned to face her. "I feel I have stolen it from you. I so wish we had come together before Julian was arrested. I hate it that you were forced into this."

"It's all right, Manfried," she assured him, "It's all right."

"No, my dear one, let me say this. I want to say this from the deepest part of my heart and soul, and I want you to think about it. This is my Christmas gift to you. Whenever you want to go away, you may go. I totally and completely release you from our agreement. I can't live with you like this, knowing the sacrifice you made, and the advantage I took of you. I will give you money to live in your own apartment, and you can choose the life you want, and deserve."

Nanette reached over and took his head in her hands, kissing away his tears, realizing how much she had come to love this man, but also concerned about what the future would bring.

"You saved Julian's life," she reminded him, "That was an eternal gift to me, and I needed no more. But you have given me so much more. And just think, if we hadn't met, regardless of the circumstances, where would I be now? With La Splendeur closing, and the other cabarets struggling, what would I do? Where could I go?"

She paused for a moment, thinking of how to say what she was thinking.

"Do you remember that evening, just after I agreed to come to you, when I told you I had no family but Julian? Do you remember what you said to me?"

"Of course I do," he replied with a smile. "I said, "And now you have me"".

"Yes, and I didn't fully realize it then, but I do now, just how fortunate I am, because I have you."

"Then you don't want to leave?" he asked.

"No, I truly do not want to leave you. I feel safe, and happy being with you. I don't want to be anywhere else, or with anyone else."

He kissed her, deeply and earnestly.

"Joyeux Noel," she whispered.

"Froehliche Weinachten", he replied.

CHAPTER 12

D ESPITE THE SHADOW of occupation, and the rumblings of the war, April in Paris was everything the poets wrote about. There were many more sun-filled days, and the parks, despite their benign neglect, still produced the scented air of a million blossoms. Nanette and Manfried spent time in the gardens whenever time allowed, although he was now going to his office on Sunday mornings with greater frequency. While he never spoke of the war's progress, nor did she ask, she sensed that the allies were gaining the upper-hand.

The Nazi-controlled press reported little news about German defeats, but their were articles noting the increased allied attacks along the French coast, and inland as well. While doing her volunteer work, her so-workers, ignorant of the fact that she lived with a German officer, often whispered about raids which the Luftwaffe were powerless to stop. She saw some women reading a single news-sheet, which she learned was printed by the Resistance. It told of the bombing of factories, rail-yards, and communication networks. The city of Tours was greatly damaged, and the railroad marshaling yards at Pierre-des-corps were decimated.

One unfortunate effect of the bombing, for French civilians, was the loss of electrical generation. All winter long, families had fought to keep their homes warm and lighted. With the loss of rail transportation to bring coal to the cities, the German High

Command ordered the seizure of hundreds of trucks, cars, and even bicycles. This created a panic throughout the region, leading to appeal after appeal by tradesmen whose livelihood depended on transportation. Some exceptions were finally made, but the overall effect of the order was a deepening hatred of the occupiers.

The officers of the German Paris Command knew an allied invasion was inevitable. Nazi defenses along the coast, referred to as "the Atlantic Wall", were bolstered and manned with more battalions. The stinging German defeats by the Soviets in the east, the loss of German bases in North Africa, and the allied landings in Italy, were signs of the declining power of Hitler's forces.

Few Frenchmen knew of these allied victories, or of the unremitting bombing campaign against the industrial areas inside Germany. During a five-day period in February, the allies had targeted aircraft factories and ball-bearing plants, followed by raids on the major Nazi-controlled oil refineries in Ploesti, Rumania. Dams in the Ruhr Valley, which had provided electrical power for German industry, were destroyed. Perhaps one of the greatest psychological blows to the confidence of the German people in their war effort, was the bombing of Berlin, with a great loss of life.

Nanette's mind was seriously conflicted. Of course she wanted the occupation to end, the war to end, and peace to reign once more. Her dilemma was that she hated the Germans, but loved a German man. What an allied victory would mean for Manfried was a question she tried to put aside, but one which hounded her constantly. For now, her only future was bound up with his. She could envision no other alternatives, but the uncertainties of the situation meant she could see to farther than the next day or the next week. Therefore she must take life one day at a time, and enjoy what each day offered.

By the end of May, Manfried's time on the job had grown to over eighty hours each week. He left early each morning, returning weary in the evening, with just enough time to eat before going off to sleep. Nanette did all the cooking now, and frequently had to eat alone. Manfried tried to reserve Sunday afternoons for Nanette, but they no longer took their walks. The increasing number of attacks on German soldiers on the streets of Paris, and the beatings of French women who consorted with German soldiers, led Manfried to fear for Nanette's safety. He said nothing to her about this, saying he was simply too tired for long walks.

One evening, concerned for his health, and the state of affairs on Paris streets, Nanette asked him if he could share his concerns with her.

"You have to learn sooner or later," he admitted, "so I might as well tell you now. Germany is losing the war. Despite the bold pronouncements from Berlin, and the posturing of our generals, there is no hope. I know I can trust you to keep this to yourself. Our Luftwaffe is kaput. We are expecting an invasion any day, and I don't believe we have the power to stop it."

"I don't know what to say," replied Nanette, "except that I will be glad when there is no more war. For you, for me, for your family, and for all families."

Manfried shook his head.

"I don't know why we got into this war. Well, yes I do. At first, I did understand. Germany was so humiliated after the Great War, and life was so hard, our leaders promised us a new creation. When people are drowning, they take whatever life-line is thrown to them. And life did become better for all of us. We had good employment, new conveniences, ample food. But now, the dream has become a nightmare."

Nanette put her arms around him, and kissed him.

"So, you must work so hard, even though it may do no good."

"I must work hard because our orders are to defend Paris at all costs. Every day, I go on an inspection tour of the city to see what preparations are being made, and every day the demands from Berlin grow heavier. It's impossible to meet them."

"And the General," asked Nanette, "how is he holding up?"

"I like General Boineburg. He is a good man, good to his aides, and good to me. But he is an old man and he sees what he wants to see. For him, these years in Paris have been a long holiday, lived well. He loves it here. It is as though he believes the war will never come to this place."

"So," she replied, "the work must be done by you and your fellow officers."

"By us. And it is almost too much to expect. I have ideas to improve things, but they fall on deaf ears. So, I do my job, and dislike it mainly because it steals the time I want to be with you."

They embraced, kissed, and went to their bedroom together, making love, and clinging to each other in a way they had not done in weeks.

The thunderbolt struck in the early hours of June 6th. Manfried had worked very late the night before, only getting to sleep around midnight. When the phone rang at 5 A.M., Nanette had to resist the temptation to let it ring. Manfried heard it, answered, and immediately leaped out of bed and began to dress. He was told to report to headquarters immediately, in a car already dispatched to pick him up.

Nanette looked at him sleepily and asked what the emergency was.

"It begins!" he said anxiously. "Paratroopers have landed on the Normandy coast in large numbers. All our units are on highest alert. I must go. I don't know when I will be back. I love you."

He buttoned his tunic, got into his overcoat and hurriedly left, his car already at the curb.

The allied night-drops were followed by the landings all along the coast of Normandy, 150,000 men, in thousands of ships. The German defenses were pounded by offshore warships, and supported by allied aircraft, unhindered by an absent Luftwaffe. It was nevertheless a bloody assault, and the allied drive into France moved ahead slowly, assisted by the French Resistance wherever their leaders found opportunities.

Nanette saw little of Manfried for the next week, and, when he did come home, he arrived late and left early. But as the German defenses stiffened, and the allied drive across France was slowed, he was able to do with shorter hours on the job. He explained that his office had done all they could from here, and now had only to wait for what was to come.

The Nazi leadership at OKW West, however, was not satisfied that everything had been done to build Paris defenses. Hitler himself, rabid about holding Paris at all costs, decided that the weak and relaxed leadership of General Boineburg had to be replaced by someone in whom he had absolute confidence. He ordered Dietrich von Choltitz, an nobleman from a long line of Prussian military officers, to Paris immediately. Von Choltitz, of a short and portly build, had a record of unflinching devotion to the Third Reich, and of brave determination. He successfully led the first German attack on Holland, early in the war. At Sebastopol, on the Black Sea, he commanded a force of 5,000 men in a siege of the city. When the city fell, he had fewer than 500 of his men left, himself wounded.

General Boineburg received the notice on August 3 that he was to be replaced, and that von Choltitz would arrive in six days. When the two men met, the meeting was perfunctory, Boineburg's staff ill at ease with this man, whose stiff and cold demeanor was such a contrast to that of their former commander. He seemed the perfect Nazi.

Before the meeting ended, the old General expressed the hope that von Choltitz would save the city from destruction in the event of a collapse. Von Choltitz made no such promise.

When Nanette learned of the change of command, she asked Manfried what it meant for him.

"I know already that I am to stay at my post. Choltitz has brought his own orderly, but my knowledge of the city's defenses is needed. He has already given me new orders."

Manfried hesitated, then decided to share with Nanette the orders that were as distasteful to him as he knew they would be to her.

"Our immediate task is to carry out orders given many months ago, which Boineburg failed to implement. We are to mine all the bridges over the Seine, and place explosives in all parts of the city, including at the factories and main buildings."

"How terrible," she shrieked, "But surely not the Eiffel Tower, or the Louvre, or the Arc de Triomphe!"

"All of them." replied Manfried, sorrowfully, "And all the power-plants and utilities. Hitler wants the city razed."

Nanette collapsed into a chair, crying.

"But why?" she asked through her tears. "You have the city, you've had it for years. Why must it be destroyed? If the British and Americans come, can't you just move your army out?"

"Why? Because the Fuhrer, whom I believe has gone mad, has given the order. He has always been a jealous lover. If he can't have Paris, neither can anyone else."

"And so, you must follow these wicked orders," she said bitterly.

"I, or someone else," he replied resignedly. "We can only hope and pray there is a way around it. But I don't know what that can be."

"Then, God help us," exclaimed Nanette.

General von Choltitz wasted no time setting things in order. One of his first commands was the confiscation of weapons from the entire Parish police force. He could risk no uprising from that quarter. In the hope of impressing the citizens of the city with the might of his forces, he staged a military parade along the main avenues. In a little over two weeks, Paris had become a city in despair.

Nanette sat at the window of their apartment, tired of reading, tired of sitting, tired of waiting. As the allies advanced eastward from Normandy, the prisoner of war camps set up by the Germans were abandoned, the inmates shipped to Germany. Nanette's volunteer work thus came to and end. Her worries about her brother Julian deepened. Would he too, be sent to Germany? She felt depressed and hopeless, like one of the characters in a book she was reading about the French Revolution. She got up, and looked at her face in a mirror. She had lost a good deal of weight, both from worry and from a poor diet. A lack of exercise had weakened her muscles, and she knew she must do something. But it was a vicious cycle: low energy led to less activity, which led to listlessness. Manfried was not faring much better, even with the influence and contacts he had. Supplies of nutritious food had simply dried up.

Less than one-hundred miles away, Julian lay on his bunk, listening to the sounds of the camp. If food and fuel were in short supply for the average citizen, they were doubly so for the prisoners. Julian had subsisted on a thin gruel and pieces of dry bread for weeks. The cold, damp days of spring had blessedly given way to warm, then hot, summer days, making life a bit more bearable.

The door opened, and a man Julian knew as Alain, entered and flopped on his bunk.

"Have you heard the news?" Alain asked."

"I don't know. What news is that?"

"I hear they're shutting this place down, sending us off. With all the bombings and such, the allies must be getting ready to move in. Anyway, as I hear it, we're shipping out soon, probably off to the German wonderland, the land of milk and honey."

They both sat quietly, pondering what such a move might mean. If they did go to Germany, would they ever return? The sound of an approaching train interrupted their thoughts. They ran to a window and looked out, seeing an engine and a long row of box-cars, rolling through the gate.

"Oh my God," exclaimed Alain, "Here comes our transportation. First-class cattle cars, complete with shit and piss. What a lovely way to see the countryside. I do hope the food is good and the wine properly chilled."

Julian liked Alain. He had kept the days and nights less miserable by his comedic banter. A Communist, one of thousands in the camp, he had been a radio-station engineer before the war, losing his job when the station was closed. Soon after the occupation began, when the Soviets broke their treaty with Germany and joined the allies, Communists all across France were arrested and sent to the camps. Alain was in the first group to be housed at Choisel.

"I wonder how much worse German camps will be than this." mused Julian

"Well, I'm certain they won't have sausages and beer waiting for us," replied Alain. "If the war is taking its toll on their population the way it is here, we'll be lucky to survive the war."

Julian felt a chill come over him. It was enough to be a prisoner, but to be one in a foreign land, must be hell, he thought.

"Damn, they're wasting no time!" exclaimed Alain, as he saw a large group of prisoners from the far side of the camp being lined up to board the cars. He watched as the men shuffled forward, those hesitant, prodded by the guards. They stepped on an overturned crate, and climbed or were pulled into the cars. Julian could hardly

believe the number of bodies being squeezed into each car, and
worried what their—and his—fate would be.

A guard entered Julian's barrack, shouting for attention,
startling a half-dozen sleeping men. He read several names from a
clip-board, Julian's included, and ordered them out. Alain and two
others were left behind, all Communists.

"Maybe I'll take the next train," quipped Alain, as Julian shook
his hand. "They always reserve the best for last."

Men were pouring out of all the barracks in Julian's sector now,
hundreds of them, heading for the tracks. They shuffled along,
heads down, terrified at what fate had in store for them. As each
was checked off a list, they boarded the cars, Julian climbing into
one nearly filled with the bodies of half-wasted men like himself.
The men sat or stood, with space between each other, but as more
bodies were forced in on them, they were forced to stand, pressed
together like pages in a book.

When the car was filled to the satisfaction of the guards, the
doors rolled shut, men already gasping for air. The car had four
screened windows, and Julian prayed that the train would soon
move out so the air rushing past might enter and relieve the stifling
heat.

One of the men, boosted up so he could see out of a window,
shouted:

"The others. They're taking the others!"

"What do you mean?" asked another.

"They're taking them to the wall," came the reply.

A groan swept through the car, then loud sobbing. The "wall" was the term for the killing ground, where prisoners were shot.

Julian forced his way to one of the windows, asked for a boost, and looked in time to see his friend Alain being herded with others toward the dreaded place. Alain held his arms wide, his face looking skyward, as if to say, "Isn't this a beautiful day to die?"

The train rolled out within the hour, the sound of the rifle-shots still echoing in the ears of the now silent passengers. At the same time, trucks, filled with the camp guards and officers, drove out through the gates. A skeleton crew was left behind to dispose of the bodies of those executed. By nightfall, the camp, which for four years had housed three-thousand prisoners, of whom only eleven-hundred still lived, became deserted.

The train chugged across northern France, joining the main line, from Nantes to Strasbourg, at Angers. Julian was unaware, as the train passed through Cande, how close he was to the place of his birth. The route would take them on a detour around the bombed-out city of Tours, through Arlen, and over the Seine at Troyes. The old, steam-powered engine, made numerous stops to take on water. At each stop, the human cargo shifted into new positions, the men allowing those in the center of the crush, to have their place nearer the windows. It was an inhuman, miserable journey, replicated by scores of such trains, and hundreds of thousands of such prisoners, all across France.

The car which held Julian was quiet except for the snores of the lucky ones who could sleep, and the crying of others.

"Have you ever been to Germany?" asked Julian of the man pressed against him, hoping to relieve the boredom with conversation.

"Many times," the man replied. "I sold wine to the Boche for twenty years."

"Why were you taken?" inquired Julian.

The man, whom Julian hadn't met before, although he had seen him in the camp, smiled.

"I got a bit greedy," he said. "I was selling on the black-market, and when my supplies got low, I began to water down the wine. Unfortunately, an S.S. officer, who knew his wine well, bought some, and traced it back to me. The next day, I was arrested. By the way, I'm Edgar."

"I'm Julian."

"And what about you, Julian. How did you come to be in this elite company?"

"Mistaken identity. They thought I killed an informer."

"And, of course, you're innocent, like all of us. But if you really did it, congratulations. I wish I had shot a few of those traitors myself. It would have made this worth it."

Darkness settled over the land, a moon-less night with the smell of rain in the air. As the wheels of the train clacked on the rails, the prisoners swayed from side to side with the cars, their minds beyond the point of care of reasoning. They crossed the heavily guarded Seine bridge at Troyes well after midnight, their stomachs churning with hunger, their throats parched. Some men slept as they stood, held upright by the bodies around them. There was a noticeable change of terrain now—the flat, rolling farmland of the Northern Plains—giving way to the hilly terrain of the Champagne Region.

As they neared the bridge over the River Aube, there was a sudden screeching of brakes. Julian's car shook violently, then crashed over on its side, sliding forward, breaking free from the others cars, careening down an embankment. The men on the downside wall of the car were crushed by the mass of bodies thrown against them, screaming in the malevolent darkness. The car came to rest against a large boulder, its side splintered open, spilling a dozen men onto the ground.

There were loud, popping sounds and the staccato of machine-gun fire. The S.S. guards, housed in a passenger car near the end of the train, swarmed out as their car was hit by bullets and grenades. Up ahead, a thunderous explosion lighted the sky, as the engine was hit. In the melee, Julian grabbed Edgar's arms, and yelled, "Let's Go." They climbed and stumbled over the bodies of others, some unconscious, some too weak or stunned to move.

As the pair ran, delicious, fresh air filling their lungs, they heard shouts in French from their left. A man, waving a flashlight and carrying a rifle, gestured for them to come his way. He pointed them to a farm-house across a field, telling them to go there and wait. They ran through a crop of rape, hearing behind them the ongoing clamor of a gun-fight. By the time they reached the house, most of the shooting had stopped, only single shots punctuating the silence, as the Resistance killed the last of the guards.

Out of breath, Julian slumped to the ground in a courtyard outside the house. In the next minutes, other escapees joined him and Edgar. They waited until two men, one of whom had sent Julian there, arrived.

"This is it then," one of the rescuers said. "We better get moving."

"Wait," cried Julian. "What about the others. There were hundreds of us."

"We know. Some of you are at a place on the other side of the tracks. We had hoped to free more."

"What happened to them?" asked Edgar.

"Only two of the cars burst open, and before we could unlock the others, the guards machine-gunned them. When we killed all the bastards, we looked inside. It was a slaughterhouse. But now we have to go quickly."

Several vans stood by, more than they needed. Six of the twelve escapees went into each van, the vehicles going off in different directions. Bottles of water, bread and cheese, were offered to the men, gratefully received and instantly devoured. They drove for about an hour, stopped, and let two of the former prisoners out. The process was repeated once again, then a third time, when Julian and Edgar were dropped off outside a mill, alongside a stream. The van driver wished the two men well, and drove off.

A middle-aged woman came out of the house.

"So, you are my new workers," she said with a smile.

Julian and Edgar looked at each other, laughed, and said:

"Yes, Madame, we are here to work."

And that's what they did, from the next day forward: learning how to run the mill, prepare the grain, and make repairs. With warm beds, decent food, and fresh air to breathe, life had definitely become more pleasant, and more hopeful.

———— ⊛ ————

Nanette grew increasingly worried about Manfried. He spent precious little time in their apartment, frequently sleeping at his office. When Nanette did see him, he appeared pale, and obviously thinner.

"Can you tell me what is happening?" she asked one evening when they were able to have a meal together.

"Everything is in a turmoil," he replied, discouragement showing in his voice. "Unlike Boineburg, the little General doesn't share much with his staff. But I know he is under a lot of pressure from Berlin."

"Pressure to do what?"

Manfried breathed deeply, shook his head and answered.

"We are ordered to hold the city to the last man. And, if we cannot hold it any longer, to destroy it completely. I told you before about the mines, but I never thought he would carry it out."

"So, he will not surrender." she said. "What a foolish man. What a waste of life."

"No, he is not foolish," Manfried asserted quickly. "You don't know how difficult his position is. He was singled out by the Fuhrer to do this job. It was a great honor, as well as a great responsibility. Too much, I think, for one man."

"Honor, you speak of honor!" she said angrily. "What honor is there in commanding a city of fearful, starving people? What honor is there in destroying what it took centuries to build? Honor is cheap when it is bought with the lives of innocent people one doesn't care about."

She rushed out of the room, falling on her bed, sobs racking her body. In a few minutes, she heard the apartment door slam shut. For the first time in their relationship she had given voice to the feelings bottled up for years. But she felt ashamed for taking it out on Manfried. He was a soldier, but she had come to know him as a person, oblivious of that title, and had loved him for who he was, rather than hating him for what he represented. She continued crying, her mind dreadfully tired, and her malnourished body weak. Weariness overtook her, and she slept.

It was dark when she awoke, popping sounds coming from the street outside the apartment.

There were no streets lamps, but from her window she could see a small group of German soldiers rushing past the building, pursued by a large band of men, firing rifles. She gasped, as three of the soldiers fell, while the others turned a corner, and ran on. When some of the men—she was certain they were the

Resistance—came to where the soldiers lay, they shot two who were wounded. From them, they took their weapons, helmets, and ammunition pouches, and ran off.

Nanette hurried down the stairs to the entrance and peered out. No-one was in sight. She cautiously walked toward the bodies, seeing blood forming circles around them. It was clear that they were dead, but she couldn't pull herself away from the sight. These were the first deaths she had witnessed, filling her with a sense of horror and pity. The face of one of the dead was visible, and she could see he was only a youth. No wonder they had run as they had. They were probably terrified.

"What a waste," she thought. "A life barely lived, dead in a foreign land, no mother to hold his head, no family to lay him to rest. And all for the evil desires of a mad-man."

Slowly, others, mostly women, emerged from their homes, coming to view, as Nanette had, the bodies of the enemy. One woman came close, looked down at one of the bodies, and spit on it. Another untied a pair of boots and removed them, then rushed off. Before others could do any more, the sound of a large motor coming toward them dispersed the crowd. Nanette returned to her room, still in shock from what she witnessed.

CHAPTER 13

WHILE THE FORCES of the Third Reich struggled to block the advance of American and British forces from Normandy, seven French and three American divisions landed near Cannes. The Wehrmacht was ordered to evacuate southern France, to take up new defensive positions to the north and west.

By this time, numerous Resistance groups, joining the FFI—the Free French of the Interior, led by military officers—moved rapidly to take control of abandoned town and cities in the wake of German retreats. After establishing new administrations, they began a program which would last for years, and bring injury to the very soul of France. It was called, "The Purge".

Charles de Gaulle, the leader of the Free French Forces abroad, had established his headquarters in Algiers. He worked with his staff for months, devising plans for a provisional government once France was liberated. One aspect of those plans called for the immediate formation of tribunals, to try those who had collaborated with the Nazis. Monkey trials had been carried on secretly for years in Vichy, by the Resistance. In most cases, the accused were offered no-one to speak in their defense, and executions followed summarily. With the departure of German troops from Vichy, and along the south coast, arrests and trials became more prevalent, posing a problem for the justices whom the Gaullists brought to put in place.

In Paris, von Choltitz greeted with consternation the arrival of an officer sent by Hitler himself, to oversee the destruction of the city. The man, a demolitions expert, had orders to verify that the forty-five bridges across the Seine were properly mined, along with the infrastructure of the city. Von Choltitz had no option but to allow the man to carry out his orders, but gave him a strict command that no demolitions take place without his personal approval.

Choltitz looked at a map of the city, his eyes running along the river, counting its bridges near the center. He envisioned what it would be like, with all the spans destroyed, and all the museums, monuments, and cathedrals reduced to rubble. It was a sobering and troubling thought. Even in the short time he had been stationed here, he had looked with awe on the majesty of the city, and the turbulent history which it had endured. But he was a soldier, and he had a duty to fulfill.

From the west, less than fifty miles away, the allies were advancing rapidly. German troops, retreating in their wake, poured into Paris, swelling the defense forces of Wehrmacht and Waffen S.S. to over 22,000. Choltitz and his staff directed the billeting of the troops, and their placement at strategic points around and in the city. It fell to Manfried Zeller to advise the unit commanders where to best position their troops, and to determine what measures needed to be undertaken to strengthen each post. As he toured these locations, he observed with dismay the continued placement of demolitions, something he was helpless to stop.

The mayor of Paris, installed by the Nazis at the start of the occupation, also noted the preparations to destroy the city, and agonized over the thought of his beloved Paris becoming a pile of rubble. He asked for and was granted a meeting with the General, during which time he begged Choltitz to withdraw his troops, and declare Paris an open city. Choltitz told him that he was a man under orders, and orders had to be obeyed.

After the mayor left, the General stood on his balcony, looking over the house-tops of the city. He felt a stirring inside, a feeling of pity, not only for the inhabitants of Paris, but for the city itself. His feelings now were nourished by those he experienced after his meeting with the Fuhrer, before coming to Paris. He realized then, that Hitler was going mad. And now, for the first time in his long and obedient career, he was questioning his orders.

That same morning, miles away, another General struggled with the question of how his forces should proceed in the coming days. Dwight Eisenhower, Supreme Allied Commander, had drawn up plans to by-pass Paris on his army's drive toward the Rhine. The prospect of fighting in the streets and narrow alleys of the city was one he sought to avoid. Ringing the city with his forces, and cutting off German communications and supplies, would spare countless lives, of both citizens and soldiers.

His problem was that his French allies didn't see it that way. De Gaulle insisted that Paris be liberated, and that it be done quickly, before the Germans had a chance to destroy it. He also had an ulterior motive. Once liberated, he would assert his own authority, and form a new government.

Complicating matters, for both the Americans and the French, was the presence of a strong Communist element in Paris, determined to pre-empt a takeover by the Gaullists. They planned to foment an uprising in the streets, at which time they would occupy key offices, and place themselves in power. Both they and de Gaulle's followers knew that whoever controlled Paris, controlled France.

The FFI was planning its own call for an uprising, but were waiting for an assurance that the approaching allies would supply and support them. However, when they learned of the Communist plan, they immediately issued their own call to arms. Hundreds of men and women took to the streets, erecting barricades, attacking German posts, and driving the Nazi occupiers out of certain offices. Fighting became fierce throughout the city, with home-made explosives setting German tanks and vehicles aflame. The Prefecture of Police, where Dani had recently assisted, was held by the FFI and under fierce assault by the Germans. For hours the partisans battled to hold their position until reinforcements arrived.

General von Choltitz knew he must come to a decision quickly. If the High Command learned of the revolt, they would insist that the demolitions begin immediately. His first thought was to request a truce to play for time. With the Swedish Consul General, Raoul Nordling, acting as an intermediary, a five-day truce was agreed on by both sides. The General now had to decide what to do with the time.

He had less time than he thought. The fragile truce lasted so briefly, people hardly had time to catch their breath before fighting resumed. Tanks of a S.S. Panzer brigade rumbled through the streets, fore-runners of a larger force Choltitz believed was on its way to the city. Battles between the Germans and their attackers were sporadic but ongoing, through both day and night. General Choltitz knew that, when his reinforcements arrived, he would have no choice but to make a final, all-out stand within the city. If Paris was to be saved, only an immediate assault by the Americans could make it happen. He called on Raoul Nordling for another meeting, to do the unthinkable: he would ask his enemy to help him.

Many miles to the east, Julian and his friend Edgar sacked the last of the day's milling. There hadn't been much, only the meager remains of last year's harvest. They heard the sound of a vehicle coming, looked at each other anxiously, then went to a window to see what type of vehicle was approaching. They recognized the van, belonging to Rol, a member of the Resistance. He brought news of insurrections happening all across France, of the heavy bombing of the German heartland, and the rapid advance of the allied forces toward Paris.

"What do you know of Paris?" asked Julian.

"Fighting in the streets, fires, bombs, German tanks. But none of our army there yet."

Julian thought of Nanette. He desparately wished he could contact her, but had no idea where she was. A few weeks before, he had asked Rol to call Jean Barras at La Splendeur. He tried, but was told the number was no longer in service.

"There is work for us to do," Rol told them. "We have gathered enough arms and men to mount an attack on the air-base near Chaumont. With the three of us, we have over one-hundred."

Julian was quiet for a moment, then said:

"Rol, I have never questioned the orders of our leaders, but I am trying to understand why we would launch an attack now. If our armies are not yet to Paris, would it not be more helpful to wait until they come closer, and coordinate our efforts with theirs?"

"I argued for the same thing when I met with our leader, but she we need to let the army know they can count on us as a forward element."

"Did you say "she"? Asked Julian, incredulously.

"Forget that," exclaimed Rol.

"But you said—."

"Forget it! Are you with us, or do you want to continue milling grain?"

"Of course I'm with you. When do we go?"

"And you?" asked Rol of Edgar.

"Yes, count me in, but I am a terrible shot with a rifle. I can throw grenades, though."

"We'll find something for you to do," Rol replied. "We go in two days. Be ready at two in the morning. We attack at four. Someone will be here for you. Wear something dark, and don't shave between now and then."

He withdrew a small pad from his breast pocket.

"Oh yes, Ask your boss for some thin rope. We'll need about sixty feet, to bind twenty Nazis, if any survive."

Rol turned and walked out, leaving Julian and Edgar to consider what they heard, and to prepare themselves for a battle.

———— ∞∞∞ ————

Raoul Nordling was nervous and anxious about the mission General von Choltitz asked him to perform. With the guarantee of a safe passage through German lines, Nordling and his party, including a high-ranking member of the Paris Communist Party and an allied double-agent, prepared to travel west. They were to search for Eisenhower's headquarters to plead for an immediate advance on Paris. As they were ready to leave, Raoul Nordling had a heart-attack. His brother took his place.

Flashing their documents and talking their way through several check points, the group found allied headquarters, and presented their information to Eisenhower. He conferred with another general, Omar Bradley, and decided to act. De Gaulle had been arguing for an attack on Paris for days, and this new information both confirmed his warnings, and opened a way to make the incursion proceed. General Le Clerc, commanding the French 5th Armored Division, would lead the attack, backed by the US 4th Infantry Division. Time was of the essence, von Choltitz had warned them. To delay, and give time for German reinforcements to reach the city, would require him to stand and fight, and set off the demolitions.

From his bunker in Berlin, Hitler repeatedly called General Model, commander of German forces in the west at OKW, demanding to know if Paris had been destroyed, as he had ordered. He screamed and raged, frustrated that his generals were not showing the loyalty he deserved. Model promised that he would see to it that von Choltitz would get the support he needed, but knew there was little he could do. The additional infantry division closest to Paris was three to four days away. He phoned the commander of a tank battalion supposedly nearing Paris, to urge full speed, only to learn that the battalion existed on paper only.

Von Choltitz' decision to forestall the demolition of the city did not mean he would let the city fall without a fight. He ordered Zeller to again inspect their defenses, especially at critical entry points and important bridges. Even as Zeller went about doing that task, forward elements of the French and American forces were nearing the westernmost gates of the city. Fighting began, intensifying by the hour. Zeller heard the explosions, looked to the sky in hopes of seeing German planes, but realized the situation was hopeless.

Late that afternoon, von Choltitz called Zeller into his office for a report on the disposition of their forces. Zeller produced a detailed map, showing all the fortified positions. The General studied it wordlessly, then looked at Manfried, and said:

"It won't be enough, but it is the best we can do."

He went to a cabinet behind his desk, drew out two glasses and a bottle of schnaps, filled the glasses, and handed one to Zeller.

"You have been a good soldier, Zeller. You have done your job well, but you and I know it is a losing battle in a losing war. Let us drink to honor, duty, homeland."

Manfried, shocked to hear his General in such a state of resignation, lifted his glass and drank.

"Zeller, I need you tonight, to gather my papers and destroy them. But first, go and spend time with your woman. Then, tomorrow, you must leave."

Manfried looked into the eyes of his commander, the hero of Sebastopol, a superb leader of men, and now, a man showing compassion.

"I will leave here in a few minutes and return at nine." Zeller said. "Is that acceptable?"

"Yes, report to me when you return. I will have a letter for my family I wish you to deliver. I'm going now to have dinner with my other officers."

The General used the occasion of the dinner to say farewell to his men, thanking them, as he had Manfried, for their loyalty. At that very hour, the forward echelon of the combined French and American force entered the city. They had come in time. Paris would be spared.

Nanette was hungry, more hungry than she could ever remember. The shops where she had recently bought food had closed. She had asked passers-by on the streets if they knew where other shops might be, but they too were empty.

She hadn't seen nor heard from Manfried for two days, and was afraid to call his office, when she knew he was so occupied. The sounds of explosions filled the night, frightening her, making her wish he was there with her. The ringing of the phone startled her. It was Manfried.

"The General is having a dinner with his officers," he said, "but I was excused to spend time with you. I will bring some food from the kitchen of the party, and we will have a nice meal together. I will be there at six."

"Oh Manfried, I am so glad to hear your voice. I have been so worried," she gasped. "I will look for you."

She decided to dress for the occasion, in one of her best dresses. As she tried on one after another, she cried with despair. They were all two sizes too large, her body reduced to mere skin and bones. She finally found one that she was able to adjust to almost fit, took special care of her hair, and got out their last bottle of wine, which they had been saving for a special time.

True to his word, Manfried arrived on the hour, worn and tired himself. They kissed warmly, then stepped into the shower, their bodies pressed together is a desperate embrace, letting the barely warm water wash over them, as their senses became aroused. They stepped out, dried off, and he carried her to their bed, shocked at how little she now weighed. They laid together, their kisses furtive, and she opened herself to him, offering what she had to give in a gesture of surrender and love.

"This doesn't substitute for dinner," she said mischievously, when they finished.

"Really?" he asked.

"It was delightful, but my stomach still begs for food," she replied.

"Then, let us eat. I have brought the best Paris has to offer. But not quite yet."

He rolled over and took him in her arms again, in an embrace as strong as she had ever felt. He entered her a second time, and in a moment, produced for both of them, an explosion of pleasure.

As they lay, exhausted and happy, Manfried told her the time for a heavy decision was nearing, and they had to discuss it.

"The city is lost to our forces," he told her, "And tomorrow many of us will be leaving for Germany. It is a bittersweet thought for me. I want to be close to my home and family, but I can't bear the thought of being without you. Our time together has been the happiest time in my life. You have been my oasis in the bleak desert of this war. How can I leave without you? So, I want to ask if you will come with me, to be my wife, to bear our children."

Nanette's soul was pierced. She had often wondered how she would face this hour when it came, knowing that this interlude could not last forever. And now the time of decision had arrived. There was no question of her love for Manfried. But was it strong enough to carry her away from her native land, to the land of the enemy? She had not gone to England with Emile because she wouldn't leave France and Julian. Were things different for her now? She didn't know, and couldn't give him an answer. And told him so.

"I knew this time would come," she said, "And yet, I don't know my own mind. Now that I know there is a deadline, if that is what tomorrow is, I must use this night to decide."

"We should have spoken of this sooner," said Manfried, "It's my fault. But I didn't want this to end. So, I ask you to consider three possibilities. The first, I come for you in the morning, and you go with me. The second, you remain here, and when the war is over, I return to look for you, praying in the meantime that God will keep us both safe. And the third, we part now, giving thanks for the love we have had, always cherishing this time in our heart."

"Thank you for that, Manfried. It does make things clearer to have those choices. But I still need the time to consider them all. Can I tell you in the morning, when you come for me?"

"If you need this night to decide, of course you can. And I will love you, whatever choice you make."

"Then let's have our banquet, and enjoy these minutes to the fullest."

They dressed, then went to the kitchen. Nanette was about to light candles she had placed on the table, when the lights on their street suddenly went out. She lit several, giving the room an unexpected feeling of comfort and warmth, while outside the battle raged and explosions filled the night. Sitting close together, they ate. It was the most delicious and satisfying meal they had in a year, but they both wondered in their minds, if this would be their last supper together.

———— ⌘ ————

The tribunals set up by the French in the wake of the allied victories across France became more widespread. Collaborators large and small were brought to trial, with punishments ranging from immediate executions to imprisonments. Those who had aided the enemy fled when they could. Others stayed and faced the wrath of the Purge.

One who attempted to flee was Paul Moreau. He had profited greatly from his dealings with the Nazis, and knew he would be a hunted man. He made his way to a small village on the southwest coast, hiring a boat and its captain to take him to Portugal. The captain told him to board, and that they would leave in two hours. When he returned, with other men, Moreau learned that the captain was a member of the Resistance. Moreau was arrested, a large sum of money with him confiscated.

After a week of severe interrogation, Moreau confessed to his role as a black marketeer, a supporter of the Nazi' cause, and betrayer of his fellow countrymen. As with all the new tribunals, careful records were kept, enumerating his crimes and the people he involved, or injured. Following testimonies by a score of hostile witnesses, and no-one to speak in his defense, the three judges voted for the death penalty. He was executed a day later, mourned by no-one, forgotten by all.

———— ⌘ ————

Julian and Edgar were ready to be picked up at the mill at the arranged time for the attack on the German airfield. Neither had been able to find much sleep. The dressed in dark clothing, had bottles filled with water, and the rope Rol had requested. Two o'clock came and went, then two-thirty, causing both men concern.

"Do you suppose they were discovered?" asked Edgar.

"Possibly. But maybe it's only a flat-tire or some engine trouble," replied Julian, who didn't believe his own speculations.

Neither spoke again for a few minutes, both becoming nervous already, wondering how they would feel if the attack did begin as planned.

Outside, the moon was dark, the night warm. It was very calm, while their insides were churning. They stood by the door, Edgar smoking, Julian chewing his fingernails.

"How the hell long must we wait?" complained Edgar, becoming increasingly impatient.

"As long as it takes," answered Julian.

"Tell me more about your sister," Edgar asked. "Is she really as beautiful as you told me?"

"She truly is. A stunning looker. She worked in the fashion business, designing dresses, and sometimes she modeled them. Later, she was a singer in a Paris cabaret. The star of the show. Lots of men wanted to date her, but she is very particular."

"Well, maybe when this shit is over, you could introduce me to her. I'm not such a bad guy, do you think?"

"You're all right Edgar. If we get through this together, I promise to introduce you."

They were both into their thoughts when the headlights of a car tiptoed across the field. The van drew up next to the mill, and stopped.

"What happened? Have we been discovered?" whispered Edgar to Rol, as the man stepped out of the van.

"A change of Plans. The Germans abandoned the airfield during the night, heading to the Vaterland."

Julian and Edgar looked at each other, their faces a mixture of disappointment and relief.

"You said, "A change of plans", is there a new objective?" asked Julian

"If you have anything else you want to take with you, get it now. We're not coming back here. We're going to Paris!"

CHAPTER 14

N ANETTE SLEPT LITTLE that night of August 24, asking herself, and praying to the saints, for an answer to her dilemma. The sounds of battle were all around, causing her to wonder how Manfried planned to make what was turning into an escape. She rose with the sun, bathed and dressed, still in a state of anguished indecision. She knew that, if she chose to go with Manfried, she had better have her bags backed.

Look into her armoire, her eyes ran across the array of beautiful dresses she had loved to wear, and in some cases, designed herself. Each dress told a story: the sad recollection of Paul Moreau's party; the exciting experience of her first dinner in Paris; the amusing memory of Manfried's first invitation to her, which she had refused. The dresses, like her past, would remain here, whatever she decided.

The shrill ring of the telephone made her jump. Knowing who it was, she lifted the receiver and said simply:

"How soon?"

"Fifteen minutes. Be on the steps, we must hurry. I love you." The line went dead.

Fifteen minutes! Such a short time left to make the second most important decision of her life. The minutes ticked away as she continued to pack, selecting the most practical clothing she had, a few toiletries, a photo of Julian.

She looked at the photo for a long time, wondering, as she had so often, what had become of him, whether they would ever be together again, how they would find each other if they both survived, especially if she did go with Manfried.

If, if, if! She knew she would probably be safer in Germany, but how could she live among the very people who sought to destroy her nation? Regardless of what she had done, she would always be French.

But to stay meant to face the consequences of her actions, and she knew they would be severe. French women who accommodated German offices were especially hated. To remain, meant humiliation and possible personal injury. And, where would she go? How would she support herself?

Already she could hear the steady beat of machine-gun fire getting closer. The streets outside her building were deserted. People were staying inside their homes, some of their windows shuttered, aware that errant shots could kill as well as those carefully aimed. Windows rattled as an explosion shattered the air. She looked out to see a group of German soldiers rushing down the street.

Now ten minutes. She could imagine the panic at German headquarters, the officers surely aware that their control of Paris was about to end. She wondered how much of the city would be destroyed in the coming days, and whether the mines and explosives of which Manfried had spoken, would be detonated.

Her hands were shaking so much that it became difficult to fold and pack her clothing.

Now five minutes. Nanette knelt and prayed:

> Mary, Mother of God, assist me in my time of need.
> Help me to make the right decision, for I am lost.

Another explosion, louder than the first, interrupted her pleas. She grabbed hold of the single piece of luggage, and moved quickly down the steps toward the entrance. Leaving her bag inside the door, she stepped out.

O God, do I go or do I stay. You know me better than I know myself. What shall I do?

She heard the sound of an engine to her left, and saw an open German command car with two occupants racing down the street toward her. At the same time, two blocks away, and out of sight of the oncoming car, she saw a tank with a white star on the side, swing onto the street facing her, on a collision course with the German car. She excitedly tried to wave Manfried off, swinging her arms wildly, but he stood up in his vehicle, and waved back.

As the car came to a stop below Nanette, she yelled:

"No, Manfried, you must go on."

Manfried, confused at first, simply stared at her, his arms spread, imploring her to come down and join him. It was his driver who saw the tank. He pulled Manfried down into his seat and put the car in gear for a quick escape. The vehicle stalled, and Manfried leaped out, stumbling and falling to the pavement. In that moment, Nanette screamed, as she saw the tank recoil, sending a shell toward the car. The explosion was deafening, filling the air with flames, smoke and debris from the demolished car. All the windows in the building facing the street were shattered. Nanette was thrown back violently against the door, breaking through the glass, landing on the floor, as the huge chandelier broke loose from the ceiling, smashing into thousands of pieces.

The decision had been made for her.

Fighting intensified all across the city as French and American forces encountered the Germans in their fortified positions. Slowly and painfully, the Nazis were routed, and one after another sector of the city fell into Allied hands. When citizens saw their rescuers gaining the upper hand, they flowed out of their houses and apartments to cheer, throw flowers, and wave the tri-color, so long hidden. Fighters of the FFI moved into and occupied main buildings, and gave directions and advice to the advancing soldiers.

Fighting was especially heavy on the rue de Rivoli, in front of the Hotel Meurice, where von Choltitz had his headquarters. American and German tanks fought a pitched battle, until the Panzers were finally put out of action. A quiet settled over the street, now filled with bodies, and the debris of smashed vehicles. Inside his office, von Choltitz packed a few things in a travel case, and awaited his fate. It was given to a French lieutenant to make the arrest, with the demand that the General surrender the city and order his men to stop resisting. That accomplished, von Choltitz, and what remained of his staff, were escorted from the building to a waiting half-track.

A large crowd gathered outside the Meurice as soon as the shooting stopped. The people began howling at the sight of the man who represented the tyranny they had endured all those years. It took the French captors all they could do to restrain the crowd, and get the Germans safely into the vehicle.

The surrender did not end the fighting immediately. Pockets of German resistance fought on until the evening hours. Then, finally, there was calm. The city exploded in a frenzy of relief and ecstasy as the news of the surrender spread from one sector to another. Church bells, which had rung when the Allies first entered the city, now rang again, and what seemed like the entire population, filled the streets with singing, dancing, and flag-waving. Citizens climbed onto the allied tanks, hugged the soldiers, decked them about with flowers. Bottles of champagne, long hidden, were brought out and shared with the victors. The nightmare had blessedly come to an end.

Julian, Edgar, Rol, and two others in the van, rushing toward Paris, heard the news of the surrender on one of the few radio frequencies they could receive. Paris was liberated. They cheered, despite their disappointment in not having had a part in the rescue of the city. What they would do now, was an open question. Rol said they would await further orders from the Resistance leader, whom they would meet at a rendevous, just outside Paris.

Their journey had been a long and circuitous one, using small roads to avoid German patrols, and what turned out to be a rush of Germans moving east. Once, seeing a long line of headlights in a valley, moving in their direction along the same road, they drove into a farm, waiting two hours for the procession of vehicles to pass. They drove on, swinging around Paris on the south, stopping finally at Sevres, where three other vans were parked, in a church-yard. Rol told them to wait, climbed out, and entered the church. Two minutes later he reappeared, gesturing for them to join him.

"Maybe we'll get some answers now," said Edgar, hopefully.

Inside the doorway was a set of stairs, leading to a barely-lit room below, where twenty or so others had gathered. What Julian heard next came as a surprise, but not a total one. For it was a woman's voice that thanked them for their willingness to come on the aborted mission.

"I know some of you may feel cheated by the early surrender of Paris. We would all have liked to be able to tell our children that we were there. But events happened so rapidly, that we were all caught off-guard. But hide your disappointment, and rejoice with me that our beloved city has been spared, and is free."

She said that last word with such emphasis and emotion, that they all began to chant:

"Free, free, free!"

As she continued speaking, and Julian's eyes adjusted to the dim light, there was something familiar about this woman. As she went on, he edged a bit closer to get a better look . . .

"With the liberation, the round-up of collaborators has already begun in earnest. We have been asked to assist the Paris command in this task, by guarding those arrested, and keeping order in the streets. This is a distasteful job, and anyone who wishes instead to return home, is welcome to do so. You have already proven your worth to France. I will stay here for a while to let you decide what to do. Whomever decides to leave, does so with my blessing."

Those words made Julian absolutely certain that he knew who their leader was. He walked over and stood beside her.

"Hello, Julian," she said, "It has been a long time, and a trying time for you. I am glad you are safe, and that you have been one of us."

A broad smile was all he could muster, as tears filled his eyes, and he gave her a warm hug. He held on to her for a moment, then stepped back, amazed at her change of appearance. Even in her military clothing it was obvious she had trimmed down her weight, and her shortened hair gave her a vibrant, youthful look.

"Sister Danielle, you are an angel sent from heaven," he said.

"Not a sister anymore," she replied, also smiling, "and please, just call me Dani. When this terrible occupation began, I knew my duty to my country was as important as my duty to God. I left holy orders and eventually became what you see here, a miserable sinner in need of God's grace, but a sinner who did some good for France."

"I'm speechless," declared Julian. "We have so much to talk about."

He paused, looked into her eyes, and asked:

"What do you know of Nanette?"

"Probably less than you. After I left Cande, I was unable to have contact with any friends, and I moved about quite often."

"Yes, I suppose you would have had to," remarked Julian. "I want desperately to find my sister, and I hope I can do so once we reach Paris. But with all the turmoil there, it will be difficult. Her last employer was the owner of a cabaret. If I can find him, he may have some idea where she is. If I remember correctly, his name was Barras. Will you help me find her, Dani?"

"You know I will. I have many contacts there, and also a place for us to stay while we search."

"Wonderful," exclaimed Julian. "I am so happy that we came together like this. I have been blessed with good friends, always surprising me. For instance, when I was arrested by the Gestapo, they sentenced me to death for a murder I didn't commit, although I was involved, which I never confessed. I was terrified beyond belief, and thought there was no hope. Then, a former friend, someone who I thought had turned against me, came to my rescue. He used his influence to have my sentenced reduced to confinement in the camp at Choisel."

"Amazing," responded Dani. "Is it someone I might know?"

"Believe it or not, it was Paul Moreau!"

"Moreau?" replied Dani, shaking her head in disbelief. "I have never known him to do anything for anyone, unless there was something in it for himself. Are you certain it was he?"

"That's what I was told. I too was incredulous. The only thing I can think of as his motive was perhaps a feeling of guilt over having me fired. I don't know how he even learned that I was in Nazi custody, let alone ready to be shot. But he undoubtedly had friends in the Gestapo, and maybe they told him since, I was living in Nantes."

"Guilt?" replied Dani. "One has to have a conscience to have guilt, and I doubt that Moreau ever had one. But then, stranger things have happened these last four years."

"Including what you did," Julian said.

"Yes, including that," said Dani, with a laugh. "Now we have to go."

CHAPTER 15

N ANETTE AWOKE IN darkness, in the bedroom of a downstairs apartment, occupied by an elderly woman to whom she had spoken only a few times before. Her head throbbed, and she felt a burning sensation across her back. It was difficult to move, but she made a determined effort to sit up. Her movements alerted her hostess, who came immediately into the room, carrying a lamp.

"Don't try to stand," the woman, whose name was Marie, cautioned. "Your back is bandaged from wounds you received from broken glass, and you have a bad lump on your head."

Nanette looked around the room, as much of it as she could see in the dim light, realizing she was not in her own room.

"Where am I?" she asked. "How long have I been here?"

"Since very early this morning," replied Marie. "There was an explosion. It threw you into the glass of the entrance door, and you fell there."

Through the dullness of her mind, Nanette began slowly to remember what happened.

"Oh my God," she cried, "Manfried, he was in the car. I must see if he is all right."

She tried to rise, but fell back, a blackness covering her mind, and she slept.

Night had turned to day when she opened her eyes again, and the pain was still there. She reached around to her back, touching the mass of dressings, carefully placed. She called for Marie.

"Ah, you are awake again! Do you feel any better."

"My head is a bit clearer," Nanette answered. "Who bandaged my back?"

"The doctor came. I called him as soon as all the people left from the street, and things became more calm. He has been here twice to check on you. A concussion, he called it, and many, many cuts. But they are not so deep."

"You are so very kind, I don't know how to thank you," said Nanette.

"I may be the only kind person you know," replied Marie. "They were upstairs, in your apartment, looking for you."

Nanette gasped, her head beginning to throb again with pain.

"Who was looking for me?"

"The Resistance, I am sure of it. They looked quite rough."

Then Nanette understood. Of course they would come looking for her, the whore of a Nazi officer, a collaborator. The words were sour on her tongue, and she knew they would keep looking until they found her. She couldn't stay in this apartment; it would only mean trouble for Marie.

The next morning, still sore, but feeling able to move about, Nanette readied to move to her own apartment. Before leaving, she asked Marie to recount the events following the explosion. She had to know if Manfried was killed, and if so, where his body was taken.

"I was just getting out of bed, when I heard the explosion. Fortunately I has here, in the back of the apartment, because all my windows in the front were broken, and sent glass across the room. I put on a robe and ran to the front. It was very difficult to see anything. The air was filled with smoke from the burning car, and men from the tank were swarming around it. Then another car came, not a tank, but a small one, the kind the Americans have. Two men jumped out and I saw them pick up two bodies, alive or dead, I couldn't tell. They drove off, then the tank went away. People from other houses came out to look, and when they went away, and the fire burned out, I brought you in here and called the doctor. You know the rest."

"Thank you, Marie." said Nanette. "I will never forget your kindness. But now I must go to my own apartment. I don't want you to be in trouble."

She began to walk across the room, when her head began to spin. She took hold of a chair, fell forward, and landed on the floor. Marie ran over to her, helping her into the chair. She then ran to her kitchen and returned with a wet cloth, which she placed on Nanette's forehead.

"No, my dear girl," she said in a motherly tone, "I think you had better stay another night. No-one knows you're here, and they won't trouble an old woman like me."

Dani, Julian, and the others drove into Paris, passing the detritus of battle, some vehicles still emitting smoke from their burned carriages. While there was a great deal of evidence showing street battles, they were surprised and pleased that the destruction to apartments and work-places was more limited. It was late when they reached a Roman Catholic hostel, worn and exhausted from lack of sleep and expending so much nervous energy. The director of the hostel knew Dani, welcoming her and her friends warmly. They were shown to their rooms, and fell asleep quickly despite sporadic sounds of gunfire from various sections of the city.

They met for breakfast the next morning, learning that Dani had been on the phone early, searching for the FFI headquarters. The director of the hostel had told her that the city was in an uproar, with the German surrender, and the news of the impending arrival of Charles de Gaulle. He gave directions to the address Dani had learned from another Resistance leader, a building near the Hotel de Ville, which was the city hall.

Their arrival was again greeted by someone who knew Dani well, a long-time Resistance fighter, who called her Voltaire, which was her code-name. Dani explained that the five of them had come to assist however needed, and that she and Julian were also seeking Julian's sister.

"We have plenty of work to do," the man told her. "We are working under the jurisdiction of the CPL, the Paris Committee of Liberation, rounding up collaborators from lists given us by the local leaders, and it is a slow process. If you want to help, we'll assign a local operative to each of your men. We always go in pairs. You, Dani, can help in our office, working on some paper work."

They all approved the idea, Dani and Julian agreeing to meet at two that afternoon to begin the search for Jean Barras, and hopefully, to locate Nanette.

Julian was paired with a man named Marc, who, like himself, had once been captured by the Gestapo, but managed to escape. He was a rough-looking fellow, his nose showing it had obviously been broken, and the tone of his voice making Julian feel uncomfortable. Marc shared that he had already arrested five collaborators, three men, and two women.

"What do we do when we find them?" asked Julian.

"If they resist, we use force—as much as needed—and sometimes a bit more," replied Marc, with a sadistic smile. "The women usually just cry, especially when we get them onto the street and strip them."

"Strip them? What do you mean?" asked Julian, not liking the thought of working with this man.

"Well, just their blouses and brassieres," said Marc. "The people love it. And then, when we shave their head, the crowds go wild."

Julian was quiet, repelled by the thought.

"You think it's cruel?" asked Marc, sensing Julian's discomfort. "Think of what some of them did. Some betrayed their neighbor to the Nazis. Some lived like queens with their Nazi lovers, while people starved. Don't feel sorry for them, my friend. They'll get a year or so in prison and then go free."

Julian weighed what Marc said, thinking it would be more palatable coming from someone who didn't enjoy his task so much.

They walked for about half an hour, then came to a street with two addresses Marc had been given, only half a block apart. They approached the first address.

"This first one's name is Claude," said Marc. "I'll do the talking. Next, we'll go to see, ah, Andrea, in 1305, apartment 6."

The two men entered the first building, knocking on the door of apartment 3. As it opened, Marc quickly stuck his foot in the door, shouting:

"Claude Joule, I arrest you in the name of the people of France for collaboration with the enemy."

Joule tried to close the door, but Marc had it blocked. He shoved it fully open, stepped in, and grabbed Joule before he could run to another room. They fought, but when Marc landed a solid blow on Joule's face, the man collapsed and begged Marc to stop.

The struggle attracted the attention of other residents, who opened their doors to look out. Marc shoved Joule into the hallway, as the neighbors began to shout.

"Yes, good! Take the betrayer away. His Nazi friends are no longer here to help him."

One of the women took Julian by the sleeve. He turned to face her.

"That swine told the Nazis that my husband was working with the Resistence, which was completely untrue." she said. "Joule was angry with us because he wanted our apartment, which is larger, and we refused to move. They took my husband and beat him. His arm was broken. That's the kind of man Joule is." She spit on him as Marc dragged him down the hall.

They went onto the street, people following.

"Remove your trousers, Monsieur Joule," said Marc, "or I will remove them for you."

Joule began to loosen his belt, then suddenly tore himself away from Marc, and bolted. He ran through the gathered crowd, knocking down a woman bystander. Marc gave chase.

"The other one, Get the other one," Marc shouted to Julian.

Julian watched him go, thinking it would be good to be away from Marc, whom he clearly disliked. He also didn't like the mood of the crowd, deciding to wait until it dispersed before going to the other address, which was close by. He turned, looking in the direction of the address given him, noticing a figure rush inside a doorway. He casually moved toward the building, and upon inspection, found it was the address given him, for a woman named Paulette Deseaux. He climbed the short flight of steps and knocked on the door, receiving no answer. He decided to act boldly.

"Mademoiselle Deseaux, I know you are in there," he shouted. "If you want your door smashed in, fine, otherwise, open it now."

After a moment, the lock on the door clicked, the door slowly opened, and a young woman stood there, shaking.

"May I help you?" asked the woman, whom Julian judged to be not more than twenty.

"No," replied Julian, "It is you who needs help."

"I don't understand," she replied.

"I am coming in," asserted Julian, "Please don't stand in my way. You are Paulette Deseaux, are you not?"

"Yes, and who are you?"

"I represent the people of France," answered Julian, with as much authority in his voice as he could muster.

Unfolding a document Marc had given him, he read the charge.

"You are accused of consorting with the enemy."

He pushed himself past her into the small, but neatly kept apartment.

"Show me your bedroom." he ordered.

"My bedroom? Why do you want to see my bedroom? I live here by myself. I have done nothing wrong." she asked, anxiety growing in her voice.

"Show me." he ordered again.

She led him down a short hallway to a room with one large bed. Julian walked in, looked around, then opened a drawer on the dressing table. Inside was some lingerie, under which lay a photo of Paulette. She was shown standing, arm in arm with a German officer. Julian held it up for her to see. She finally broke and began to sob.

"Please Monsieur," she pleaded, "you must understand. Things were difficult. I had no other choice. I had no job, no friends to help. If you arrest me, they wild do terrible things to me. I have seen it, like that man just minutes ago."

"He damn well deserved it, and so do you." declared Julian.

"How do you know? What right have you to judge me? You weren't here." she said angrily.

"You don't know what it was like to be hungry every day, freezing in winter, clothing turning to rags. It was something I had to do to survive, nothing else."

She became less defensive now, almost aggressive.

"And what were you doing." she asked. "Running away like all the other men? Refusing to make a stand for our freedom?"

Julian, himself now angry, grabbed her tightly by the arm.

"Don't talk to me about freedom. I don't owe you an explanation, but I'll tell you this to make things clearer for you. I was with the Resistance in Nantes, arrested and sentenced to be shot. Only through the efforts of other resisters, I was rescued, and continued to work with them. So don't accuse me of being a coward."

She was silent for a moment, then said:

"We have all suffered, in different ways, Monsieur. Can the suffering and the blame now come to an end? Can we be one people again, or must we let the Nazi curse forever infect our souls? For if we do, then they will have won, no matter how the war ends."

He let go of her arm, seeing there the red mark his grasp had caused, and realizing how much he must have been hurting her, both in body and soul. He thought of Nanette and what she might have had to do to survive. He tried to push from his mind the thought that she might be like this woman, a bird caught in a web, crying, until someone, anyone, came to free her, or to encircle in a net more insidious and spirit dissolving.

He looked into her pleading face, filled with an intensity that stirred his soul.

"I will not take you in," he whispered gently, "I will mark you as having fled, and no-one else will come for you. But you have to leave this house. Do you have somewhere to go?"

"I was planning to leave tomorrow; to go home."

Her voice broke with emotion as she said the word, "home", giving Julian the sense that there must be a lot of sad history in her past, and that going to the place she called home might be another painful experience in her young life.

"Good." he said, finally. "Leave as soon as you can, and try to stay out of the sight of your neighbors. Someone reported you, and may do so again. If you have to stay here tonight, keep the lights out, or draw the curtains."

She thanked him, kissing him lightly on a cheek.

"I am not a bad woman." she said.

Julian returned to the office where Dani was still hard at work, and gave his report on Paulette Deseaux. On the incident document, he had written, "Unable to find. Reportedly has fled."

Seeing Dani, he called to her. She turned, waving some papers in her hand, eager to speak to him.

"I have news," she declared, "Some good, some bad."

"What is it?" he asked.

"We have found Barras. However, he is in prison, and I don't know if we will be able to see him."

"Is he nearby?"

"Yes, in the old Fresnes Fortress. He was arrested more than a year ago. I was told that when he was forced to close his cabaret, he began trading in black-market goods. The police took him, and he was sentenced to two years in prison. I 'm trying to use one of my contacts to get us into the prison."

"Barras is our key to finding Nanette," said Julian, "When will you know if we can see him?"

She looked at her wrist-watch.

"I expect a call in about an hour. Why don't we get something to eat, then come back here."

The call came shortly after they returned, informing them that one of them could see Baraas late that afternoon, but only for a few minutes.

"Let me talk to him," suggested Julian, "Nanette surely told him she had a brother."

Dani hesitated, wondering if Barras would be truthful if the news were bad, but then agreed.

The Fresnes prison was centuries old, a forbidding fortress surrounded by gray walls and iron gates. On the street in front of the main gate, were the burned-out carcasses off allied tanks, hit by a German artillery piece, before the gun was destroyed. The Gestapo has used Fresnes as a place of torture, as others undoubtedly had in times past. Only weeks before, 3,000 male and female political prisoners had been loaded into cattle-cars for transportation east.

Julian waited while Barras was sent for, praying that the man could, and would help him.

Barras arrived, wearing worn prison clothing, needing a shave, his hair dirty and disheveled.

He looked questionably at Julian, who was probably the first visitor he had in a long time.

"Who are you?" the man snarled.

"My name is Julian Lemond, I am the brother of Nanette, who used to sing in your cabaret."

Barras looked at Julian, a slight smile breaking his face.

"Nanette, beautiful Nanette," he whispered, so softly that Julian could barely hear him.

"So, you do remember her? Do you know here she went after she worked for you?"

"Beautiful Nanette," is all Barras answered, as if in a stupor, or a deep revery.

"Yes, my sister was beautiful. Now listen to me. I want to find her, to help her. Do you know where she went."

Barras looked Julian directly in the eyes, as if searching there for something lost. He didn't speak for more than a minute, and Julian hoped the man was dredging up a memory locked away for these terrible years.

"She's gone. She went away," said Barass finally, but sending a wave of fear through Julian.

"Gone where?"

"Beautiful Nanette. She's gone. She doesn't sing for us anymore. And now, no-one comes," said Barras, softly, sadly.

"Where, where did she go?"

Baraas' eyes widened, as if a tiny fragment of memory, a disturbing fragment, returned to disturb and anger him. He stuck his index finger out, as if pointing to someone he imagined was there.

"She went with him. One day she was singing for us, the next day she was gone." he said, his voice edgy with fear and hate. "He took her, and she doesn't sing for us anymore."

"Monsieur Barras, please listen to me," said Julian softly, but sternly, trying to keep his frustration and impatience in check. "Who did she go with? Do you know the man?"

Suddenly, as if a shot of adrenalin had filled him, Barras stood, knocking over his chair, bringing a guard running.

"That Nazi bastard, he lured her away," Barras shouted, waving his fist in the air. "He took her, he took her."

Then he collapsed, his energy spent. Julian hurried to him, and, with the guard, they set him back in his chair. His breath was coming in short pants, as if he had not exercised this much in years.

Julian's face had gone pale, the implications of what Barras said boring into his heart. His worse fears seemed to come about. If what the man said was true, his dear sister, the one person in the world he truly loved, had done the unthinkable. If Barras was right, Nanette had become like the young girl he met earlier in the day. She had consorted with the enemy.

It was obvious to him that he would get no more out of Barras. Julian thanked him, but his words were unheard, as they carried him, nearly unconscious, back to his cell. But now, at least, although it hurt Julian to think of it, he did have a lead. He knew the Nazi with whom Nanette left the cabaret had to be an officer. Enlisted men had neither the privileges nor the money to frequent the better cabarets. But where would he go next? He decided to ask Dani her thoughts on the matter.

When he found her again, still doing paper-work at the police station, she rose and gave him a hug, which came as a surprise to him. But it was welcome. The conversation with Barras had struck him hard, and the warmth of her body, and the compassion behind the embrace, was a comfort. She had noticed right away, the troubled expression on his face.

"Julian, what is it? Did Barras have anything useful to tell you?"

"Useful? Yes, I think so. But devastating."

"Sit, and tell me."

Julian repeated what Barras had told him, which brought tears to her eyes, as she shook her head from side to side.

"Oh Julian, that doesn't sound like Nanette. Do you believe he was telling the truth?"

"Yes, I do. It was the way his eyes looked, and his voice—at first so soft and hesitant—then in a state of rage, as he spoke of the German luring her away."

Dani was quiet for some time. In the background, were the sounds of cell doors clanking, of people coming and going, cursing, shouting, weeping.

Dani, like Julian, found it difficult to imagine what might have compelled Nanette to leave her job and go with a German officer. Although the very idea was repugnant to them, they had been out of touch with her for a very long time. Could it be possible that life as a cabaret singer in the midst of Paris's relentless hedonism changed her? It was a thought which horrified them. Both wanted desperately to push such an idea out of their mind, but there was nothing positive to balance such a line of reasoning. They must find her, and learn the truth, no matter how bitter its taste.

"I've spent the day calling around to the churches in the area," said Dani, "hoping Nanette might have spoken to a priest on some occasion, and that he might remember her. I had no luck."

Julian took a deep breath, and blew it out, running his hand through his hair.

"Then, where do we go next? How do we find a Nazi officer who had a French woman companion? There must have been dozens of them."

"I have an idea," said Dani. "Let's start with the very top. Let's try to find the name of the officers on the General's staff. They would certainly have the most money. And we can work our way down from there."

"That sounds good, but how do we do that?" asked Julian.

"We contact the army—French or American—and ask who those top officers were and what happened to them. Some of them may still be here, in prison. It's too late now, but we can get an early start in the morning."

They found a small café, which had just reopened, amid the broken windows and debris on the sidewalk outside. It offered only some bread, cheese, and wine, but the two felt happy being together, sharing the simple meal. They talked more about old times, catching each other up on the events in their lives, smiling, laughing, joking. In the midst of this difficult time, their hour together was an oasis of happiness. As they left, and walked toward the hostel, their swinging arms met, and they took hold of each other's hand, bringing a measure of healing to their injured hearts.

Julian spent a restless night at the hostel. He tried to think of more pleasant things, like the little dinner with Dani, but his mind continued to replay his conversation with Barras and those horrifying words the man spoke: "That Nazi bastard, he lured her away". It was well into the early morning hours before his tortured mind gave way to sleep, and he had to be awakened by one of the hostel attendants, at Dani's request.

After a quick breakfast, they went to the Hotel de Ville. The front wall of the huge building was pock-marked from thousands of rounds of small arms fire. It was crowded with soldiers and civilians, carrying out broken furniture and smashed fixtures, further evidence of the battle which had raged over this important location. At a temporary entrance, Julian told a French army private his mission. The soldier seemed disinterested in what Julian had to say.

"As far as I know," the Private said, "the Boche General is long gone. Who knows who remains."

"What of his staff? Might any of them still be here?" asked Julian.

"How would I know?" replied the soldier, shrugging his shoulders.

"Well, who the hell does know?" bellowed, Julian, banging on the table with a fist.

The shout caught the attention of an American Captain standing nearby. He spoke French, asking the Private what the trouble was. The young man told him, and Julian added a bit more information.

"You must go to the that office across the square," said the Captain, pointing to a building some fifty yards away. "The records of whom we have taken captive and are holding, are there. Ask for a Major Rance."

Julian and Dani thanked him and went to the place he directed them. They told their story a third time, only briefly, to another non-com, who would not summon the Major without some explanation. He asked them to wait, returned in two minutes, and told them Rance would see them as soon as he finished some business. The Major came to a doorway and motioned for them to join him in a small office a few doors away. They took the seats offered to them.

Julian, attempting to establish rapport with the officer, introduced himself and Dani, then explained the role they had played with the Resistance. Rance was impressed, telling them that he had been in France since Normandy, and how his unit had been guided by a Resistance group as they made their way across the country. He spoke a name, which Dani recognized, telling him that, before she was given her own cell to lead, she and the other person had worked together.

"So, how can I help you?" asked the Major, smiling and seemingly interested.

Julian told him about their search for his sister; that they had learned she might have lived with a German officer; and wondered if any of General Choltitz' staff might be imprisoned in Paris.

"Let me get this straight," said Rance, rubbing his forehead and looking at Julian. "You want to find a Nazi officer, so you can locate your sister, who may have been his mistress? Is that it?"

Before Julian could reply, Dani broke in.

"This is true, but we suspect there may be extraordinary circumstances regarding her life with him. She was definitely not the kind of person who would have taken up with a Nazi without some special reason."

Rance moved his hand over the stubble on his chin. He was darkly tanned, with heavy creases around his eyes from squinting in the sunlight. There was no doubt that he was a field officer.

"This I can tell you," he said, "General Choltitz and his closest aides have either been killed, or taken to a camp outside Paris. Some lesser office personnel are in the city prison, awaiting transportation. It wouldn't hurt to let you speak with some of them. Maybe they'll give you a lead."

"Can you arrange that? We would be most grateful," said Julian.

"Yeah, since I helped capture them. I have some business to attend to at the prison anyway, so if you will wait about fifteen minutes, I'll get a car and take you there."

Rance returned as promised, leading them outside to where a Jeep with a driver was waiting.

He offered Dani the front passenger seat, while he and Julian sat on the hot, steel seat in back. When they arrived at the prison, the Major spoke to one of the guards, and ten minutes later the three visitors sat in a room, across from four German officers, all lieutenants, one of them quite young.

Rance, who spoke perfect German, told them they were seeking the name of an officer, possibly on the General's staff, who had a mistress named Nanette. Using Rance as his interpreter, Julian added a description of his sister, citing the cabaret in which she had worked.

The four Germans sat stock-still, refusing to admit if they knew anything. Rance looked at Julian, who showed his disappointment. After another try, which yielded nothing, they got up and left the room, feeling quite defeated. As they reached the end of the hall, they heard a commotion behind them. Turning, they saw one of the guards restraining the youngest of the prisoners, who had thrown a punch at the guard. Rance, Dani, and Julian shook their heads and continued toward the prison entrance. Just as they were about to leave, a guard called to them, and gestured for them to return.

"One of the Nazis said he has something to tell you," he said.

The three rushed back and went to a small holding cell, where a prisoner, a bit roughed up, was sitting. They recognized him as the one who had attacked the guard.

"I had to do it," he told Rance in a whispered voice, "To get away from the others. They harass me all the time. But I think I can help you."

Rance told Julian and Dani what the man said, then asked him: "What do you know?"

"Please, I must first ask, if I can have a cell away from the others? They hate me."

Julian looked at the Major, who explained the German's request.

"Can you do it?" asked Julian, of the man's request.

"Sure, no problem," said Rance, who then turned to the soldier.

"Yes, we guarantee it. Now, what do you know?"

"First, the officer's name was Zeller. He brought the same beautiful woman to several parties, so she must be the one you are seeking. We all envied Zeller, but he was a very private person. After one of the parties, we saw it was raining very hard. The General told me to get his car and drive Zeller and his woman home, before coming back for him. Where Zeller lived, was across the river. I remember it was an old, but very fine hotel."

Rance indicated for the man to stop for a moment, while he told the others what he had heard.

Then he nodded for the lieutenant to continue, asking if he could give directions to the place.

"It was some time ago, so my memory is foggy. But the building stood out."

"How do you mean, "stood out"?

"It was in the middle of the block, facing an oncoming street. Above the entrance was a tall window, and inside one could see a magnificent chandelier, which lit the whole street."

When Rance interpreted for Julian and Dani, Dani exclaimed:

"I know the place. I've been there! It's the Hotel Duc de St. Simon. I know it because it is only two blocks from the secret headquarters of the Paris Resistance."

Rance and Julian looked at each other, astonished at the irony of what Dani said. Could it be that Nanette and her officer lived within shouting distance of the Resistance leadership?

They rose, and readied to leave, Dani assuring them she could lead them to the hotel. Then, Julian turned toward the German. He offered his hand to the young soldier, and said one of the few German words he knew.

"Danke!"

They raced across the city as quickly as traffic would allow, dodging the wreckage of battle, often having to detour around streets too filled with debris. Rance was himself caught up in the excitement of the search, urging his driver on. When they tried to turn onto the rue de St. Simon, they found portions of the street blocked by the remains of a German staff car, realizing it lay directly in front of the hotel. They parked and walked to the hotel, past pieces of building material littering the street.

"My God," exclaimed Julian, "Did a bomb do this?"

"Most likely a shell from one of our Shermans," replied Rance. "They do tend to bruise things a bit!"

One of the things bruised, was the entrance to the hotel, its elegant door broken and hastily replaced with a substitute. The window above the door was gone, the glorious chandelier a pile of sparkling ruins in the foyer. A woman peered out at them from a second-floor window, then quickly let the curtains fall.

"Someone's still living here," remarked Rance.

"Yes, let's pay her a visit," suggested Julian.

They climber the stairs to the second floor and knocked on the door to the flat in front. An elderly woman, clearly very nervous, answered, and asked who they were, and what they wanted.

Rance stepped forward, letting her see his uniform, hoping that would relax her and make her more cooperative.

"We are looking for a woman who lived here with a German officer," Julian said. "Do you know which flat was theirs?"

"Two above this one," the woman replied. "Others have been here before you, also asking about her."

"Others? Do you know who they might have been?"

"They were rough-looking. Maybe FFI, maybe Resistance. I don't know. I told them she was no longer there. Then they went upstairs, and soon left. As I told them, she wasn't there."

"Mademoiselle," said Julian gently, "We are friends of the woman, and wish to help her. Have you any idea where she might be?"

"On the day of the big explosion, which broke many windows, as you can see," she said, pointing to the smashed panes, "I heard the woman come down the stairs. I looked out and saw she was carrying a valise. A minute later was the big crash, and then people rushed out into the street. It was smoky from the German car that was on fire. A big tank with a white star on the side came along. The soldiers, I think they were like you," she said, pointing to Rance, "jumped out, and found two dead Germans on the ground. They were from the car. Then a truck came, and carried the bodies away. We were all frightened to death."

"The woman," asked Dani, "Did you see her again? Did she go outside?"

"I did not see her again."

Julian asked for a pen, which Rance provided, and wrote a brief note on a scrap of paper. He wrapped the paper around a ten-franc bill, and handed it to her.

"If the woman, who is my sister, comes back, please give this note to her. It's very important that she get it. The ten francs are for your trouble."

The woman smiled, promising that she would do as Julian asked. He thanked her, and the three went up to the fourth floor. They knocked on the apartment door, not expecting a response. They tried the door-knob, finding the door unlocked, and went in. Evidence of the explosion littered the floor of the front room. In the bedroom, where nothing seemed to be disturbed, Dani opened the doors to the armoire, then turned to the others.

"This was where she lived, all right. Look at the dresses."

Julian came over and looked. Standing beside Dani, tears flowing down their cheeks as they touched the delicate fabrics and felt the presence of their loved one.

"We must find her," declared Dani, "We simply must."

Before leaving the building, they knocked on the door of the other apartments on each floor, and had no response. Yet they felt as if they had made a great stride forward, and their hopes were lifted.

Marie watched carefully through the cracks in her boarded up front window, as the three moved down the street. She heard Nanette rustling in the bedroom and went to her.

"I heard knocking at your door," noted Nanette.

"Yes, others were here, looking for you, I am sure. I heard them at Mademoiselle Molet's flat above, talking to her. After a while, they came here, two men and a woman, but I didn't answer their knock."

"Thank you, Marie. I owe you so much. But I know I can't stay much longer. I really was glad to have this last night here, but I do feel stronger now, and must get back to my room. I can't hide forever, and I have no other place to go."

Marie walked over and sat beside her on the bed.

"My dear girl," she said, "I think what you did was very wrong in many ways, but I will not presume to judge you. Sometimes we simply do what we must. And then, things catch up with us, and we must pay for our deeds. But you are young, and I can see you are intelligent. You will get through this. Despite everything, you are still a daughter of France."

Nanette began to cry, both at the warmth of this kind woman's words, and at hearing again those words which Emile had used years before: "Daughter of France". Was it true, or had she broken that tie, given up that birthright? No, she must not allow herself to believe that. Whatever might come, however much she may have to struggle, she would hold on to that claim, and not let anyone take it from her.

She wiped away her tears, learned over to kiss Marie, then stood, straight and tall.

"Now it is time for me to go. No word of thanks are enough to repay you, Marie, but you will be in my heart forever."

Nanette went up the stairs, as quietly as possible, hoping not to alert the other tenants of her return. Everything in the flat seemed to be quite as she had left it, except for the broken glass in the front room. As she entered the bedroom, she saw one of Manfried's shirts on a hangar, and began to cry. Was it possible that the love of her life was dead and gone from her forever? The thought of being alone again, after the happiness they had shared, was too much to grasp. She didn't know where or to whom she would now turn. A bleak and exhausting thought. She told herself she must rest a while longer, then decide if she had the strength to venture out in search of food.

Twice during the day, she heard crowds passing by, shouting obscenities at what must have been people caught up in the purge. The scene repeated itself in all parts of the city, and across France, people identifying collaborators, and some falsely accusing others in reprisals for past wrongs. Not since the Revolution at the end of the 18th Century, had such a reign of terror pitted one citizen against another. Before it ended, nearly 60,000 citizens would be rounded up and held for trial.

As the sun set, and twilight crept over the city, Nanette noticed that the streets had become quiet. She decided to leave her flat in search of food. She hoped the German retreat might have enabled some shopkeepers to reopen and bring out hidden supplies. She crept down the stairs and out onto the street, then walked painfully for fifteen minutes, finding such a shop. Although the choices were few, she was able to find a few things to give her sustenance. She kept her head down, as she nervously selected what she could carry in her net bag—some soup, bread, and tinned fish. There were only two other customers in the store, and she didn't think anyone recognized her. Except the woman behind the counter! When she was ready to pay, the woman seemed to look at her quite intently, but said nothing. Nanette left the shop, glancing over her shoulder several times on the walk home.

She breathed a sigh of relief as, with one final look to see if she had been followed, she entered her building and climbed silently to her apartment. Putting away the food, she kept out a can of soup for supper, feeling at last that she could relax.

CHAPTER 16

MAJOR RANCE DROPPED Dani and Julian at the hostel, neither of them wanting to go back to the FFI headquarters anymore that day. There was too much on their minds . . .

"I ve been thinking," said Dani. "Nanette left nearly everything she owned in her flat. If she is still in the city, hiding somewhere perhaps, she may have nowhere else to go for the long term, and have to come back . . . The rent on the flat is probably paid until the end of the month, if not longer. Why don't we go there and wait for her?"

"Brilliant!" exclaimed Julian. "Do we go there now, or tomorrow?"

"Well, I've already paid for tonight at the Hostel, so why don't we stay until tomorrow. Besides, I would really like to find a clothing store and get something different to wear. If you would like to do the same, I have money enough for us both. And then we should eat. I'm starving."

"I would love it, Dani, but I feel like a parasite, living off your generosity."

"Nonsense," she cried, "You deserve to have some good things happen to you. Please, don't think that way. Let's just enjoy the peace and freedom we have for a while."

After asking around, they were able to find a store selling men's clothing, and, just a block away, one for Dani.

They shopped separately, agreeing to meet when they had finished in a small café nearby.

Julian bought a pair of trousers, underwear, socks, a pair of shoes, and two lightweight shirts. He finished before Dani, went to the café, and ordered some wine. It seemed to be taking Dani a long time to shop. And then Julian remembered how it had been when he once went with Louise to find a new dress.

Julian ordered some bread to go with his wine, and was eating, when the café door opened and a young woman entered, carrying a few sacks. His eyes grew large, as he realized that the very attractive woman who had entered was Dani. For as long as he had known her, back in Cande, when she wore the habit, and recently, when she had on men's clothing, he had never seen her in a dress. It seemed astonishing! She wore heels, and a light summer dress, over a slim, well-toned body, with a touch of color on her cheeks. Somehow, she had managed to fix her hair in a female fashion. In his enthusiasm to greet her, he went to get up, knocking over his chair and nearly spilling his wine.

Dani laughed as she came to his table.

"Let me introduce myself," she said with a wide smile. "I am Danielle Dupree, lately of Cande and points west. And you, Monsieur, who might you be?"

"Ah, Monsieur Julian Lemond, lately of Choisel, and points east." replied Julian, cracking up with laughter, and, at the same time, becoming aroused by the appearance of this lovely woman.

"Please, join me at my table, and tell me more about yourself, Mademoiselle. Or is it Madame?" he asked jokingly.

"Perhaps in time I shall tell you," she replied, lifting her nose in a mock show of superiority.

"Then, what must I do to learn you secret?" he asked.

"Ply me with wine, and I will tell all," she said, both of them bursting out in laughter.

She took the chair Julian held out for her, still laughing so much, it brought tears to her eyes.

He drew his chair closer, and, deciding to take a big risk, leaned over and kissed her on her cheek. She turned her head slightly, so that their lips touched, ever so briefly.

"I'm so glad we are getting to know each other better," she said. "I have been lonely, and I think you have also. And now, we don't have to be, anymore."

They ordered from a menu which surprisingly offered several choices, drank wine, and relaxed in the atmosphere of budding love, which had been so absent in their lives for so long.

After they had eaten, they walked hand in hand to the hostel, carrying their packages, telling each other what they had bought beside what they were wearing. Julian thanked her again for the money to buy the clothing, and for the nice meal.

"I do have some savings in a bank in Cande," he told her, "from my job in the factory. As soon as I can get there, I insist on reimbursing you."

"If you insist," she replied, "but please, don't let it be a source of concern."

They said goodnight, gave each other a kiss, and went to their respective rooms, which were shared with other visitors.

In the morning, they had a small breakfast, when the telephone rang, and the director of the hostel indicated it was for Julian. Very puzzled at who knew he was there, Julian took the receiver.

His face turned pale, and, after asking a few questions, he put the phone down and returned to the table.

"Julian, what is it. Is it something about Nanette," Dani asked.

"It was the woman I gave the note to. Somehow, Nanette returned to her flat last night without being seen. Then, just a few minutes ago, a group of men came into the hotel and took Nanette away. We must hurry."

They ran to the street in a state of panic and hailed a cab. But before directing the driver to Nanette's flat, they realized that made no sense, and told the man to take them to the Prefecture of Police. They held onto each other's hands as the rode, both silently offer up a prayer. Going inside, they spoke to an officer on the duty-desk, introducing themselves, Julian telling him they were looking for a woman recently brought in.

"Nanette Lemond, is that the name," asked the officer, looking at his intake sheet.

Tears came to Julian's eyes as he heard her name, and nodded to the man.

"Is she all right," asked Dani.

"Yes, yes, just a little shaken, but all right. You know, the men who round up collaborators are not the most gentle sort, and if there is a crowd around, they like to show off their trophies. I guess they did attempt to bare her breasts, which is the usual practice, but it seems she had some prior injuries, so they were not so hard on her. I put her alone in a room. You can see her."

"You go first, Julian," said Nanette. "The shock will be enough. Then I'll come in when you tell me."

Julian agreed and went with an officer to a room in the back. Nanette was looking out of a small window. She turned as the door opened, gasped, and ran across the room to embrace her brother, whom she hadn't even known was still alive. They held onto each other so tightly that it was painful for her, but she didn't want to let go. All she could think of to say was, "Thank you God, Oh thank you," as tears of joy flowed down her face.

Julian released her and stepped back, seeing in her wan face the pain and embarrassment this moment brought, along with the joy.

"I think I'm dreaming," he said." I have thought of you every day, not knowing if this day would ever come, and here we are, together again."

"How did you ever find me?" she cried, still astonished.

"We have so much to catch up with," he said, "and it will take time. But there is someone else to see you. Can you stand another surprise?"

"Yes, but let me kiss you, and tell you how I missed you.

They embraced again, and she kissed his cheeks and ran her fingers through his hair, as if needing to touch him to believe he was really there.

"My big brother," she said through her tears, "Always coming to my rescue. Now, who else could be here?"

"Wait, and you'll soon see."

When Julian returned with Dani, Nanette was uncertain who the woman was. It was only when Dani spoke her name, that she shrieked with joy, nearly overwhelmed with emotion. After hugs and kisses, she had to sit, her emotions spent.

"Danielle," cried Nanette, "I didn't know who you were. I'm sorry. You look so, so different. On the street I wouldn't have known you."

"Yes, well, it's a long story, which we will tell you when we can."

Without warning, Nanette began to sob uncontrollably. Julian knelt beside her, putting his arm around her.

"I am so ashamed for you to see me in this place," she whimpered. "I have done a horrible thing. I don't know if you can forgive me."

"Of course we forgive you, both I and Dani, ah, Danielle. Now don't think about such things; just be happy with us that we are together, and believe that we will look after you. You will have to stay here until we can see what can be done. Will you be all right?"

Nanette nodded, trying to wipe away her tears.

"Then we will go and see what we can work out with the police. We'll be back soon."

She nodded again, got up thanked and hugged them both.

Back at the front desk, Julian asked if there was a chance she might be released in their custody, citing her injuries.

"That is not for me to decide," replied the officer. "We don't really have a word to say in the matter. We're only holding those arrested until the place is found to house them until their trial. She'll probable be moved later today, or tomorrow.

"Where will she go then?" asked Dani.

"She will be turned over to a Committee of Liberation, which sets up the trials. In a matter as simple as this, it will be a quick trial. They have dozens of them each day for women who consorted with the enemy. There was actually no law against it, so the courts had to come up with some new provisions, and new penalties. But it is all being worked out."

Julian didn't know whether to be glad or sorry about what the officer said.

"Do you know how long it might be before her trial is held," he asked.

"I can only guess," said the officer, "but two or three days at the most."

"You said you have no authority to let her out on parole." said Julian. "Who do we have to see about allowing her to be in out custody until the trial."

"That would be the leader of the Liberation Committee for this area.," replied the officer. "I can give you his name, but be aware that he is very much overworked just now. It may take some time before you can get an appointment. Let me see. Ah, yes, it is Charles Darlan. Here is his number."

He wrote the number on a slip of paper, handing it to Julian.

The two went again to see Nanette, telling her what they had learned about the time she would have to wait before the trial. They asked if it was all right for them to stay in her flat while they waited with her, and she thought it a good idea. She asked them to look in on her neighbor, Marie, to thank her for her kindness, and let her know what was taking place. They agreed, kissed her, and left.

Julian and Dani went to Nanette's hotel, stopping in to see Marie, and express their thanks for giving Nanette such loving aid. They also stopped on the floor above, thanking that woman for the call which told them of Nanette's arrest. Then they went to Nanette's flat, found enough for a light lunch, and tried to arrange an appointment with Darlan. The person answering the phone said Darlan was out of the office, but a message would be left for him to return their call. When asked when that might be, they were told "in a day or so".

"I don't know that we can do much else until the trial," said Julian. "It's hard to just sit and wait."

Dani was quiet for a while, then said: "Julian, a thought just occurred to me, that I want to follow up. Will you be upset if I leave for a while, to try to work some angles?"

"Of course not, if it is something you think might help Nanette. Can you tell me more?"

"Not just yet. I don't want to build false hopes. I just ask that you trust me, and let me try."

"I trust you more than anyone. I don't know how long you plan to be away, but I will miss you. These last few days have been so wonderful, despite the circumstances."

"Thank you, Julian. I feel the same. I'm going to put some things together to wear, and be on my way. I'll be back as soon as possible."

When she had packed, and readied to leave, Julian took her in his arms and kissed her.

"I'll miss you. Come back soon," he said.

───── ⌘ ─────

While Dani was gone, Julian spent part of his time sitting by the phone, awaiting Darlan's call, and some to visit Nanette. He learned, however, that she had been transferred to a jail known as the "Depot". He went to that location, on Quai de l'Horloge, but was unable to get permission to see his sister. Showing his disappointment, he pressed the officer to whom he spoke, asking if he could give him any information about her fate. He learned that Nanette's trial was scheduled for two days later, at ten in the morning. That was the information he had wanted so badly, and hoped that Dani, wherever she was, would return in time.

He was restless the whole following day, frustrated at not having access to Nanette, and upset that there was no word from Dani. He had no doubt that her mission was vital in her eyes, but wished she had told him what it was she was seeking, and where she had gone. On the morning of the third day, the day of the trial, Dani was still not back. Julian dressed, leaving a large note for her to see as soon as she came into the flat. He hoped she would get back before the trial began.

Julian found the building where the Paris Court of Justice was located, arriving a half hour before the time scheduled, hoping to see, and possibly speak with, Nanette. What he found instead, was another trial underway, where a woman accused of being the mistress of a German officer, and of speaking publically against France, was convicted and given a one-year prison term. She left the courtroom in tears to begin her sentence. Julian was stunned, and hoped Nanette would not share the same fate.

Julian found a seat among a spattering of people, some of whom were friends and relatives of others standing trial, and others who viewed the trials as spectacles of enjoyment.

When someone acting as a bailiff called for the next case, A female warder led Nanette into the room. Appearing both tired and worried, she looked around the room, smiling when she saw Julian. The court was presided over by three judges rather than the usual five. This was a measure forced on the judicial system by a lack of suitable magistrates, since many of them had served the Vichy Regime, and were excluded from further service.

Along with Nanette was a harried looking defense lawyer, who had met Nanette only ten minutes before. Nanette had told him she thought Julian would be there to speak in her defense, and she pointed to him as she took her seat The lawyer came over to Julian, introduced himself, and wrote Julian's name, being careful to spell it correctly, and how Julian was related to the accused.

One of the judges looked at the papers before him, read the accusation against Nanette, and, after swearing her in, spoke to her directly.

"You are Nanette Lemond?"

"I am, your honor," she replied in a whisper, her eyes downcast, her beauty hidden by disheveled hair, and eyes rimmed with dark circles.

"You have been charged with consorting with the enemy. How do you plead?"

"She pleads not guilty, due to extreme hardship," responded her lawyer.

"Very well. I have before me an affidavit from the Paris Police, and signed by two witnesses, certifying that you lived for a period of one or more years as a mistress to a German officer. Do you deny the accusation?"

As her lawyer was about to reply, the judge waved him off.

"Let the woman respond on her own. It is a simple question. Mademoiselle. Lemond, do you deny the accusation?"

"No, your honor."

"That much is settled then," said the judge. "Now let us hear about the so-called extreme hardship. Who wishes to speak on her behalf?"

Julian raised his hand, and was acknowledged by the judge, who asked him to come forward, where he was sworn. He gave his name and relationship to Nanette.

"What is it you wish to say?" asked the judge.

"I have known my sister all her life, and she has been, and is, a kind and generous person, who loves her country. As a member of the Resistance in the Nantes region, I fought against those who collaborated with the Nazis, and have nothing but loathing for all of them. Here in Paris, since the liberation, I have helped find and arrest our nation's betrayers. In so doing, I have learned about the difficulties single women faced, especially those thrown out of work by . . ."

"Stop," interrupted the judge.

"Monsieur Lemond, as you said, you are but a visitor to Paris. Those of us who lived here during the dark years don't have to be told about the conditions here. We know they were harsh, but there are thousands of young women who survived without the help of the Nazis. If this is all you have to say in your sister's defense, we will save time by telling you, it is no defense at all."

He looked at Nanette's lawyer.

"Have you any other witnesses?"

"No, your honor."

"Then my colleagues and I will confer and render our verdict. We will recess for ten minutes."

As he rose to leave, a man entered and hurriedly brought a message for the judge, who studied it for a moment, then made an announcement.

"It seems that we have another witness for the defense, who will be arriving shortly. Since it is nearly noon, we will recess until two o'clock."

Nanette's lawyer looked at her quizzically. She shrugged her shoulders to show her ignorance about this mystery witness, then left the room with her warder.

Outside the courtroom, Nanette was seated in the hallway, with a guard beside her. Julian was allowed to approach and speak with her. She spoke first.

"Julian, where is Danielle? I thought she would be here."

"I thought so too. She told me she had something very important to do, and went off. That was two days ago, and I haven't had a word from her. I'm really worried for her safety. I wish she were here."

"Have you any idea who this new witness is?" asked Nanette.

"I'm as puzzled as you," he replied, "unless it's that neighbor woman who helped you."

"I doubt it. For one, Marie probably doesn't know about the trial, and for another, what could she say? But thank you, Julian, for trying to defend me."

"It wasn't much of a defense. I guess we'll just have to wait to see who comes."

He was thinking about, Dani, but wondered what she could to what had already been said. It seemed as if the judge didn't want to hear from character witnesses alone.

Julian stayed with Nanette as a court attendant brought her something to eat, which she shared with him. Neither of them was very hungry.

"Julian," said Nanette, "I am so sorry to involve you in this after all that you have gone through. You must have been terrified at the thought of being shot. When I got you letter from Choisel I was so relieved to know you were alive. Can you tell me how you escaped and came to be here?"

He suddenly looked up at her in surprise. "Nanette, how did you know about that?"

"About what?" she asked.

"About my death sentence?"

She realized her gaffe, and had to think quickly.

"Ah, someone—I can't remember who—told me. I think it was Danielle. Yes, I'm certain it was she."

"But Danielle wasn't in Cande. By then she had already left to join the Resistance," replied Julian, a suspicious look on his face.

"Then she must have heard it from someone, and then called me," suggested Nanette.

"It's just strange that she didn't mention it to me. I didn't know she even contacted you after she joined the Resistance. That would have been very risky for her."

"I wish we could get on with this trial," said Nanette, trying to avoid any more questions about the subject.

Julian let it go and Nanette thought his silence meant the matter was settled, but for Julian it was not. He had a feeling she wasn't telling the whole truth, and worried about that. He wished Dani were here so she could verify what Nanette said. He was angry that Dani had run off as she did, leaving him to wonder what was so important to take her away for so long. He stewed in his thoughts for a few minutes more, when the bailiff announced that the judges were ready for the trial to resume. Julian hoped against hope that the mysterious witness would have something convincing to say in Nanette's defense.

When Nanette was seated again, the lead judge called for the new witness. The door to the room swung open, and Dani walked in, dressed in her military garb. Nanette showed surprise, Julian relief. Dani was sworn in, asked to state her full name, which was Danielle Simone Dupree, and her relationship to the accused. She also put into the record her service as a Resistance section chief.

"What do you wish to present on behalf of the accused?" asked the judge.

"You honor," began Danielle, "I have just returned from Nantes, where I examined the circumstances surrounding the arrest and conviction by the Gestapo of Mademoiselle Lemond's brother Julian."

Before she could continue, Nanette rose from her seat, eyes blazing, and shouted: "Danielle, you must not speak of it!"

At the outburst, Julian looked from Nanette to Danielle, quite baffled by his sister's words.

"Quiet, quiet!" ordered the judge. "Mademoiselle Lemond, you must not speak unless told to.

Go on, Mademoiselle Dupree."

"I have learned from the records, of which I have a copy for the court," continued Danielle, "the details of Julian's betrayal, arrest, sentence of death, and subsequent removal of the death sentence."

Nanette began to sob, crying out: "No, Danielle, No, please."

The judge gave her a stern look, which silenced her, allowing Danielle to continue.

"While it may be painful for Nanette to acknowledge, and for her brother to learn, I believe the interest of justice is served by what these documents reveal." she said, not unaware of how painful this must be for her dear friends.

She then gave an account of Paul Moreau's betrayal of Julian, and his demonic plot to advance his own interests with Zeller, which resulted in Nanette' sacrifice, to save Julian's life.

When she finished, Nanette was in tears, and Julian stunned beyond belief. The courtroom was quiet as a tomb, those present shaking their heads, astonished by the details of the story.

The judge looked directly at Nanette.

"Is what Mademoiselle Dupree said, an accurate account of events?" He asked.

Nanette simply nodded, without speaking. The three judges put their heads together in a whispered conversation. They opened the folder which Danielle had given them, reading through the documents, and shaking their heads in consternation. Their deliberations went on for several minutes, leaving the principals and the spectators in a state of tension. Outside, a rescue vehicle raced by, its sirens blaring. Everyone in the room seemed restless, wanting to hear the judges to announce their decision. A clock chimed in the hallway, causing people to instinctively look at their time-piece. There was more whispering among the judges, then nods, seeming to indicate that they had come to some agreement.

"This man Moreau," one of the judges asked. "Where is he now?"

"Perhaps in Hell," replied Danielle. "He was captured, and after confessing his guilt, was executed."

The room remained very quiet, the lead judge jotting down some notes, then conferring again with his fellow judges, before writing his name on the bottom line of an official document. He looked up, ran his gaze from Julian to Danielle, and then to Nanette, overlooking Nanette's lawyer, who was superfluous at this point. They all held their breath, awaiting the verdict.

"The accusations against you, Mademoiselle Lemond, are serious. However, given the circumstances of this case, and your heroic measure to save your brother's life, the court has voted leniency. There will be no punishment for your actions. You are free to go."

Julian leaped up from his seat and ran to Nanette, who was crying and shaking her head. He took her in a strong embrace, kissing her wet cheeks, and uttering his thanks over and over. Danielle waited a few moments, then joined them.

As the courtroom began to empty, Nanette's lawyer obtained from the judge a writ, outlining the decision of the court, and protecting her from any future prosecution. He gave it to Nanette, who thanked him for his services. The three then moved outside the building, where they found a bench, and sat together, still amazed and shaken by Dani's revelations.

"Nanette, my dearest, why didn't you tell me?" asked Julian.

"What purpose would it have served?" replied Nanette. "It was something I had to do, as you would have done for me."

"But all those years. It must have been horrible for you, living like a slave to that man." said Julian.

Nanette paused, torn between two responses. If she told Julian it had been a difficult time for her, it would only add to his feeling of guilt. If she revealed her love for Manfried, she feared it would upset him to realize his sister had anything but hatred for the Nazi officer who held her.

"It wasn't horrible," she decided to say. "I was treated well and no demands were made of me."

"What kind of person was he, to do such a thing to you?" asked Dani.

At that, Nanette broke down completely, her body racked with sobs. Dani hugged her and said: "Oh Nanette, I am so sorry to bring up hurtful memories. You're free now, and safe."

Nanette continued to cry, shaking her head, her mind in a turmoil. She knew it would be a betrayal of her love for Manfried, and of his love for her, to have them think of him as a monster. She could not let that happen. As she began to regain control, she reached out a hand to Julian, and to Dani, and began to tell her story.

"The man with whom I lived was Manfried Zeller. I met him at the cabaret where I worked, and he frequently asked me to go out with him, which I refused to do. When he learned of Julian's arrest and death sentence—probably from Moreau, after what Dani uncovered—he told me he might be able to help. The Nazis do take care of their own, and Manfried explained that he could plead for Julian's life, if Julian was a relative of someone close to Zeller. He told me that, if I agreed to be his consort, he could make his appeal on that basis. I agreed, knowing that he was taking some risk, since we were not yet living together. I also saw no other way to save Julian."

She paused, catching her breath, so grateful that Julian held onto her hand, massaging it gently as she spoke.

She continued: "So, I went to live with him, and what I said was true. He made no demands on me, except to live with him and accompany him to parties. He provided me with money to buy food and clothing, and was always very kind and gentle. As time went on, despite my hatred for the Nazis, I began to know him as a person, and a very caring one. Forgive me, Julian, but he was like you in so many ways, that I couldn't help but comparing him with you."

She stopped, squeezing Julian's hand, looking at his and Dani's face to gauge their reactions. They both seemed genuinely sympathetic to her story, so she went on.

"After being with Manfried for nearly a year, sleeping in separate bedrooms, he received word that his only brother had been killed. The brother was younger than Manfried, and Manfried, like Julian for me, looked after him. Manfried was devastated, and I began to realize how he felt about Julian and me. He seemed so helpless in his grief, as I had in mine, that my heart began to melt. It was then that discovered what I thought was impossible. I truly loved the man."

She began to cry again. Julian put an arm around her, his own emotions churning, his mind trying to take hold of all she was telling them. She continued, speaking through her tears.

"Please don't judge me too harshly for this, but I have to tell you that our last year together was a time of new happiness for me. I had no idea where Julian was, or if he was even alive. Our parents were gone, and I had no home to return to. I felt alone and adrift, with nowhere to turn, and then Manfried came into my life, and German or not, he was someone who cared about me, and who offered a future for me. Then, he too was taken away, and I thought I was alone again. But you came, both of you. I miss Manfried terribly, but you lessen my pain with your love. And, that's my story."

No-one spoke. Julian only held onto Nanette, feeling her pain, wanting to make things better, knowing it would take a long time for healing to occur, but wanting to let it begin now . . .

"Will you forgive me?" asked Nanette, looking from one to the other.

"You are forgiven loved and cherished. I owe my life to you," said Julian.

"There is nothing to forgive, but if you think so, I forgive you and love you," replied Dani.

"What you told the court about Moreau," Julian asked Dani, "Was he really the one who betrayed me?"

"I'm afraid so. He told the Gestapo that he had seen you in a car on the night of the butcher's killing, and they followed up from there."

"I can't believe how easily I was duped into thinking Moreau was acting on my behalf," said Julian. "I guess I was so relieved to have my death sentence overturned, that I would have believed anything. But in the end, he proved to be what everyone always thought he was, a selfish miscreant who only looked after himself."

They remained on the bench for a while, then went to Nanette's apartment, where they had some wine, and relaxed before tackling the bewildering question of what to do next. Dani shared some additional information she had learned while in Nantes.

"While in the Nantes area, I noticed a great deal of activity in rebuilding the city. Once the Germans left, people began thinking about the future and what would be needed. I think, Julian, that you will be able to find a job there very soon."

"I was wondering about that," replied Julian. "It would be wonderful if my former boss went back to his previous manufacturing. I'll bet the Nazis left him some great machinery. I would love to go back soon and see what might be available. What are your thoughts, Nanette?"

"To be truthful, I haven't been able to think beyond each hour. When I was taken to jail, I really believed I would be sent to prison. Now, I feel like a new life has been given to me, but I don't know what to do with it. I agree that going back to Nantes, or Cande, might be a good thing. I have some money that Manfried gave me before—before he left. It could sustain us for a while. However, I ask you to please help me do one thing before we leave. I want to know if Manfried lived or died."

Julian looked at Dani, and she at him. They had a difficult enough time finding Nanette. How could they possibly learn anything about a German officer, who may or may not have been killed? But, if Nanette needed this to close the book on her recent past, they would do what they could to help her.

"That American, Major Rance, maybe he can tell us where to look for information," suggested Dani.

"Good idea," replied Julian. "He was the one who helped us find you," he said to Nanette. "We'll go to him tomorrow, and ask for his help."

They did that, or tried to, but learned that Rance had moved out with his company. They made inquiries at the office from which he had worked, but no-one seemed able to give them what they needed, or to tell them where else to inquire. Seeing that they were at a dead-end, they sadly gave up their search. Nanette took the news bravely, and began to pack for the move back to Nantes.

CHAPTER 17

ALTHOUGH THEY AGREED to return to Cande or Nantes, getting there was a problem. Dani no longer had use of the van in which they arrived, having turned it over to the FFI. They learned that it would be weeks before trains were running west again, since so many miles of tracks had been destroyed during the fighting. Nanette told them the rent on the apartment had been paid through the end of September, so they had at least three weeks of housing about which they had no worries. They would all stay there until word came that the trains were running again.

The allied advance across France had been rapid during the summer months, and landings around Marseilles enabled the U.S. 7th Army to press north along the Rhone and as far as Strasbourg.

But the joint forces in northern France began to meet heavy resistance in the mountains and forested regions east of the Meuse River. Expectations that the war might be over by the end of 1944 now seemed very dim.

Charles de Gaulle, working day and night to form a new government and organize France's diverse factions in a party of unity, ordered the FFI to integrate its members into the French army. He also made a plea for members of Resistance groups to continue their struggle by joining the army. When Julian heard this, he knew he had to seriously consider doing as the General asked.

"I did little enough up to this point, especially since the attack on the airfield was aborted," he told Nanette. "I know men are needed for the final push, and I would like to see the war through to its end by contributing what I can."

Nanette felt she couldn't muster enough of an argument to counter Julian's views, and Dani didn't think it was her place to offer any advice on the matter, although her emotional attachment to Julian made it hard for her to be silent. Julian sensed what Dani was feeling, and decided to discuss it with her that evening. The occasion came when they excused themselves from Nanette, and went walking, arm in arm.

"Dani," began Julian, "I realize my idea of enlisting changes things, and I want to hear what you have to say about it. But, before you speak, let me say something, and I will say it simply and briefly. I love you, and, if you will have me, I want to spend the rest of my life with you. Germany can't hold out forever, and, when we defeat them, I want you to be my wife."

Dani stopped, reached up, and kissed him warmly.

"I was hoping you would say those lovely words," she replied. "I love you too, with all my heart. The thought of you going into the fight frightens me. Still, I know it is where you should be, and where I would want to be if I were you. To answer your question, yes, I will have you, and will wait for you as long as it takes."

They returned to the apartment, telling Nanette of their promise to each other, which she received with great joy. When Julian explained that he would leave in the morning, Nanette smiled at

Dani, gave her a wink, and said she would be gone for at least two hours, visiting her friend Marie. Neither Dani nor Julian objected.

Julian's leaving forced Dani and Nanette to reconsider their plans to move to Cande. They spoke with the manager of the hotel, who agreed to extend the lease on the apartment until as long as they wanted to stay, at a rent they believed they could afford. Their next task then, was to find jobs, rather than sitting around the apartment waiting for the war to end. They also needed the income.

Dani decided to see if anything was open at police headquarters. Her request was welcomed, and she was offered a position, manning the front desk at one of the city's eighty police stations, freeing men for street duty. It was work she enjoyed, and the policemen she came to know respected and admired her for her resistance activity as well as her skills working with people.

For Nanette, finding something was a bit more difficult. She decided against trying to find a job at a cabaret, wanting to put that phase of her life behind her. The free press was publishing again, and she looked in its pages for job opportunities. While there were openings for construction workers, nothing appeared for which she was suited. Then, while dressing one morning, she asked herself why she hadn't thought of making some inquiries at one or more of the fashion houses which had remained in business. She asked for and was granted an interview at a lesser known establishment which had managed to eke by through the crisis.

She met with the owner, Charles Berteau, telling him of her previous employment with Emile Terrand.

"Yes, now I remember," he said. "You and he turned out a delicious line of fashions. His departure was so rapid, I was never able to learn what had happened."

"It was something sudden and very personal," replied Nanette, without elaborating.

"Yes, well, the war has brought on many unexpected emergencies. But you are wondering if a position may be open with our firm. In general I would no, but in your case the answer is yes. I don't know what you have been doing since Emile left, but I can certainly use your talent. Just last week our design staff began brainstorming about some new lines. I would like very much to have some ideas from you. We could start you at a modest salary, and see where we go from there."

He mentioned a figure, which she viewed as acceptable under the circumstances, and told him so.

"Then," he said, "if you are ready, come by on Monday at eight, and we'll begin."

They both rose, shook hands, and he escorted her to the door, thanking her for coming. She did start the following week, overjoyed to be back in the business where she began.

The dual income enabled the women to pay their rent, put food on the table, and put money aside for whatever the future held. After a month, during which time they had two brief letters from Julian, they learned that one of the train lines to Nantes, running through Cande, was reopened. They left early one Sunday morning, planning to return the same evening, on the last train of the day. When they arrived in Cande, they found the little town to be much as they had left it, except for some artillery damage on the western side, when a fleeing German unit had made a stand against its pursuers.

Their's was a nostalgic stroll along the streets to the town center, where La Belle Femme once stood. The building was now empty. As Nanette and Dani put their faces against the glass to see if anything remained inside, they heard footsteps approaching. They turned to face the oncoming woman, who stopped instantly.

"Nanette Lemond!" she exclaimed, "Can it really be you?"

It was Irene, her father's former accountant, who had left to marry the dentist.

"Yes, Irene, it is Nanette. I have been living in Paris, and just came for the day to see the old town. This is Sister Danielle. Do you remember her?"

"Yes, I remember the name, but she wasn't the lovely woman she is now. It is so good to see you both."

"What happened to the business which replaced my father's shop?" asked Nanette.

"It's a sad story," answered Irene. "The owner got into trouble with the Nazis who wanted him to do something he disliked, and when he disobeyed the order, they closed him down. He was lucky not to be shot. The poor man only lived another year, then died. The shop has been empty since."

"What a shame," remarked Nanette, "I remember him as a kind person."

"I must tell you," said Irene, "Nantes was terribly damaged during the fighting. It will take a long time to rebuild. There is not a good dress-shop this side of Paris. Are you thinking or starting up again? I know it would be a success."

"Good heavens, no," replied Nanette. "I wouldn't know how to begin. The business end of things was always handled by Papa, as you know. And I'm not sure people have money enough for nice clothing at this time. Perhaps they might in a year or so, but by then, other shops will have rebuilt also."

"Just keep it in your mind," suggested Irene, who then waved and left.

Nanette looked at Dani, who smiled and said nothing.

"What?" asked Nanette, laughing. "Don't think of such a thing. I really do not believe a dress-shop is what is needed just now, regardless of what Irene says."

"All right," said Dani, "I won't even mention it."

They spent the day visiting old friends and neighbors, everyone pleased and amazed to see them, and to learn of their experiences. A few people they knew had died, including the bicycle riding Monsieir Durat, and many of the town's young men serving with the army had been killed. Everyone asked about Julian, happy to know he was free, in good health, and in the service. The two women took the late train back to Paris, exhausted from talking, but feeling it had been a pleasant and worthwhile journey. Nanette was glad they had come, for it reinforced in her mind the realization that she had become a city person, for whom life in Cande would be tedious.

Autumn spent itself, then fall, and winter swept in with a vengeance. It was one of the worst in years, producing strong winds, and heavy snows, especially in the east. There, in the Ardennes, on December 19th, the Germans opened a winter offensive, pouring into the battle nearly half a million men, supported by planes and heavy armor. Allied forces, caught unawares, were overwhelmed, allowing the enemy to establish a wide incursion into their lines. Murderous fighting occurred, with tens of thousands of casualties on both sides, until the "Battle of the Bulge" ended in early January. The remains of the German army retreated to their natural line of defense, the Rhine. Even this formidable barrier could not stop the allied advance, and by the first week in May, Germany surrendered. The war in Europe had blessedly come to an end.

Nanette and Dani, enjoyed their jobs, celebrated madly with all their fellow countrymen the defeat of Germany, and hoped Julian would soon be able to return. Nanette had proven herself a valuable addition to Charles Berteau's firm, earning her several raises in salary as business improved. She was immensely pleased with herself in her ability to pick up where she had left off years ago, creating designs which drew praise and admiration from her colleagues. She developed a new cluster of friends, went to parties, but continued to refuse offers from interested admirers. Her heart still belonged to Manfried, and, as long as there was hope that he might still be alive, no-one else would claim it.

Julian was relieved of duty within two weeks of the surrender. Before returning to Paris, he went to Nantes, where he found his old friend from Nantes, Robert Tolan. Tolan was working as a reporter for a newspaper, often writing on economic matters. He offered Julian a place to stay while seeking employment, which he gladly accepted. Julian's former boss, whose factory had begun making the transition back to peace-time operations, was pleased to see him, offering him a job whenever he was ready to return. Julian thanked him, told him he was very interested, and would reply within the week. With Tolan's help, Julian also found an apartment which was soon to be vacated, not far from the factory. Armed with these prospects, he returned to Paris.

His sister and fianceé were overjoyed to see him. The three went for a homecoming dinner at a newly opened restaurant, splurging on an expensive bottle of champagne. As soon as they got back to the apartment, the couple began making plans for their wedding. Julian told then what he had found in Nantes, bringing shrieks of joy from Dani, who agreed that they should move there as soon as possible. They briefly considered having the ceremony in Cande, but Dani felt it inappropriate for a former nun to be married in the parish where she had served, so the idea was rejected.

"Nanette," said Dani, "We both prayed for this day, but I worry about you, and how you will get along after Julian and I move to Nantes."

"Well, I will certainly miss being with you. I have felt like I had a real sister all this time. You have been wonderful, and I wish you every happiness. But I know Paris quite well, I like my job, and the salary is good enough. Besides, Nantes is not so far away. I will visit whenever you want me."

The civil marriage was conducted by a magistrate, then the couple went to a nearby church for the sacrament. Dani had invited some of her police co-workers to the party they held afterward, not expecting much of a response, and was astounded when over twenty men and their wives attended.

Robert Tolan came to act as Julian's best-man, with Nanette as maid of honor. After the reception, the couple tearfully kissed and thanked Nanette, then left for a week-long holiday along the southern coast, with plans to stop in Nantes.

⌘

Soon after Dani and Julian left, Nanette began searching for a new apartment. She hated to leave her good friend, Marie, but had no use for the extra bed-room, and needed to find something less costly. Fortunately, she found another flat just minutes away, and closer to her place of employment.

Nanette was genuinely happy for Julian and Dani, but their departure left a large hole in her life. It was easy to tell them she would be all right, but even the first days of Dani's absence were difficult to bear. She had long talks with Marie, whom she found to be a sympathetic listener, and decided to establish some kind of routine to occupy her off-work hours. She had several times walked to the gardens of the Luxembourg Palace, and made up her mind to do it on a daily basis.

She began the routine the next morning, stopping to see Marie as she passed her flat.

"So, you are really going to become a daily walker," remarked Marie.

"Yes, and isn't it a beautiful day?" remarked Nanette. "The sun is warm, and the gardens will be as beautiful as ever."

"If these old knees of mine were stronger, I would join you," said Marie.

"Then someday we must take a cab, and go there together," replied Nanette.

She walked down her street to the busy Boulevard Ste. Germain, across the Rue de Renne, and then used less busy streets to take her to the gardens. It was close to a twenty minute walk each way, with a surprisingly large number of people already on the streets. She loved the beautiful garden statuary, especially that of Joan of Arc by Rude, and the splendid fountain of the Medici. Her favorite though, was the fountain designed by Fremiet and Carpeaux, with its sea monsters and five women holding a giant sphere. It was there she chose a bench, and read the newspaper bought along the way.

Many others enjoyed the gardens, each nodding to Nanette as they passed. She thought what a beautiful and peaceful place this was, and had been, even during the course of the war. It was her have, her escape, place to meditate. A few minutes later, an aux pair, with two children in tow, greeted her, accepting the invitation to sit with her, while the children ran around the fountain, chasing and screaming in delight. She smiled at them, wondering if God, in his mercy, would ever see fit to give children of her own. The two women chatted, then said good-bye, as the children began to become over rambunctious.

Nanette turned to the newspaper, which reported on decisions among the allies on the partition of Germany, and the fate of Berlin. Another article told of the tremendous problem facing the victors as concentration camps in Germany and Poland were liberated. Hundreds of thousands of refugees had no place to go, putting a great strain on available food and clothing supplies. She shuddered to think of those poor people who had suffered so much, and whose suffering would continue for some time. Despite what she had been through, she felt she was among the most blessed and fortunate.

And yet, Nanette still felt an ache and a longing for something she couldn't describe. Sitting there, in the warmth of the sun, the realization of what was missing took shape in her mind. She had been overwhelmed by the forgiveness Julian and Dani offered her, but she suddenly knew what she needed was the blessing of a higher power.

On the western edge of the Gardens was a beautiful church she had passed many times. She folded her newspaper, walked the short distance to the entrance, and went in. She saw a priest go into an empty confessional, entered, and spoke the words she hadn't used for many years:

Father, I have sinned, and seek God's forgiveness.

It was a long and tortuous confession, describing her final years as a cabaret singer, and her illicit love affair, broken by periods of crying and sighing. The kindly priest led her along patiently, until she reached the end of her story.

"My dear girl," said the priest, stunned by the full impact of her story, "I believe you have been more sinned against than sinning. Perhaps you have already been told that, yes? But it is not enough. What do you wish to do?"

"Penance, Father. I ask for an act of penance to perform, and I need to hear and believe that God has truly forgiven me."

There was a moment of silence and some slight movement, as the priest wiped the tears from his eyes. Then he said, "God has given you a talent, which can be used for good. Each Saturday evening for the next three months, I want you to be here to begin the Mass with singing. I want you to use your voice to glorify God. I will have our music director meet with you to select works appropriate to the ecclesiastical seasons. That will be your act of contrition. Do you agree?"

"Oh Father, I agree with my whole heart. I used to do it a long time ago, and I want to do it again. Tell me when to begin."

"Very well. Come see me in my office tomorrow morning at this time, and we will make the arrangements."

Nanette thanked the priest, leaving the confessional in a state of euphoria and joy. Outside, the sun seemed brighter, the songs of the birds louder, the smell of the air fresher. She danced down the steps of the church and went to her job, already humming a tune.

Yes, she would sing, songs of thanksgiving, songs of joy, songs of deliverance.

She met with the priest and the music director as promised, and was given three pieces, from which she would chose two for the coming Saturday. She asked if she might sing as one selection, a Protestant hymn she once learned as a youth: Amazing Grace. The organist said he too knew it, and they agreed it would be her second song. The week passed quickly, her evenings made less lonely as she rehearsed her music, both songs already familiar to her. She was a bit nervous as she arrived for the Mass, getting there thirty minutes beforehand to coordinate details with the organist.

———⊶∞∞⊷———

On the outskirts of Paris, approaching from the east, a passenger train meandered its way through cities and towns, losing and gaining riders as it went. A cabinet in the third car was occupied by a tall man, who watched the scenery pass. His reflection in the glass of the window showed scars from several wounds, which, despite their cruel appearance, did little to hide the handsomeness of his features.

The man was on a quest, a search to find the person more dear to him than life itself. For more than a year he endured pain, privation and humiliation by dreaming of the day when he and his beloved might be together again. He had few clues as to her whereabouts, nor did he know if she still lived. He had called the number of the apartment they once shared, finding the telephone out of service. He tried contacting the place where she last worked, but the business had closed. Love and hope were the only things which sustained him and drove him on.

As he arrived at the Les Invalides station, he stepped out, and moved into the waning sunlight. Bittersweet memories flooded his mind. He was in the place where love was found and lost, and where injuries had nearly cost him his life. The next few days would be crucial to his future; whether he would spend it in joy or in loneliness. It was coming on evening, and he had one last, possible place to search. He headed for the Luxemburg Gardens, admiring as he made his way, the buildings once so familiar to him. The sights brought a sense of melancholy, a wishing that he might have come to know these streets and avenues in happier times. His pace was slow, his cane lending support to a weakened leg.

The gardens seemed fresh and welcoming, the fountains playful. He stopped at his—their—favorite fountain, sat for a while, reminiscing, seeking, hoping. Bells from a nearby church brought him out of his reverie, and he listened to them in a way he never had before. Something deep inside him felt the bells calling, inviting him to come. He thought it a strange feeling, and yet was drawn to get up and move in their direction. He hadn't been to Mass for a very long time. Perhaps he would find in that holy house a measure of comfort he could not find elsewhere.

—⊗⊗⊙—

As the last echoes from the bells began to fade, Nanette stood before the congregation, and gave a nod to the organist who began to play the first of her songs. Soon her voice filled the nave with melodious beauty, the worshipers looking at each other in astonishment and approval. After the first song there was a pause, then she began with the second piece. Halfway through she saw the form of a man walking down the aisle, his cane clicking ever so softly on the stone floor. Her eyes went wide, and her heart began to thump. She was barely able to finish the verse she was singing:

"I once was lost, but now am found,
was blind, but now I see."

She finished, and walked down the aisle, trying not to run, saying to herself, "No, it can't be. It just can't be, but Mother of God, let it be him," as tears began to blur her vision.

When she was twenty feet away, Nanette could see the familiar smile, the loving features, his scars of battle. And she knew! He rose, took her by the hand, and, mindful of those around, led her out of the church, where they stopped. She came to him, swallowed by his arms in a warm and loving embrace. Neither spoke, just luxuriating in the familiar feel of each other, and the realization that a million prayers and dreams had become reality. They held on for minutes, not finding the words to express what was inexpressible.

Finally, they stood back, holding each others hands, he taking in her restored beauty and obvious good health. She returned the look, seeing his scars, imagining the pain he had felt, knowing without a doubt that which his eyes told her, that his love was as deep as hers.

"I have waited a long time for this moment," he said. "Tell me if it is real."

"It is real, and it is wonderful." she said, kissing him. "God is so good. All my prayers have been answered."